IN SEARCH OF A KILLER

Lucy poked her head into Bob's office. "Bob? I'm done here, but I'd like to look at Sherman's house. Is that okay?"

"Good idea," said Bob, opening his drawer. "I've got a set of his keys here. It's on Oak Street, number 202."

"Thanks," said Lucy, taking the keys.

"I'm the one who should thank you," said Bob. "I really appreciate what you're doing."

"I don't know what Rachel told you, but I'm not a professional investigator. There's no guarantee that I'll be able to figure out what happened."

"I know, I know," said Bob.

"I just don't want you to get your hopes up," she said, meeting his eyes. "You've got to face the fact that you may never know what happened."

He nodded.

Lucy sighed. "And if he was murdered, well, you've got to realize that most murder victims are killed by someone they know."

Bob swallowed hard. "By someone I know?"

"Most likely," said Lucy. "Do you still want me to go ahead?"

Bob looked her straight in the eye. "Absolutely," he said.

"Okay," agreed Lucy, but as she limped down the steps to the parking area she wished she had a little more to go on than a gut feeling that Sherman Cobb hadn't committed suicide . . .

Books by Leslie Meier

MISTLETOE MURDER

TIPPY TOE MURDER

TRICK OR TREAT MURDER

BACK TO SCHOOL MURDER

VALENTINE MURDER

CHRISTMAS COOKIE MURDER

TURKEY DAY MURDER

WEDDING DAY MURDER

BIRTHDAY PARTY MURDER

FATHER'S DAY MURDER

Published by Kensington Publishing Corporation

A Lucy Stone Mystery

BIRTHDAY PARTY MURDER

Leslie Meier

KENSINGTON BOOKS
Kensington Publishing Corp.
http://www.kensingtonbooks.com

KENSINGTON BOOKS are published by

Kensington Publishing Corp.
850 Third Avenue
New York, NY 10022

All Kensington Titles, Imprints, and Distributed Lines are
available at special quantity discounts for bulk purchases
for sales promotion, premiums, fund-raising, and educa-
tional or institutional use. Special book excerpts or cus-
tomized printings can also be created to fit specific needs.
For details, write or phone the office of the Kensington
special sales manager: Kensington Publishing Corp., 850
Third Avenue, New York, NY 10022, attn: Special Sales
Department, Phone: 1-800-221-2647.

First Kensington Hardcover Printing: August 2002
First Kensington Mass Market Printing: May 2003

10   9   8   7   6   5   4   3   2   1

Printed in the United States of America

For my cousin Margery Baird

Chapter One

Sherman Cobb wasn't feeling well. In fact, he hadn't been feeling well for quite some time. He couldn't even remember the last time he woke up in the morning feeling rested and refreshed, ready to face whatever the new day brought. That was why he was sitting in Doc Ryder's waiting room, expecting the worst.

He'd first visited the doctor a few weeks ago, complaining of pain and tiredness. "Ordinary enough symptoms," Doc Ryder had said in a reassuring tone of voice. But when the doctor palpated his abdomen, Sherman was sure he'd noticed an expression of alarm flicker across his face. It was quickly suppressed, but Sherman had noticed it and Doc Ryder's usually brusque and hearty tone became cautious and guarded as he ordered a battery of tests. "Nothing to worry about—just to be on the safe side," he'd said, but Sherman hadn't believed him.

Deep inside, he knew something was wrong, just like some women can tell they're pregnant long before the strip turns blue on a pregnancy kit. He didn't know how he knew, but he could feel death overtaking him, like the gradual chill you feel when the furnace goes out. First your hands and feet feel cold; then you notice you can't seem to get warm and the radiator feels cool to the touch. You check the thermostat and notice the temperature has fallen a few degrees; the oil tank must be empty or perhaps the pilot light has blown out. You go down to the cellar to investigate.

That's what he'd done. He'd come to the doctor to find out what was wrong. But no matter what it turned out to be, he knew it wouldn't make any difference. His pilot light was struggling to stay lit, but he knew it was just a matter of time before he finally ran out of fuel.

He sighed and reminded himself that he'd cheated the grim reaper a few times in his life and could hardly complain that his chit had finally come due. He'd had a good life, a productive life. He'd had his share of success; he'd known great happiness. All told, he thought, there was only one thing that he wished had been different.

Maybe it could be, he thought, wondering whether he should simply leave things be or should try to change them after all these years. And if he did, would there be enough time?

Pausing at the kitchen door with an armful of lilac blossoms she had just cut, Julia Tilley realized Papa was angry about something. In her twenty years she had become an expert reader of his moods, always watching for the slightest flicker of his mustache, the curl of his mouth and the lowering of his brows. Not that such acute awareness was required today—she could hear his voice reverberating through the entire house, like thunder.

Julia hesitated, unsure what to do. The lilacs would certainly wilt unless she got them into water very soon. On the other hand, Papa's anger seemed to be directed to her older sister, Harriet, and Julia was content to leave it that way. She certainly didn't want to draw his attention by going inside the house.

Moving quickly, she picked up the old enamel bucket that held kitchen scraps and carried it out to the compost heap next to the garden, where she emptied it. She then took it to the pump and filled it with clean water for the lilacs. She set them in the shade and sat down on the porch steps, wondering what to do for the duration. She could walk down the drive to the mailbox, hoping Papa's tantrum would be over by the time she returned, or she could stay here on the stoop and—well, not exactly eavesdrop because that would be wrong, like opening someone's mail—but perhaps a phrase or two would come to her and she could figure out what all the fuss was about.

"Damned scoundrel . . . a Communist . . . filthy New Dealer . . ."

So, it was about Thomas O'Rourke, the young man her sister Harriet had been seeing. Julia had suspected as much. He was a labor organizer and a big supporter of Mr. Roosevelt's New Deal. Papa, a Maine Republican, had no doubt that Mr. Roosevelt's policies would ruin the country.

"I love him, Papa, and you're not going to stop me."

Julia's eyebrows shot up in amazement. Harriet was daring to argue with Papa.

"Don't you dare talk to me like that, young lady," was Papa's predictable response.

"I'm not young, Papa, don't you see? I'm thirty years old. I've always done what you said and what has it gotten me? I'm an old maid—too good for anyone in this town, that's for sure."

Julia considered this. It was true, she realized, with a jolt. None of the farmers and small tradesmen who lived in Tinker's Cove would want a college-educated wife like Harriet. Or herself, for that matter.

"Is that what you want? To marry some man and become his laundress, his cook, his concubine?" Papa practically spat out the words.

On the stoop, Julia hugged herself. She could see Papa's expression as clearly as if she were the object of his wrath. The bristly eyebrows, the narrow nose and hollow cheeks, the frowning mouth. How could Harriet bear to confront him? How could she stand his disapproval?

"Yes, Papa," replied Harriet, coolly. "That's exactly what I want, more than anything. I want to feel Thomas's arms around me, his lips pressed against mine. I want to give myself to him. I want to bear his children."

Julia's jaw dropped, and apparently, so did Papa's. There was silence. A long silence. Julia sat very still, watching the swallows' swooping flight above the neat rows of baby lettuce in the vegetable garden.

When Papa finally spoke, his voice was as cold and hard as ice.

"Understand this: If you marry Thomas O'Rourke, you are no daughter of mine and you will have nothing that is mine. Marry him and you will become dead to me."

Julia's lips twitched, hearing the awful words.

Rachel reached out to gently shake Julia awake, but hesitated. Miss Tilley was almost ninety years old and, like a lot of very old people, didn't sleep well at night. It seemed a shame to disturb her, even if lunch was ready. She had made up her mind to turn down the pot when Miss Tilley's eyes sprang open.

"Ah, you're awake," said Rachel. "Are you ready for lunch? It's your favorite, shrimp wiggle on toast."

Julia Ward Howe Tilley blinked and looked around. She'd been dozing, she realized. Papa was long gone, and dear Mama. And Harriet was dead, too. Julia stroked her arthritic fingers and furrowed her brow. She was the only survivor, the last remaining member of her family. Or was she? What if Harriet had given Thomas O'Rourke a child? Her heart beat a little faster at the thought.

Chapter Two

Finally, a sunny day, thought Lucy Stone, wife of restoration carpenter Bill Stone, mother of four and part-time reporter. Thick, gray clouds had covered the little Maine town of Tinker's Cove for most of March. According to the weatherman, it was global warming that brought one cold, gray, sunless day after another. There hadn't been much warm about it, but it had certainly depressed everyone Lucy knew. But today the sun was shining and good spirits would be restored.

Lucy reached for her bright pink turtleneck and pulled it over her head, shook out her shining cap of hair and studied her reflection in the mirror that hung over her dresser. Were those gray hairs? she wondered, leaning closer for a better look. She ran her hand through her short, dark hair and gently grasped a handful so the sun that was streaming through the window could fall on it.

When did that happen? she asked herself. When did her hair start turning gray? And why hadn't she noticed? She considered yanking out the gray hairs, but there were too many of them. She would have to get some hair color. Or should she leave it be and let her hair lighten naturally? She remembered her mother, who had always insisted her hair was as dark as ever, long after it had faded. No, she decided, she wasn't ready for the salt-and-pepper look.

As she turned her head from side to side, imagining the effect of the hair color, the shaft of sunlight fell on her face. Was that a little mustache she was sprouting on her upper lip? Lucy leaned anxiously into the mirror. No, she wasn't sprouting a mustache; it was a series of fine lines. Little wrinkles, she realized, dismayed. And there were more, around her eyes. She'd simply have to be more careful to remember to apply moisturizer, she told herself, reaching for her favorite gray slacks.

She pulled them over her legs and automatically reached for the button, but something was wrong. Had she somehow twisted the waistband? She looked down and saw a little pooch of flesh protruding between the two sides of the zipper. She sucked in her breath and zipped up the pants, then fastened the button. She carefully let out her breath and the button held. Just to be on the safe side, she pulled a long black sweater on over the pink turtleneck. The effect was slimming, but she knew it was only a temporary solution. Summer was coming, which meant shorts and sleeveless shirts and—she gasped in horror at the thought—a swimsuit.

She was definitely going to have to do something, maybe exercise more or go on a diet, she told herself as she hurried out of the house and started the car. It was almost eight and she didn't want to be late for breakfast with the girls.

Calling themselves "the girls" was a joke—but the group of four women took their weekly Thursday morning breakfasts at Jake's Donut Shack very seriously. All married with families and numerous commitments, they had discovered that breakfast was easier to fit into their busy schedules than lunch.

Pulling open the door at Jake's, Lucy headed for the corner table in the back where they always met. As usual, she was the last to arrive.

"We ordered for you," said Sue Finch. "Your regular."

"Thanks," said Lucy, slipping into her seat and reaching for the coffeepot. "I guess I'll start my diet at lunch."

"You're going on a diet? Which one?" asked Rachel Goodman, pushing her oversize glasses back up her nose. "I've heard that Zone diet is very good."

"Not if you care about your health," said Pam Stillings, adjusting her macrame shawl. Pam had gone to Woodstock and had never quite gotten over it. "You can't tell me that eating nothing but meat and cheese and butter is good for you."

"All you ever eat is brown rice and tofu," observed Sue, checking her perfect manicure. Sue was a faithful *Vogue* reader and a borderline shopaholic.

"Well, I like it," replied Pam, tucking her long brown hair behind her ear. "And it's good for you."

"I like it, too. I like everything. That's my problem," moaned Lucy. "What should I do? I could barely get my pants buttoned this morning."

"It's all a matter of mathematics," said Rachel, picking up her fork and diving into a big stack of pancakes. Rachel had majored in chemistry before dropping out of college to marry law student Bob Goodman. He was now a partner in an established Tinker's Cove law firm. "You simply have to expend more calories than you consume."

"Exercise more and eat less," translated Sue, stirring some artificial sweetener into her black coffee.

"Look at her: She lives on nothing but coffee," declared Pam, digging into her bowl of oatmeal. "You do that and pretty soon your metabolism slows down to nothing. It's smarter to eat plenty of fiber. It makes you feel full."

"Well, if I'm going on a diet, I'll need my strength," said Lucy, as the waitress set an overflowing plate, including a cheese omelet, sausage, home fries and buttered toast, in front of her.

"It's not fair," said Rachel, who was frighteningly well informed. "Did you know that our metabolism slows down seven percent every ten years? Figure it out: We need almost twenty percent less food than we did when were twenty."

Lucy resolved to eat only half of her omelet, and to skip the fried potatoes and sausage.

"That's not the only thing that's not fair," said Sue. "I'm starting to get wattles under my chin."

Lucy's hand reflexively went to her throat. Was it as firm as it used to be?

"The skin on the back of my hands is getting so thin," complained Pam. "They get all wrinkly when I bend my wrists back."

Lucy looked down at her hands. It was true, the skin wrinkled back like the Saggy Baggy Elephant's.

"Don't you hate that?" sympathized Rachel. "But what I mind most are my disappearing lips. Where do they go? No matter how much lipstick I use, they just seem to curl under or something."

Lucy extended her tongue, tentatively. Her lips still seemed to be there.

"No, the worst thing is that when I look in the mirror, I look just like my mother," said Sue.

Lucy felt a shock of recognition.

"Frightening, isn't it? Not that I plan to follow in my mother's footsteps. She's addicted to plastic surgery. Just had her third face-lift." Rachel shuddered.

"My mother weighed two hundred and fifty pounds when she died," said Sue, who probably wouldn't hit the hundred-and-twenty-pound mark on Doc Ryder's scale. "But somehow, I still look like her."

"My mother was in denial," confessed Lucy. "She dealt with aging by just pretending she looked the way she always had." She paused, remembering. "She didn't."

"My mom smokes like a fiend and drinks like a fish," said Pam, shaking her head in amazement. "The only reason I can think that she's still alive is that her liver is pickled and her lungs are smoked like hams."

"Thanks for the image," complained Rachel, pushing her ham to the side of her plate. "I've lost my appetite, thank you."

"I guess the thing to do is to learn from their mistakes," Lucy said. "Mom neglected her looks and got all washed-out looking, but I don't have to let that happen. I'm picking up some hair color today."

The others nodded in agreement with Lucy, except for Rachel, who peered at them owl-like through her glasses.

"Don't you see what you're doing?" she asked. "You're all reacting to your mothers. Sue's mom was fat, so she doesn't eat. Pam's mom smokes, so she not only refuses to smoke, she buys all her food at the natural foods store. Lucy's mom didn't take care of her looks, so Lucy's resolved to cover her gray. We need to stop reacting . . ." She paused, collecting her thoughts. Then she spoke. "Instead of reacting we need to formulate our own personal positive paradigm for aging."

The others looked at her blankly.

"What is it with her and the big words?" asked Pam. "Can any of you guys help me out and tell me exactly what a paradigm is and where you can get one?"

They all laughed.

"It's a vision, a plan," explained Rachel.

"That sounds like an awful lot of work," observed Lucy. "Maybe we just need better role models. Someone positive." She thought for a minute. "Like Miss Tilley. How's she doing, Rachel?"

Rachel provided home care for Miss Tilley, the retired librarian, who was the oldest resident of Tinker's Cove.

"She's great," said Rachel. "Same as always. You remember taking sociology in college? About inner-directed and outer-directed people? Well, Miss Tilley is the most inner-directed person I know. She just does what she does. You know, she eats the same meals for dinner every week?" Sue counted them off on her fingers. "Roast beef on Sunday, cold beef on Monday, chicken on Tuesday, shrimp wiggle on Wednesday, shepherd's pie on Thursday, chicken à la king on Friday and baked beans on Saturday."

"Actually, I didn't take sociology," said Pam. "And if I had, I probably wouldn't remember it anyway. But I guess I'm inner-directed because we have spaghetti every Wednesday."

"It just means that she doesn't care what other people think," said Sue.

"She's just herself," agreed Lucy. "There's nobody like her."

"That's exactly right," agreed Rachel. "For example, she likes to wear a certain style of shoe. She's worn it for years. Gets two pairs every year mail order from the company. Well, they finally discontinued it. So she was looking through the catalog and these sneakers that light up when you walk caught her eye. For kids, you know. Well, she decided she had to have them. I told her they were for kids, that she'd look ridiculous. Didn't faze her in the least. She told me she doesn't have much excitement in her life anymore and she was going to get the sneakers. And she did."

Sue was incredulous. "She's wearing sneakers that twinkle when she walks?" she asked.

Rachel nodded. "She likes them so much she ordered two more pairs, in case they discontinue them."

"I'll have to stop by and visit," said Lucy. "This I've got to see."

"How old is she anyway?" asked Pam. "She must be getting up there."

"Actually, her ninetieth birthday is coming up." Rachel drank the last of her coffee. "I think she's feeling her age a little bit. Lately she's asked me to help her go through her closets and drawers to clean things out. She's also got a meeting coming up with Bob's partner, Sherman. He handles most of the older clients' wills and things."

"Very sensible," observed Pam. "After all, she can't expect to live too much longer."

"Ninety years," mused Lucy. "Think how much has changed in her lifetime. We've gone from long skirts and corsets to . . . Britney Spears!"

When they all stopped laughing, Sue held up her hand. "I've got an idea," she declared.

They all moaned.

"You're going to love this," she continued, gazing off into the distance. "Why don't we have a birthday party for Miss

Tilley? A really big party, you know, invite the whole town. Have the high school band and the chorus. She could arrive on a fire engine. After all, she is the town's oldest resident and she was the librarian for so many years, absolutely everybody knows her."

"We could do a 'This Is Your Life' show," suggested Lucy. "Bring back people from her past, successful people she encouraged."

"I don't know if she'd go for something like that," cautioned Rachel. "She's pretty reclusive; she likes her routine. She wouldn't want to miss her shrimp wiggle. Plus, she doesn't like attention."

Sue waved away that objection. "This is a woman who wears shoes that twinkle when she walks."

"I bet I can get Ted to put out a special edition of *The Pennysaver,*" offered Pam, referring to her husband and Lucy's boss, the editor and publisher of the town's weekly newspaper. "A commemorative edition chronicling her whole life. It will really be a history of the town during the twentieth century."

"That's a great idea," exclaimed Sue. "Are you all with me? May twentieth will be Miss Tilley Day!"

She raised her water glass in a toast and they all joined in. "To Miss Tilley Day!"

A brisk March wind was blowing when Lucy left the restaurant, but solar heat had warmed her car. She slid behind the steering wheel and held her face up to the sunshine as she started the engine. What a great idea, she thought. Miss Tilley Day.

As a reporter for *The Pennysaver,* she knew better than most how the pressures of modern life were negatively impacting the town. A recent proposal to build a casino had been highly controversial and divided neighbor from neighbor, the town's fishermen were struggling to maintain their traditional livelihood against increased regulation and diminishing stocks of fish, and an influx of second-home builders had driven real estate prices higher than locals could afford. The school committee was struggling to meet new, higher standards imposed by the state; the volunteer fire department was under pressure to become professional; and the town budget simply could not meet all the demands placed upon it without a hefty tax increase.

Miss Tilley Day was just what the town needed, Lucy thought. A day for year-round residents to come together before the annual onslaught of tourists and summer people and enjoy themselves. A day to celebrate their town, its history and its heritage. A day for Tinker's Cove to celebrate itself. She could hardly wait to get to work and tell Ted all about it.

But first, she had an errand. She switched on the blinker and made a right into the drugstore parking lot. Leaving the engine running, she dashed inside and went straight to the hair care aisle where she was temporarily baffled. So many choices. Scanning the rows of boxes she found a familiar brand she had seen advertised. She chose the color that seemed closest to hers and went around the corner to the skin care section. Her positive personal paradigm, she decided, did not include getting old without a fight.

Chapter Three

Another sunny day. Blustery, but that was expected in March. Bob Goodman zipped up his jacket on Tuesday morning and opened the front door, hanging on to the knob so the wind wouldn't catch it, and carefully closed it behind him.

Climbing into his brand-new compact SUV, he inhaled the new-car smell. Gosh, life was good, he thought, as he waited for the motor to warm up. He patted the steering wheel fondly. He loved this car. It was irrational, he knew, but it had been love at first sight. And fortunately, he was now in a position where he could indulge himself. Not that he was a millionaire or anything, but the law practice was doing very well. The family finances were on a sound footing, even with the hefty tuition he was paying Harvard College to educate his son, Richie.

It was worth it, of course. Richie was a smart kid and he was doing very well, showing no sign of a sophomore slump. His grades were good but, even more important to Bob and Rachel, he seemed happy and engaged in his studies. He had even undertaken an independent project, cleaning and cataloging a dusty collection of Greek vases he had discovered in the basement of his dorm. Probably collected and abandoned by some nineteenth-century rake, thought Bob, with a chuckle.

He slipped the car into gear and purred down the driveway. This car was so sexy, he thought, smiling with satisfaction. Not only did he have a sexy car, he had a sexy wife. Rachel was so beautiful, and last night she had been in a particularly affectionate mood. He remembered running his hands down her long back, her soft lips parted to receive his kiss, the way she moaned with pleasure when he lifted her hips.

Hearing an angry beep, he firmly put those thoughts out of his mind. He had better pay attention to the road. But honestly, who could blame him for loving his wife? And he did love Rachel, even more than he had when they were first married. He loved the quiet way she took care of him, making sure his clothes were clean and cooking dinner for him every night. He loved her kindness, the way she had simply started taking care of Miss Tilley after she had that awful accident. Rachel hadn't gone in and taken charge like some Lady Bountiful; instead she'd tactfully overcome the stubborn old woman's resistance by paying regular visits and bringing her freshly baked cookies or running an errand for her, as any friend might. Soon she'd become a fixture in the retired librarian's home, providing meals and chauffeuring her around town. Now, she even got paid, through the town's senior services program.

Bob glanced at the dashboard clock and saw that he was early, so he decided to run the new car through the automatic car wash. There was still a residue of salty slush on the roads and he wanted to keep the finish looking new as long as possible. The car wash was a popular place this time of year and he had to get in line.

While he waited for his turn, he thought about the party Rachel and her friends were planning for Miss Tilley. Rachel had told him about it over dinner, growing excited as she described the "This Is Your Life" program they were planning. He liked the idea; in fact, he wouldn't mind participating.

Goodness knows he felt indebted to Miss Tilley, who had taken an interest in him when he was a small boy.

He could remember searching through the stacks in the old Broadbrooks Library, looking for popular biographies and war stories. She had never criticized his choices, but had offered suggestions of her own. "Ah, you like plenty of action? Maybe you'd like to read *Ivanhoe* or *The Three Musketeers*?" Soon he'd given up the slim, watered-down books written for his age group in favor of long and complicated stories by Dickens, Scott and Dumas. He'd rapidly become a fast and discerning reader, a skill that had carried him through college and law school.

He slid the car onto the automatic track of the car wash and enjoyed the sensation of being dry and comfortable inside as the car was sprayed with water and pelted with detergent and wiped with whirling wheels of cloth. Then the light turned green and he drove out into the sunlight, flicking on the windshield wipers.

His good fortune had continued, he acknowledged, when Sherman Cobb had hired him as a summer associate while he was still in law school. Sherman hadn't limited him to title searches and running errands but had entrusted him with real cases, sending him into court to argue for bail, restraining orders and child support payments. That summer had changed him forever, convincing him that a small-town legal practice was preferable to a high-paying job with a white-shoe law firm in Boston. When Sherman had asked if he'd consider joining the practice, he'd accepted without hesitation.

He'd never regretted that choice, he thought, pulling into the driveway by the COBB AND GOODMAN LAW OFFICES sign. Oh, he probably could have made a lot more money in Boston, but here in Tinker's Cove he'd been able to make a real difference in many people's lives. He'd helped them buy houses, he'd arranged their estates, he'd gotten them out of trouble. Occasionally, he'd made sure they didn't get away with something they shouldn't. Even after more than twenty years in practice, he still looked forward to going to work every morning.

Today was no different. He couldn't wait to dig his teeth into that wrongful injury suit. But first, he resolved, he'd stop in Sherman's office and thank him for bringing him into the practice. Goodness knows, it was long overdue. Oh, sure, there'd always been an understanding between them, but he'd never actually told Sherman how grateful he was and how much he'd enjoyed working with him all these years. And lately, he'd noticed Sherman hadn't been quite himself. Probably feeling his age.

It was exactly the things you didn't say that haunted you later, thought Bob, pulling open the outside door. Once inside the vestibule, he felt a small sense of alarm when he noticed the office door was open. Not ajar, wide open. This was unusual, and he quickened his pace as he proceeded into the reception area. There, a wastebasket was tipped over in the middle of the room.

He stopped and righted it, setting it back in its place by Anne's desk. Then it occurred to him that he wasn't behaving very intelligently if the office actually had been burglarized and he stuffed his hands into his pockets so he wouldn't touch anything else. He looked around for further signs of a break-in, but nothing else seemed to be disturbed. Using a handkerchief, he pulled open the top drawer, where Anne kept the petty cash, but it hadn't been touched. The only thing that was amiss was the door to Sherman's office. It was open.

Taken by itself, that wasn't terribly unusual. What was unusual was the fact that the light was still burning. Sherman would never have left the light on.

Maybe the burglar had been after something in Sherman's office. But what? There was nothing of value there. On the rare occasions when a client had entrusted them with stock certificates or Grandma's diamond lavaliere, they had always arranged for the transfer to take place in the bank so the valuables could be stored in a safe deposit box.

Bob realized he was hedging. He didn't want to go into

Sherman's office. He was afraid of what he would find. Angry with himself, he straightened his shoulders. How bad could it be? Overturned files, papers spread everywhere, he could deal with that. If the office had been defaced in some way, well, they employed a cleaning service. There was absolutely no reason for this sense of dread that was paralyzing him. He forced himself to take a deep breath, exhaled and walked through the doorway.

Sherman was seated at his desk, with his head resting on the blotter.

Bob felt as if he had been hit with a jolt of electricity. Why had he dithered so? A heart attack, a stroke, seconds counted. He ran to the desk and reached for Sherman's wrist, hoping for a pulse, but Sherman's arm was stiff and cold. Bob's gaze went to Sherman's face. He could see his right eye, partly open, and a pool of congealed blood spread out beneath him on the blotter. Bob dropped Sherman's arm and stepped backward, fighting nausea.

Panting, he reached over Sherman's body for the phone. He had almost touched it when he saw the small handgun lying beside it. He snatched his hand back and reached instead into his pocket for his cell phone and dialed 911.

"It looks like a clear case of suicide to me."

Bob stared in disbelief at Lieutenant Horowitz, the state police detective who investigated serious crimes in the region. Over the years the two men had developed a cordial working relationship based on mutual respect. Bob had been relieved when Horowitz appeared just as Sherman's body was being taken away, convinced that the detective would not rest until he'd tracked down the murderer. Now he couldn't believe the words coming from his mouth.

Horowitz fingered the small white card he was holding and tapped it against his other hand. "He had an appointment with Doc Ryder last week. You know anything about it?"

"He never said anything. Maybe a checkup or something?"

Bob sat while Horowitz punched the keypad of his cell phone and listened numbly while Horowitz questioned the doctor.

"The doc says he had pancreatic cancer. He refused treatment. Not that it would have done much good. Nothing they could do. He only had a couple of months at the most."

Bob absorbed the information. Pancreatic cancer. He hadn't had the faintest idea.

"He never said a word to me about it."

Horowitz put a hand on his shoulder. "Lots of times they don't, you know. Once they accept that it's inevitable, they just decide to end it all without any fuss. Nice and neat. It's a way of taking control."

Bob's ears roared and he put up his hands to cover them. He didn't want to hear it, to admit it. Horowitz was wrong. He didn't know Sherman; he didn't know the first thing about it.

Horowitz stood, his hands in the pockets of his tan raincoat, and studied Bob. "Are you going to be okay?" he asked. "Do you want a ride home or something?"

"No, I'll stay," said Bob, "if that's okay with you."

Horowitz held up a hand. "It's fine. We're done here."

"You're done?"

Horowitz nodded. "Crime scene boys dusted for prints, they bagged the gun for forensics, but I don't think there're going to be any surprises."

He paused in the doorway, as if he were reluctant to leave. "I'm real sorry about this, you know," he said, his voice tired.

Bob looked at the detective's gray, world-weary face and wished he could wrap his hands around his neck and shake him. That was crazy, he knew, but this whole thing was crazy. He wanted to erase Horowitz, erase the entire morning and go back to yesterday when Sherman was still alive.

"Thanks," said Bob. "Call me when you get the medical examiner's report?"

"Sure thing."

Then Horowitz finally left and he was alone. He sat at his

desk and looked at the blank legal pad in front of him. He drew a line down the middle, intending to find a way to make sense of it all. On one side he wrote "cancer." What should he put on the other side? He didn't know. Sherman had no family. He'd always put his work first. But to someone faced with cancer, he doubted work would continue to seem very important.

Bob propped his elbows on the desk and buried his head in his hands. Why hadn't he said something when he'd first noticed Sherman seemed distracted? He'd attributed it to his age, but now he knew it was cancer. Sherman had been in pain; his suffering had driven him to commit suicide.

No more problems for him, snorted Bob, *but a whole lot of problems for me.*

Instantly, Bob felt guilty and ashamed. Sherman would never have left him in this mess unless he'd been in despair. And that was what hurt the most. He'd thought Sherman was more than his partner, he'd thought Sherman was his friend. Why hadn't he turned to him—if not for support and comfort, at least to say good-bye?

Sherman always said good-bye. He had never once left the office ahead of Bob without poking his head into Bob's doorway to let him know he was leaving.

Bob took off his eyeglasses and rubbed his eyes, remembering the Sutcliffe case. All the evidence had weighed heavily against Tim Sutcliffe, who eyewitnesses agreed had robbed the Quik Stop one steamy July night, shooting the clerk and leaving her for dead. Even Bob had figured Sutcliffe was really guilty, given his extensive record. But Sherman had plugged away, persistently questioning the eyewitnesses and proving, one by one, that they hadn't really seen the robber that well. Only the clerk had remained certain it was Sutcliffe. And then, just when the case was to go to the jury, hadn't somebody else confessed to the crime?

No, thought Bob. Sherman never gave up, even when it seemed hopeless, and he wouldn't have killed himself. Which meant somebody else had to have done it.

Suddenly, Bob remembered the overturned trash can and

the unlatched door. Of course. Someone had come in last night when Sherman was working late and shot him. Then they'd left the gun so it would look like suicide. He reached for the phone, intending to call the police, when a surge of grief hit him. He'd missed his chance to tell Sherman how much he appreciated all he'd done for him.

Chapter Four

"**Y**ou *can* fight the aging process!" promised the perky little blonde on the TV screen. Perfectly proportioned and perfectly tanned, she bared her perfect white teeth in a perfect smile and nodded, making her perfectly bleached blond curls bounce.

"Is she for real?" asked Sara. Lucy's thirteen-year-old daughter was lounging on the sofa with an open bag of M&Ms on her stomach.

Zoe, who was in second grade, was perched in front of the family computer, playing an action game. Lucy's older kids, Toby and Elizabeth, were away at college.

"I'm not looking for a relationship here," panted Lucy, straining to follow a complicated combination of steps. "I just want to lose ten pounds."

Lucy was dressed in an old pair of leggings, so old the seams were splitting, and one of Bill's T-shirts. On the TV screen, Debbie was dressed in an orange bikini, only a shade brighter than her orange skin.

"You *can* lose those last ten pounds!" exhorted Video Debbie, making Lucy wonder if the TV was really a two-way communication device. Maybe Debbie could read her mind. "But losing weight is only one reason to exercise. Exercise is good for you! It helps fight heart disease, it keeps you limber, and it acts as a mental filter. Exercise makes you happy!"

"Are you happy, Mom?" asked Sara, popping an M&M into her mouth.

"I'm trying," panted Lucy, tripping over her feet as she attempted to execute a grapevine step.

"Don't stop!" cautioned Debbie. "I'll be right back for your Tummy Tune-up!"

Lucy reached for her water bottle, and attempted to march in place while she tilted back her head and drank. Water spilled down her chin.

"Way to go, Mom," observed Sara.

"Listen, this is harder than you think. Especially when you've worked all day and you're tired." Lucy paused. "How does she do it? How does she talk? I can hardly breathe."

"She's in shape," said Sara. "You're not."

"Thanks for the encouragement," said Lucy, painfully lowering herself to the floor for tummy crunches.

"This is our toning segment," said Debbie, who had perched her round little bottom on an exercise mat that was color-coordinated to complement her bikini. "Our goal here is to condition our muscles, while keeping our heart rate up. Let's begin. Now I want you to lower yourself vertebra by vertebra—but not all the way! Hold it, hold it; now bring yourself back up. Feel that?" Debbie pointed to her flat tummy with a perfectly manicured finger. "I certainly can!"

"Uhhh," said Lucy, collapsing onto the floor. A sympathetic shriek rose from the computer.

Debbie was now bringing her knees to her chin and then extending her legs, toes pointed. It looked easy. "You want your legs to float, to be weightless," she advised.

Lucy raised her head, drew her knees in and then extended them. A horrible howl escaped her lips as her legs thunked to the floor.

"Are you okay, Mom?" Zoe turned her head in concern.

"I think I pulled something," gasped Lucy, clutching her abdomen and moaning.

On the screen, Debbie was bicycling her legs. "Don't stop! It's worth it, I promise you."

Lucy rolled onto her side, curled in a fetal position.

"Now she's doing yoga," said Sara, helpfully informative.

On the screen, Debbie had twisted her legs into a lotus position.

"I know I can't do that."

"You can do it," said Debbie. "Start by sitting with your legs crossed and with time, you'll be able to do more."

Lucy sat Indian-style, rubbing her tummy.

"Now, let's stand up and try Warrior."

Debbie unfolded herself and rose effortlessly, bending her front knee and extending her back leg in a lunge. By holding on to the coffee table, Lucy was able to struggle to her feet, but Warrior position proved harder than it looked and she lost her balance and rolled back onto the floor.

"It's a good thing we got that extra-thick pad for the new carpet," she said, crawling over to the couch. "I could've hurt myself." She sat on the floor, resting her back against the sofa. "I hope I won't have sore muscles tomorrow."

"You know what the best part of the workout is?" inquired Debbie.

"The end," muttered Lucy, finding herself speaking in unison with the perky blonde on the TV. This was spooky.

"Because you've done it! You've accomplished something that's good for you!"

"I think I deserve a reward," said Lucy, reaching for the M&Ms and checking the nutrition information label. "Three hundred calories per two ounces. That's not very many, is it?"

Sara shrugged.

Lucy reached for the remote and pushed the rewind button. "I bet I burned a ton of calories in that workout. I'm sweating, you know."

"Mom, you don't have to share everything."

Lucy fanned herself with one hand and reached for more M&Ms with the other. "How many calories do you think I burned? Five hundred? A thousand?"

"Probably a million, Mom. Listen, I want to ask you something."

Lucy chewed happily. "Shoot."

"You know how my birthday's coming up?"

"Oh, that's right. You'll be thirteen! A teenager!"

"No, Mom. I am thirteen. I'm going to be fourteen."

Lucy helped herself to another handful of candy. "Are you sure?"

Sara rolled her eyes. "I know my own birthday, Mom. And I was thinking that I'd like to have a sleep-over and invite some of my friends."

"That would be nice," said Lucy. "How about having a Night of Beauty party? You could do each other's hair and nails, stuff like that."

"Cute idea, Mom," said Sara, sarcastically. "But I was thinking of something a little different. I want to invite some of my boy friends."

Lucy's eyes widened in shock. "A coed sleep-over?"

"Yeah, Mom. Everybody's doing it."

"They are? How come I haven't heard, if everyone's doing it?"

"'Cause everybody's doing it," said Sara, loftily. "It's not like something you need to talk about, you know. It's like brushing your teeth. You don't talk about it because everybody does it."

The phone rang and Zoe snatched the receiver. "It's for you, Mom."

"I don't think so," said Lucy, shaking her head and getting up slowly. If the way she felt now was any indication, she was going to be very sore tomorrow.

It was Rachel and she sounded upset.

"What's the matter?" asked Lucy.

"Something terrible has happened. Bob's partner is dead."

"Sherman Cobb?" Lucy pictured him: a trim gentleman with a distinguished touch of silver at his temples. "He wasn't very old, was he? What did he die of?"

"Not very old. In his sixties, I think, but he didn't die of natural causes." Rachel hesitated. "He was shot."

"Shot?" Lucy couldn't believe it. People didn't shoot each other in Tinker's Cove. In fact, most people didn't even bother to lock their doors.

"The police think it was suicide, but Bob and I don't think so."

Lucy hadn't thought of suicide, but now that it had been mentioned it seemed a lot more likely than murder. "Why not?"

"A lot of reasons. That's why I'm calling. Bob and I were hoping you could maybe investigate a little bit. Since the police won't."

Lucy hesitated. She'd been warned more than once to keep her nose out of police business. And her husband, Bill, didn't much like her penchant for investigative reporting, either.

"I don't know," she demurred.

"Please. You have no idea how much this would mean to Bob. Could you just stop by his office tomorrow and hear him out? Then, if you don't think there's anything to investigate, well, that'll be it."

That didn't sound unreasonable to Lucy. "Okay. I was planning to interview Miss Tilley, but I guess that can wait."

"Thanks, Lucy. You're a pal."

Lucy replaced the phone slowly, absorbing the news of Sherman's sudden death. He would be missed, she thought, as she wandered back into the family room to turn off the TV. Sara, however, was watching MTV.

"Have you done your homework?" asked Lucy. It was a reflex, really. She was really thinking about Sherman, trying to reconcile his quiet life in Tinker's Cove with violent death. The police were probably right; it was probably suicide.

"Mom, what about that birthday party? Can I have it?"

Lucy was lost in thought. "Of course," she said, talking to herself, "the police have been wrong before."

Sara didn't wait to hear the rest but jumped to her feet and gave Lucy a quick hug.

"I wonder what that was all about," said Lucy, still talking to herself as she pushed the eject button and removed the videocassette from the machine. She glanced at the sleeve as she slid the cassette inside. "Burns calories—up to 300 every workout!" was emblazoned on the front, beneath the color photo of Debbie's smiling face.

That must be wrong, she thought. She'd probably eaten more than three hundred calories worth of M&Ms and she hadn't even done all of the workout. While Debbie had been bending and stretching and bouncing, she'd been lying on the floor, moaning. And moaning, she guessed, didn't really use up very many calories.

She lifted the T-shirt and looked down at her round, bulging tummy. It was going to be a lot harder than she thought to get rid of the darned thing. And now that she'd agreed to look into Sherman's death, when was she going to find time to exercise?

Chapter Five

Bob's secretary, Anne Shaw, greeted Lucy warmly when she arrived the next morning, but her face was drawn and her eyes were puffy, as if she had been crying.

"Hi, Lucy. I'm so glad you're here. Bob's expecting you. You can go right in."

"I'm awfully sorry for your loss," said Lucy. "I know it's hard to lose someone you work with."

"Sherman was more than my boss," said Anne, reaching for a tissue. "I worked for him for almost thirty years, you know. After all that time he was my friend, too."

Anne buried her face in the tissue, relieving Lucy of the need to reply. She always wished she could get past the platitudes when faced with grief, but she could never think of anything comforting to say that didn't sound false and hollow. Sometimes she thought there was no real comfort to be offered; the pain just had to wear itself out.

She gave Anne a sympathetic nod and limped painfully toward Bob's office. As she'd expected, her muscles were protesting yesterday's workout. She knocked softly on the open door.

"Lucy!" exclaimed Bob, jumping to his feet. "Thanks so much for coming."

"Of course I'd come," she said, taking Bob's hand. "I'm so sorry about your partner. It must be very difficult for you."

"Difficult doesn't describe it," said Bob, who suddenly seemed exhausted after greeting her so energetically. He subsided into his chair, like a leaking balloon, and offered her a seat with a wave of his hand. "I really don't know where to begin."

"At the beginning," said Lucy, seating herself carefully and giving him an encouraging smile. "Just tell me what happened."

Bob ran his hand through his thinning brown hair and took a deep breath.

"I knew something was wrong as soon as I got here yesterday morning—Tuesday." He was staring at the calendar on his desk. "I can't believe it was just yesterday," he finally said. "It seems like eons ago."

Lucy nodded sympathetically. "You said something was wrong," she prompted him.

"Right," he said, sitting up a bit straighter in an attempt to pull himself together. "The door wasn't locked and the wastebasket was tipped over."

"Whoa," said Lucy. "You need to go back a bit. Why did you think the door should be locked? Wasn't Sherman's car here?"

"No," said Bob. "He lived just a few blocks from here. He usually walked. The parking area was empty."

"And you're usually the first one to arrive in the morning?"

Lucy was appalled when this seemingly innocent question caused Bob to swallow hard and blink back tears. Questioning him was going to be a more delicate task than she had expected.

"Only recently," Bob finally said. "Sherman was always first, for years and years. Then a few weeks ago he said that since he was the senior partner, he thought he'd come in a little later. I never thought anything of it, but now that I look back, it was probably the beginning of his illness." Bob stared out the window at a leafless, gray tree. "I should have known something was wrong. Doc Ryder says he had pancreatic cancer. He only had a few months, maybe not even that."

"How could you have known?" Lucy said, speaking softly. "It seems logical enough for a man who's getting close to retirement to cut back a little bit."

"Not if you knew Sherman," insisted Bob. "His work was his life. He didn't have any family, you know. He didn't go on vacations. His only interest was his Civil War reenactment group."

"Those people who dress up in uniforms and camp out pretending they're soldiers?"

"Yeah." Bob nodded, managing a small smile. "Sherman loved it. I think he was a colonel or something. It's a big deal, you know. More than sitting around the campfire. Everything has to be authentic. He'd spend months tracking down stuff like antique buttons and wool socks. They had to be one hundred percent wool, no synthetics allowed. Even the food had to be exactly right. Beef jerky and coffee and biscuits. He loved nothing better than spending a weekend camping out in the rain somewhere, marching through mud and fighting the battle of Gettysburg all over again."

Lucy chuckled, relieved that Bob was temporarily distracted from his grief. "It's hard to believe that a man who enjoyed that sort of thing would commit suicide," she said. "He seems like the kind of guy who wouldn't give up without a fight."

"Exactly," agreed Bob. "His favorite expression was 'Hold the fort!' Even sang it to a little tune, some Civil War song. He used to say it led the hit parade in 1864."

"That's all very well and good," she said firmly, "but I don't think he was killed by a Confederate sharpshooter."

"Oh, I don't know," said Bob. "That theory makes about as much sense as anything else I can come up with. I just can't think of any reason for somebody to kill him."

"No controversial cases, no nasty divorces?"

Bob shook his head. "This is a small-town law practice.

We do wills and real estate closings. Occasionally we handle a divorce or a criminal matter, but nothing like that's going on right now. I had the same thought myself, and I looked through the current files on his desk. It was all pretty straightforward stuff: a couple of planning board variances and a historical commission application, a partnership agreement, a few appeals . . ."

The phone rang and he reached for it, giving Lucy an apologetic half smile.

"Yes, Mrs. Delaporte," he said, speaking into the receiver. "It's true that Sherman has passed away." He nodded. "Yes, yes, indeed. It's a very great loss for all of us. But I can assure you that your affairs are in order and that I'm here to help you if the need arises."

Lucy could hear little squawks coming from the phone and Bob rolled his eyes.

"No, Mrs. Delaporte, I can assure you I'm fully qualified. I've been practicing for over twenty years now." He shook his head. "No, I don't have any plans to bring in a new partner."

He fell silent and Lucy's attention drifted to the diplomas on the wall, the Currier & Ives prints, the Waverly plaid curtains.

"Thank you for calling, Mrs. Delaporte. Have a nice day, now. Good-bye."

Bob replaced the receiver and turned his attention to Lucy.

"I'm afraid a lot of our older clients are going to be pretty upset—they consider me the junior partner." His face went pale and he looked down at his blotter, chewing on his lip. "Not anymore," he whispered. Then, adopting a brisk manner, he stood up. "Do you want to take a look at Sherman's office?"

"Sure. If I can."

"Why couldn't you?"

"Well, usually there's crime scene tape and it's sealed off until the police have gathered all the evidence . . ."

"Not this time. The police think it's an open-and-shut case of suicide."

"Well, that may not be so bad after all," said Lucy, wincing as she got to her feet and followed him into the adjoining office. "I won't have to worry about stepping on anybody's toes or disrupting an investigation."

"Well, here it is," said Bob, gesturing at the empty room.

Lucy glanced around. A typical office. Pictures on the wall, bookcases filled with law books, new commercial-grade carpeting in a beige Berber, a credenza holding stacks of manila folders. She took a quick breath, bracing herself to examine the substantial desk that stood in the middle of the room, but when she looked closer she saw no trace of violence. Not even a bloodstain.

"There's no—" she began.

"The police did take the blotter," said Bob, anticipating her question. "There was very little blood," he added, declining to mention that the police had told him the small-caliber bullet had bounced around inside Sherman's skull, destroying his brain.

"He was sitting here with his head on the desk?" asked Lucy. "Where was the gun? In his hand?"

"By his hand. Like it had fallen out of his hand."

"No note?"

"No. There was one of Doc Ryder's appointment cards stuck in the side of the blotter. That was all."

Lucy furrowed her brow.

"Don't you think he would have written a note?"

Bob sat down in a chair and held out his hands. "I can't figure it out. I don't believe he would have left all his business unfinished like this. He was an excellent lawyer. He did his best to represent his clients. These were long-term relationships, people he had known for years and years. And then there's me and Anne. I wouldn't have expected him to cry on my shoulder, but I think he would have told me he was ill." Bob looked at her bleakly. "If he did kill himself like this, he must have been desperate, and that's what really bothers me most. That after all these years he didn't turn to me for support."

This was too much for Lucy, who reached for a tissue herself. After she had blown her nose and dabbed her eyes, she reached for Bob's hand.

"I'll do what I can," she said. "We'll get to the bottom of this."

"Thanks, Lucy," said Bob. "You have no idea how much this means to me. If there's anything I can do to help, just ask. Anything you need, it's yours."

She smiled. "Right now, I think I'll just look around here, if that's okay with you."

"Sure," said Bob, getting to his feet. "I'll leave you to it."

Left alone in the office, Lucy perched on Cobb's chair and opened the drawers, one by one. There were no hidden bottles of liquor, no dirty magazines or stashes of drugs. Just pens and pencils, pads of legal-sized yellow paper, Post-it notes in all sizes and colors, paper clips, a stapler, ink cartridges for a fountain pen, an instant camera and some packs of film, floppy disks for his computer, a ruler, scissors. Lucy fingered an ornate silver letter opener carefully; it was sharp enough to be a murder weapon. But it wasn't, she reminded herself. Cobb had been shot.

Shutting the last drawer, Lucy stood up and walked around the office, studying the decorations on the wall. There were neatly labeled photographs of various battle reenactments, a shadow box contained lead bullets and minnie balls collected at Gettysburg battlefield, and other frames held medals and insignia. It was all interesting in its way, but didn't seem to offer any motive for murder.

Pausing at the credenza, she began looking through the files of the cases he'd been working on before his death. Stapled to the front of each folder was a form listing dates for filings, motions, pretrial conferences and even trials. A personal injury suit was scheduled for the end of the week, she saw.

Interested, she opened the file and began to read. Cobb had been retained by the defendant, who was accused of causing an automobile accident that disabled a local fisherman. It looked as if Cobb was planning a spirited defense of his client.

Lucy closed the file and picked up another; this required a filing by the end of the week. Glancing through the files, Lucy began to share Bob's conviction that Cobb would not have left so many people in the lurch, not least of all his partner. Bob was going to have a heck of a lot of work to do in addition to his own caseload.

Closing the office door, Lucy went out to the reception area.

"You know Bob has asked me to investigate Mr. Cobb's death," she began.

Anne, a trim woman of sixty, nodded her head. Her eyes were puffy, but she had stopped crying.

"Would you mind if I asked you a few questions?"

"Not at all. I'd like to help, but I don't see how I can."

"Well, I was looking around in Mr. Cobb's office and it seemed to me he had a lot of work on his plate right now. Is that so?"

"Yes," agreed Anne. "Circuit court goes into session next week, you know."

"I don't know. What do you mean?"

"Well, we have district court for misdemeanors, and superior court is for felonies and civil matters. Those are in session year-round. But say you want to appeal a case, take it to the next higher level, you have to wait for the circuit court to go into session. It happens twice a year."

"Why only twice a year?"

"Because we don't have enough population in our district to need an appeals court of our own. We share it, sort of, with five other counties. Our months are April and October."

"Did Mr. Cobb have any cases for this session?"

"He had several." Anne leaned closer to Lucy and lowered her voice. "Between you and me, this has left Bob in a terrible position. I don't know how he's going to manage to get everything done. Just getting the postponements and delays is going to be a nightmare. I mean the court clerks are being very nice and understanding, but there's so much paper-work involved. . . ." She threw her hands up in the air. "It isn't like changing a dentist's appointment, you know. There's a lot more to it."

"I can imagine," said Lucy. "Tell me, did Mr. Cobb seem agitated or different in any way when you saw him last?"

Tears sparkled in Anne's eyes. "Not a bit. He was joking with me on Friday, telling me to do my finger exercises over the weekend because we had such a busy week ahead." She paused. "If anything, you know, I'd say he was looking for-ward to it. He loved litigation and he had some cases he was really eager to argue."

"Thanks," said Lucy. "You've been a big help." She started to leave, then remembered she needed to speak to Bob. Again, she tapped on his door before poking her head into his office.

"Bob? I'm done here, but I'd like to look at Sherman's house. Is that okay?"

"Good idea," said Bob, opening his drawer. "I've got a set of his keys here, but you know, I bet the house isn't locked. It's on Oak Street, number 202."

"Thanks," said Lucy, taking the keys.

"I'm the one who should thank you," said Bob. "I really appreciate what you're doing."

The depth of feeling in his voice made Lucy uncomfort-able.

"I don't know what Rachel told you, but I'm not a profes-sional investigator," she said. "There's no guarantee that I'll be able to figure out what happened."

"I know, I know," said Bob. His eyes were fixed on hers.

He reminded her of her dog, Kudo, when he wanted a doggie biscuit. She looked away, out the window at the milky March sky.

"I just don't want you to get your hopes up," she said, meeting his eyes. "You've got to face the fact that you may never know what happened."

He nodded.

Lucy sighed. "And if he was murdered, well, you've got

to realize that most murder victims are killed by someone they know."

Bob swallowed hard. "By someone I know?"

"Most likely," said Lucy. "Do you still want me to go ahead?"

Bob looked her straight in the eye. "Absolutely," he said.

"Okay," agreed Lucy, but as she limped down the steps to the parking area she wished she had a little more to go on than a gut feeling that Sherman Cobb hadn't committed suicide.

Chapter Six

Driving down Main Street with the keys to Cobb's house tucked in her purse, Lucy found herself feeling extremely frustrated. She was already hooked on this investigation and desperately wanted to take a look at the house, but she knew she couldn't do it today. She was already running late—on Wednesday, deadline day—and would have plenty to explain to Ted.

When she got to *The Pennysaver* office, however, there was no sign of her boss. Only Phyllis, the receptionist.

"About time you got here," observed Phyllis, poking a pencil into her bun and peering over her rhinestone-trimmed half glasses. "Did you pull a muscle or something? His nibs is having a fit."

"I worked out with a videotape yesterday," said Lucy, grimacing as she hung her jacket on the coatrack. "Where is he, anyway?"

"Over at the police station, trying to get something on this suicide." She clucked her tongue. "Poor man. What a shame."

Her sad tone piqued Lucy's curiosity.

"Did you know Sherman Cobb?"

"Oh, yes. I even dated him," said Phyllis, lowering her

head and smoothing her beaded turquoise cardigan over her ample bust.

"You did? When?"

"Quite some time ago. Let me think. I guess back in the eighties sometime."

"Wasn't he quite a bit older than you?"

"Well, I wasn't getting any younger. I remember thinking that a twenty-year difference wasn't all that much. I mean we were both grown-ups." She sighed. "He was a lovely man."

Lucy did a quick calculation. She figured Phyllis was now in her mid-fifties, which would put her in her thirties when she dated Cobb and he would have been in his forties, maybe his early fifties. Not unreasonable.

"Was it serious?" Lucy asked.

"I had high hopes in the beginning," replied Phyllis, "but it didn't work out. It was like my mother said, I had him hooked but I couldn't get him in the boat."

"Afraid of commitment?"

"I don't think so," said Phyllis, shaking her head and making her earrings jangle. "I finally decided he was simply a confirmed bachelor. He had a well-ordered life and I don't think he wanted to risk any changes."

"Do you think he really killed himself?"

"I don't know, but I can tell you this: I don't think he would have wanted to become dependent upon anybody else."

Lucy was just coming out of the bathroom, where she'd downed a couple of aspirins, when the bell on the door jangled and Ted strode into the office looking like a haunted man. A man haunted by a rapidly approaching deadline.

"Well, nice to see you decided to drop in," he said sarcastically, tossing his jacket at the coatrack and missing. He left it lying on the floor and went straight to the old rolltop desk he'd inherited from his grandfather.

Lucy's hackles rose. "I was working on a story."

"And what story was that? Something I assigned?"

"Uh, no," confessed Lucy. "I was talking to Bob Goodman. He wants me to investigate Sherman Cobb's death. He doesn't believe he killed himself."

"Yeah, well, that's not what I'm hearing from the cops. So unless there are some new developments, I don't want you working on this on my time. I need you too much for other things," he said, handing her a stack of faxes.

"And here's today's mail," said Phyllis, passing over a pile of press releases.

"Oh, goody," said Lucy, feigning enthusiasm. "Breaking news: The VFW is having a roast beef dinner on Saturday. Just like the one they had last Saturday and the one they'll have next Saturday."

"A complete roast beef dinner?" asked Phyllis, feigning excitement. "With mashed potatoes and gravy, vegetable, salad, dinner roll, dessert and choice of beverage? Six dollars for adults and four dollars for kids ages five to twelve?"

"How did you know?" asked Lucy, her eyes wide in fake amazement. "ESP?"

"Yeah, that must be it. ESP," said Phyllis, turning to answer the phone.

At her desk, Lucy thumbed through the pile of press releases and sighed.

Finally headed for home later that afternoon with a car full of groceries, Lucy detoured down Oak Street past Cobb's house. Number 202 was a white clapboard bungalow with dark green shutters and a neatly clipped forsythia bush that was just coming into bloom. The clipped forsythia intrigued her; what sort of person trims a forsythia bush? Maybe Phyllis was right and Cobb was some sort of control freak.

She always let hers grow freely, setting out exuberant shoots of blossoms that nodded in the spring breezes. On the other hand, lots of people did trim their forsythia bushes into neat balls, or squared them off at the top. If only she could take a peek inside the house, she thought, slowing the car.

A glance at the dashboard clock told her she didn't have time. She had to get home and cook supper for the family. And tonight, following Video Debbie's advice, she had splurged on a beautiful piece of salmon. Low-calorie salmon chock-full of healthy omega acids that were good for the heart. She was going to serve it with a huge salad, small baked potatoes and lovely fresh asparagus. It was a meal that would make a dietician smile. It was a meal that would fuel the body without adding unwanted fat; it was a meal fit for a gourmet. A fit gourmet.

"What is that smell?" demanded Sara, as Lucy unwrapped the groceries.

"Fresh salmon," said Lucy, smacking her lips.

"It smells like fish," complained Sara.

"It is fish."

"I'm not gonna eat fish. Especially not pink fish."

"Try it, you'll like it," said Lucy, who was listening for the crunch of tires on gravel that indicated Bill was home. "Do me a favor and set the table?"

"Zoe!" yelled Sara. "Mom wants you to set the table."

Lucy gave Sara a look. "You can help her, and make the salad, too."

Sara started to protest but, hearing her father's quick honk announcing he was home, reconsidered and carried a stack of plates into the dining room.

"Honey, I'm home," chorused Bill, imitating Desi Arnaz.

Lucy couldn't help smiling. With his full beard, plaid flannel shirt and work boots, he didn't look much like the dapper Desi. She raised her cheek for a kiss.

"What's for dinner?" he asked.

"Have I got a treat for you: salmon, fresh asparagus, baked potatoes and salad."

Bill wrinkled up his nose. "Salmon?"

"You'll love it."

"If you say so," he said, dropping his lunch box on the counter and reaching into the refrigerator for a beer.

Then he took his usual place at the round, golden oak table

in the kitchen, pushing aside Lucy's purse to make room for his elbow. As he shoved it over, the keys to Cobb's house fell out of the outside pocket.

"How was your day?" he asked, picking up the unfamiliar keys and fingering them.

"Busy," said Lucy, as she washed the asparagus and began trimming off the ends. "How was yours?"

"Usual," he said, taking a long pull on the cold beer. "What are these keys for?"

"Sherman Cobb's house," said Lucy. "Bob and Rachel don't believe it was suicide and asked me to poke around a little bit."

Bill sighed in frustration. "What do you want to go and do that for? Haven't we been through this a million times? Why do you have to keep sticking your nose into police business, huh?"

Lucy felt her back stiffen. "Because my friends asked me to, that's why."

Bill set his can down with a thunk. "And you have to do everything that anybody asks? You can't ever say no?"

"Apparently not." Lucy's temper flared as she set the asparagus pot on the stove. He had a valid point and she knew it. She also knew she had something else to confess. "I'm working on learning how to say no but I haven't quite got there yet." She took a deep breath. "I told Sara she could have a sleep-over for her birthday party. Is that okay with you?"

"Sure." Unwilling to continue the fight, Bill retreated. "It would have been nice if you'd checked with me first, but Sara deserves a nice party." He chuckled, recalling her last sleep-over. "Those girls are so funny. Remember how they giggled and squealed over Brad Pitt? I just hope they don't keep us up all night."

"It's not just girls this time," said Lucy, shoving the salmon pan under the broiler. "She's invited some boys."

"Boys? What do they want boys for? They like to fiddle with their hair and try makeup and polish their nails. One year they polished my nails, remember?"

"Sara says all the kids are doing it."

"Well, they're not doing it here," said Bill, flatly.

"Why not?" shrieked Sara, storming into the kitchen through the swinging door. She'd obviously been listening on the other side. "Mom said I could, didn't you, Mom?"

"I did," admitted Lucy. "But you have to admit you got me when I was distracted. You kind of took advantage of me."

"You said I could!" repeated Sara, in the triumphant tone of a prosecuting lawyer who has caught the defendant in a contradiction.

Lucy's eyes met Bill's. *Help me out here,* she silently telegraphed him.

"Dad! Mom said I could and that means I can, right? I've already told all my friends and they all want to come. I can't go back now and say that my parents won't let me. I'll look like a jerk."

"It doesn't sound like a good idea to me," began Bill in his reasonable voice.

"Why not?" demanded Sara, ripping open a bag of salad and dumping it into a bowl. "What's the big deal? Toby's my brother and he lives here when he's not at college. And his dorm is coed, and so is Elizabeth's. And all my friends have brothers and sisters. I mean, people don't divide up their families. Boys in one house, girls in another." Sara paused for breath. "I mean, what is with you people? It's a coed world, you know."

Bill cleared his throat and Lucy glanced at him. He looked like a drowning man.

"Sara, I don't think you should talk to your father in that tone of voice," said Lucy, throwing him a lifeline.

"I'm responsible for what happens in my house," said Bill, sitting up a little taller. "I don't think mixing boys and girls together all night is a good idea."

"You don't trust me," wailed Sara.

"Of course I trust you," said Bill.

Lucy knew he was done for. He'd let the lifeline slip from his fingers and it had floated out of reach.

"Then I can have boys at the sleep-over?"

"I guess so," said Bill, surrendering to his fate.

"Dinner's ready," said Lucy, lifting the salmon onto a platter.

It had been a surprisingly pleasant dinner, thought Lucy, as she cleared the dirty dishes. They'd gotten the controversial stuff out of the way before sitting down at the table. And Zoe had been so cute, talking about how the pet mice had escaped their cage and run around her second-grade classroom. Amazingly enough, the heart-healthy, low-calorie salmon had disappeared without any complaints. It was an unfamiliar food and even Lucy had to admit she preferred flounder or cod, but little Zoe had finished her piece without protest.

Lucy had stacked the plates and was reaching for the crumpled paper napkins when she discovered the truth. Both girls had hidden their portions of fish in their napkins . . . and so had Bill. Ten dollars' worth of fish was going to the dog. A very heart-healthy dog.

She was loading the dishwasher when the phone rang. It was Sue.

"Just wanted to make sure you're coming to breakfast tomorrow," she began. "I've got some exciting news about Miss Tilley Day."

"Really? What?"

"No fair," said Sue, in a teasing voice. "You'll just have to wait like everyone else. So be there."

"I wouldn't miss it for the world," said Lucy.

"How's the show coming?" asked Sue.

Lucy swallowed hard. "Not well," she admitted.

"Lucy! You haven't forgotten, have you?"

"No, I didn't forget. I was going to interview Miss T this morning, but I had to go see Bob Goodman instead. He wants me to investigate his partner's death."

"Do you have time for that? On top of the party and all?" inquired Sue. "Maybe you'd better leave this one to the police. After all, we don't have that much time left. Only five weeks."

"I know. I'll get right on it. First thing tomorrow. After breakfast."

"See you then," trilled Sue.

For a fleeting second Lucy envied Sue her leisurely lifestyle. Wouldn't it be wonderful, she thought, to have oceans of time? Kudo nudged her knee, reminding her it was time for him to go outside. She reached down and scratched him behind the ears, then opened the door for him. Upstairs, she heard the girls squabbling. In the TV room, she heard the fanfare that announced Bill had switched on the evening news. Her life wasn't perfect, she decided as she went to join him, but she wouldn't have it any other way.

"I guess we won't be having salmon again," she said, taking her usual seat on the couch. "I gave the leftovers to the dog and he's in danger of exploding."

"Better him than me," said Bill, who was stretched out in a recliner with the newspaper.

"You know, I'm sorry about throwing the sleep-over at you like that. I didn't mean to say it was okay without talking to you first. I got distracted and—"

"That's what she does," interrupted Bill. "It's divide and conquer."

"And she never gives up until she gets what she wants."

"She's really getting to be a handful," observed Bill. "I blame you. If you don't watch it, that girl's going to be out of control."

Lucy knew he wasn't really serious, but she threw the ball right back at him anyway. "Me? What about you? Girls need a strong father."

"I couldn't agree with you more," said Bill. "But I'm getting too old for the job. I can't keep up with her."

Lucy looked at him, taking in his work-roughened hands and his grizzled beard. It used to be a rich, chestnut brown.

"All joking aside, it's true that we're getting older. Both of us. Sometimes I worry about you, working all alone. What if you fell or something? Not to mention those power tools. If you had an accident, how would you get help? Don't you think maybe it's time to hire a helper?"

She got up, intending to get the remote, but he grabbed her by the waist as she passed and pulled her into his lap.

"Don't you worry. I'm not over the hill yet."

"Ow!" shrieked Lucy. "That hurts. I've got sore muscles from my age-defying workout."

"My back's a little stiff sometimes, I admit it," continued Bill, nuzzling her neck. "But everything else works just fine."

"I know." Lucy smiled naughtily. "Later for you, mister, but please, be gentle."

Chapter Seven

The girls met for breakfast as usual on Thursday, but there weren't very many laughs. Pam's allergies were flaring up and she was miserable with a runny nose and red, puffy eyes. "It's these spring flowers," she explained, as she accepted a tissue from Sue. "I'm going to stop at the drugstore first thing and get something."

"That's terrible," sympathized Rachel, who was taking a dark view of things since Sherman's death. "We wait all winter for the flowers, and when they finally bloom you can't enjoy them. It's not fair."

Lucy was having a hard time following the conversation because her mind kept drifting to the various projects she'd taken on: Sara's birthday sleep-over, the investigation, her job at the paper and the interview with Miss Tilley. Still determined to lose weight and get in shape, she'd ordered a low-calorie bowl of cereal with skim milk and she couldn't help feeling deprived as she saw other customers eating heaping platters of eggs and pancakes. She practically growled when Sue asked if she was still planning on interviewing Miss Tilley after breakfast.

"It's on the top of my list," Lucy informed her.

"Ouch!" exclaimed Sue. "You didn't have to bite my head off."

She was obviously determined not to let the general gloom affect her good spirits.

"Now, listen up," she said, holding up a manicured finger for emphasis. "I have big news."

"Well, are you going to tell us?" challenged Lucy, busy scraping up the last soggy flakes of cereal with her spoon.

"This is big, this is so big," replied Sue, hugging her hands to her chest. "I need a fanfare or something."

"Bupababupa ba ba!" sputtered Pam, setting off a coughing fit.

"Just tell us," said Rachel, "before Pam has to be hospitalized."

"Okay, okay. Here it is: Norah is going to put the birthday party on her show!"

Three jaws dropped open as the women considered this news. They all knew Norah Hemmings, the "queen of daytime TV," whose afternoon talk show was at the top of the ratings, because she had a summer home in Tinker's Cove. In fact, Sue's daughter Sidra worked on the show and had recently been promoted to a full producer from her previous job as an assistant producer.

"How is this going to happen?" asked Rachel. "Do we have to get Miss T to New York?"

"It won't be a surprise if we do that," moaned Pam. "Besides, I've got the high school band all signed up. How are we going to get them to New York?"

"Miss T on TV?" Lucy's mind boggled at the very idea.

"This is not the reaction I was expecting," harrumphed Sue. "I thought you'd all be excited."

"It is exciting," said Pam. "But I thought this was going to be a homegrown, hometown kind of celebration."

Lucy and Rachel nodded in agreement.

"It still is," said Sue. "Norah is going to come to us. They're going to videotape Miss T and air it as a segment on her show. It will be part of a larger theme. Vital old women or something like that. All the details haven't been worked out yet." She paused and looked at Lucy. "That's where you come in."

"Me?" Lucy's voice was high and squeaky.

"Yes!" Sue produced a sheet of paper from her purse. "Sidra faxed this to me yesterday. She needs some information so they can decide how to do the segment and she needs the answers to these questions. I thought you could sort of mix them in with your interview."

Lucy reluctantly took the fax. She was beginning to think the machine was an invention of the devil, at least in Sue's hands. As she expected, the list was long and the questions were complex, focusing on how women's roles had changed through the years.

"I'll do what I can, but—" she began.

"I knew I could count on you!" exclaimed Sue, cutting off her objections. "Now, moving right along, let's talk about refreshments. Joe Marzetti's promised us a hundred dollars' worth of groceries at the IGA—whatever we want, soda or chips or paper goods—but that's not going to be nearly enough if the whole town turns out and I'm pretty sure they will. Any ideas?"

Lucy found her mind was wandering again, drifting back to Sherman Cobb, and she was relieved when Rachel looked at her watch and pushed her chair away from the table.

"Sorry, guys, but I've got to get going. Miss T will be wondering where I am."

"I'll go with you," said Lucy, impatient to get moving. "I've got a lot of things to do today."

Since it was only a few blocks to Miss Tilley's house, Lucy decided to follow Video Debbie's advice and walked, hoping the mild exercise would stretch out and relieve her still achy muscles. Rachel drove because she would need the car if Miss Tilley asked her to run some errands, so she was already there when Lucy came up the path to the neat Cape-style house built in 1799.

Miss Tilley was sitting in the Boston rocker she favored,

but her cheeks had lost their usual rosy pink color and she seemed frailer than ever. Lucy suspected she was taking the news of Sherman's death rather hard.

"Lucy, isn't it terrible about Sherman?" she asked, as Lucy took her trembling hand and gave her a peck on the cheek.

As soon as Lucy released her blue-veined and age-spotted hand, Miss Tilley clasped it with the other and began kneading her swollen knuckles.

Lucy nodded as she took the wing chair on the other side of the fireplace. Her glance wandered to the floor and she noticed Miss Tilley was indeed wearing a jazzy pair of silver running shoes on her size-four feet. Ordinarily, Lucy would have teased her about them, but not today.

"He'll be missed by a lot of people," murmured Lucy, turning her attention to the cup of tea Rachel was offering her and doing her best to resist the gingersnaps perched on the saucer. "Did you know him well?"

"I was always very fond of him," said Miss Tilley, setting her teacup on the little antique tavern table next to her chair. "I watched him grow up, you know. He used to come into the library every week. He was a great reader. And then he went off to college and law school and I was his first client when he came back to Tinker's Cove and opened his law practice. He handled the closing for this house."

Lucy bit into a gingersnap while Miss Tilley continued.

"Honestly, I really don't know what I'm going to do now." She was agitated, practically wringing her hands. She was also shuffling her feet, setting off little explosions of colored lights that Lucy did her best to ignore. "I suppose I'll never know what it was he wanted to talk to me about. He called Monday afternoon. He was quite insistent."

"He wanted to see you? I thought it was the other way round." Lucy cast a questioning glance at Rachel, who was sitting on the couch. "I thought you wanted to get your affairs in order."

"My affairs are in order," said Miss Tilley. "Always have been, thanks to Sherman. He always handled all my legal matters, you know. I'm too old to switch now. What will I do?"

Lucy wanted to pursue the matter, but was interrupted by Rachel.

"Don't you worry," said Rachel. "Bob will take care of everything for you."

Miss Tilley grimaced. "It won't be the same. He'll do his best, of course, I know that. But Papa had a very high opinion of Sherman."

She looked up at the oil painting of her father that hung above the fireplace. He was pictured in his flowing judge's robe, holding a thick volume in one hand. His expression always reminded Lucy of the famous World War I poster of Uncle Sam pointing his finger and declaring "I Want You!" Lucy guessed the old judge didn't want to enlist anyone into the military; he wanted to swoop down like winged justice and send them to jail for a good long time.

"Papa always took an interest in Sherman Cobb," said Miss Tilley, nodding up at the old buzzard fondly. "He left him money to go to law school, you know."

Lucy looked up at the painting, wondering if she'd misjudged the old guy, and bit into the third gingersnap. She reached into her bag and took out her reporter's notebook, with the pen neatly tucked into the wire coil, and unfolded the fax. Before she could pose the first question, however, Miss Tilley turned the tables and questioned her.

"You didn't live here in 1965, the year we had the Centennial, did you?"

Lucy shook her head. Maybe Miss Tilly was getting forgetful. The Bicentennial was in 1976.

"Too bad. You really missed a swell time."

"Was that the town's hundredth birthday?" asked Rachel, also puzzled.

"No, no, no." Miss Tilly flapped her hand. "It was the hundredth anniversary of Lee's surrender at Appomattox Courthouse and the restoration of the Union."

"The end of the Civil War," said Lucy, wondering why the citizens of Tinker's Cove had felt it was something worthy of celebration one hundred years after the fact. Nobody was then alive who had fought in the war; by then it had become little more than a chapter in a history book.

"The town went all out," said Miss Tilley, smiling at the memory. "We had a big parade and a pageant on the Village Green. Sherman wrote the pageant, you know. He included the part about my grandfather, the hero of Portland, and he insisted that I play Barbara Frietchie."

"Barbara Frietchie?" asked Rachel.

"You know," prompted Lucy, who had majored in American lit. "In the poem. By Whittier."

"'Shoot, if you must, this old gray head, but spare my country's flag, she said,' " quoted Miss Tilley, repeating her line. The twinkling shoes rather spoiled the effect. "I was gray, then, of course, and the part just came naturally to me. If Stonewall Jackson had marched into Tinker's Cove and told me to lower Old Glory from the pole in front of Broadbrooks Free Library, well, I would have done just as Barbara Frietchie did!"

"I don't doubt it," said Lucy, scribbling it all down in her notebook. This was great stuff for the profile she was going to write for *The Pennysaver*. Maybe they could even use it for the *Norah!* show. "What else do you remember?" inquired Lucy, posing one of the questions on the fax. "What's your earliest memory?"

"My earliest memory," mused Miss Tilley. "I guess my sister, Harriet. With a big white bow on her head, pulling me along in a little wagon." Her eyes had a faraway look; then she frowned. "She wouldn't go fast enough. She said I'd fall out, because I was just a baby."

"I didn't know you had a sister," exclaimed Rachel. "Was she much older than you?"

"Ten years." A shadow fell across Miss Tilley's face. "She died."

"How sad," murmured Lucy, wondering if Harriet had died from some dreadful childhood scourge, diptheria or rubella, now hardly remembered except as the name of a vaccine. It occurred to her that in her ninety years of life Miss Tilley had witnessed most of the major advances that had taken place during the twentieth century. "Life has certainly changed since you were a little girl, hasn't it? I mean, was there electric light when you were a girl? Indoor plumbing? Cars?"

"We had indoor plumbing—there was a pump in the kitchen. Electricity and the telephone came around the same time. We had one of the first telephones. And dear Papa had the first motorcar in Tinker's Cove. A Ford."

"That must have created a sensation," guessed Lucy.

"Oh, it did." Miss Tilley chuckled at the memory. "Used to scare the horses something awful."

"It must have been rather uncommon for women to go to college back then," began Lucy, posing another question from the fax. "How did that come about?"

Miss Tilley sighed. "Well, Papa didn't want his daughters to have to depend on a man for their supper." Her head drooped momentarily, but she raised it to continue. The words came out slowly, with effort. "That's exactly how he put it."

Rachel caught Lucy's eye, signaling that it was time to wrap up the interview.

Lucy held out her arm, checking her watch. "Oh, dear, I hadn't realized it was so late. I'd better be going."

Miss Tilley snapped out of her doze and shifted in her chair. The shoes twinkled furiously. "That's right. I mustn't keep you."

"Thanks for the tea and the conversation," said Lucy, tucking the list of mostly unanswered questions into her notebook and getting to her feet.

Miss Tilley watched as Rachel showed Lucy to the door, raising her hand in a farewell wave. Then her hand fell heavily to her lap and she leaned back in her chair. Her eyelids drooped and her breaths became shallow.

Returning to her charge, Rachel realized she'd nodded off and covered her with an afghan. It seemed to be happening more and more. One minute she'd be talking, and the next she'd doze off. Sometimes for only a few minutes, other times for an hour or longer.

Doc Ryder had told her it was nothing to be concerned about, but Rachel wasn't convinced. She couldn't help wondering if these periods of unconsciousness weren't a prelude to a final lapse into a coma, and then death. Rachel adjusted the afghan, pulling it a little higher, then placed her cheek against the old woman's.

It was hard to sit up straight on the shiny black seat of Papa's new automobile. The leather was slippery, and Julia found herself sliding across the seat every time Papa turned a corner. She couldn't brace herself against the dashboard because it was too far away and her legs wouldn't reach; she was also too small to reach the strap that dangled from the roof. So she struggled mightily to keep her back straight, like a lady. Papa didn't approve of slouching. He certainly wouldn't want her to slouch in the automobile. He was very proud of it, and she knew she must make a good impression or he wouldn't bring her along for any rides in the future.

Papa was an important man, a judge, and Julia knew she must always make a good impression that would reflect positively on him. It wouldn't do for a judge to have a daughter who didn't know how to behave. People would lose respect for him and it was *absolutely essential* that people have respect for the law. Julia could hear him saying the words, putting the stress on the *lute* of absolutely and the *sen* of essential. Abso*lute*ly es*sen*tial. But Papa wasn't lecturing her now, he was humming a tune as he rolled along at a sedate pace in his gleaming black motorcar.

"What is that song, Papa?" she asked.

"Glory, glory, Hallelujah! His truth is marching on!" sang Papa, bringing the song to a thunderous conclusion. "Why, that's 'The Battle Hymn of the Republic.' It's a wonderful song. Most inspiring."

"I like the *hallelujahs*," said Julia. "But some of the other words are difficult. What does *vintage* mean? And what are *grapes of wrath?* Are they white or red?"

"Red," said Papa. "Most decidedly. You'll understand when you're bigger." He was silent while he negotiated a curve, then added, "You were named for the woman who wrote that song, you know. Julia Ward Howe."

"I was?" Julia was tickled. "I didn't know women could write songs."

"Julia Ward Howe is a fine poet and a fine patriot. You should try to emulate her, always."

"I will, Papa," promised Julia. "Who's Harriet named for?"

Harriet was Julia's older sister, almost ten years older and already a young lady who wore corsets and swept her long hair up in a bun on the top of her head. Julia's hair was still short because it had been cut off when she had scarlet fever a few months earlier. She admired Harriet's long hair, but she didn't miss her own because it had required a hundred painful brushstrokes every morning. She hoped it would take a long time to grow back.

"Harriet is named for Harriet Tubman," said Papa, as they drew up in front of the big white house on Main Street that was home. "Born a slave, she was a very brave woman who helped many slaves become free."

Julia pursed her lips. "What's a slave, Papa?"

Papa's back became straighter and his voice sterner. "A slave is a person who is owned by another person and must work for him. It's a great evil that ended with President Lincoln's Emancipation Proclamation."

"People can own other people?" Julia was intrigued with the idea. "If I had a slave, I could make her do my chores, couldn't I? Then I'd have more time to read."

"And why, might I ask, should someone else do your chores for you? Are you not able to do them yourself?"

"But I don't like to do them," said Julia, in a very small voice.

"Well, that's very naughty indeed," said Papa, lifting her out of the car and setting her on her feet.

Julia looked up at Papa. Her eyes went up his long woolen

slacks, over his vest with the gold watch fob, all the way up to his bearded chin. "Who are you named for, Papa?"

"For General William Tecumseh Sherman, of course."

Julia wanted to ask Papa who General William Tecumseh Sherman was, but he was already striding up the path to the front door. She hurried to keep up with him, but her legs were much shorter and she had to run. But no matter how hard she tried, she could never catch up. Even if she ran as fast as she could, getting out of breath. Papa was always ahead, just like General Sherman on his horse.

She could see him, General Sherman, high above her on his beautiful horse. The general was following a woman with a gold crown who was holding a sword high above her head as a symbol of victory. *He has trampled on the vintage where the grapes of wrath are stored, He has loosed the fearful lightning of his terrible, swift sword, His truth is marching on.*

But now the woman had whirled around and Julia could see her face. It was Harriet. Harriet was holding the sword. It was shining and gleaming, sparks of bright light were shooting off the white blade as she swung it around, faster and faster as she ran straight for the general. His horse reared up and he fell to the ground with a horrible brain-splitting thud.

Miss Tilley's eyes sprang open and she saw Rachel leaning over her.

"What happened?" Miss Tilley asked

"The teacup broke," said Rachel, bending down and picking up the pieces. "You must have knocked it off the table."

"That was a very stupid thing to do," said Miss Tilley, with a sigh of frustration.

Rachel smiled. "No harm done. It was just a teacup. Plenty more where it came from."

She patted the old woman's hand. "Ready for your dinner?"

"Yes, yes, I am," said Miss Tilley, slowly rising to her feet. "Thursday, shepherd's pie." She paused. "Next week, let's try something different. I've heard spaghetti is very tasty."

Rachel's mouth dropped open in disbelief as Miss T padded off to the dining room, her shoes twinkling as she went.

Chapter Eight

A s she walked on to Sherman Cobb's house on Oak Street, Lucy followed Video Debbie's advice and pulled in her tummy, tucked in her bottom and pulled herself up to her full height. It felt good, she had to admit.

Walking was supposed to be one of the secrets of good health; it seemed that some expert was always advising Americans to walk and bicycle more. Of course, they never seemed to take into account the fact that sidewalks and bike trails were few and far between. Here in town there were sidewalks, but they ended when Main Street turned into Route 1. In theory, Lucy could have walked or bicycled into town from her house on Red Top Road, but the traffic whizzing by made it a dangerous proposition.

Of course, before there were so many cars people had to walk more. Lucy wondered if Miss Tilley had walked a great deal when she was younger, and if it had helped her achieve her advanced age. The more she thought about it, the more she doubted it. In the twenty or more years she had known Miss T, she had never seen her walking, though she had often seen her cruising around in a massive Chrysler until an accident resulted in the revocation of her driver's license.

After that, Rachel came to the rescue, chauffeuring the old lady around town.

A wayward spray of forsythia slapped Lucy's shoulder and she paused for a moment, admiring an especially handsome patch of daffodils in somebody's yard. Here spring was literally bursting out all around her and she was too busy, too lost in her own thoughts, to notice. She resolved to pay more attention. Had the robins arrived yet? She didn't know.

Checking each lawn she passed for robins and noting the progress of emerging hyacinths and tulips slowed her steps, but not her thoughts. For some reason, she mused, she'd been convinced that Miss Tilley had contacted Cobb about updating her will. Where had she gotten that idea? She couldn't remember, but it was obviously wrong. Miss Tilley had made herself quite clear on the issue. She'd insisted Cobb had called her, requesting a meeting. Was it even about her will? Lucy wondered. Miss Tilley had boasted that her affairs were in satisfactory order. That didn't sound as if she was planning any changes. So why had Sherman Cobb wanted to see her? A good-bye visit? An expression of gratitude for the old judge's bequest? Maybe the answer would be found inside, thought Lucy, pausing in front of the modest white clapboard house with green shutters.

Things outlast people, thought Lucy, observing that Cobb's house looked just the same as always. You couldn't tell by looking at it that its owner had died and would never return. The windows didn't droop in sadness; the doorstep didn't sag in despair. Everything remained exactly as he had left it, with the lawn neatly raked and clumps of daffodils lined up against the foundation, almost ready to bloom. The crocuses were also in bloom, fragile bursts of white and purple, but he would never see them.

Lucy stood on the stoop outside the kitchen door, fingering the keys. This was creepy, she thought. She didn't even know Cobb and she was about to enter his house and go through his things. The most private details of his life would be exposed to her: the unpaid bills on his desk, his bank book and income taxes, old letters, the contents of his medicine cabinet and his laundry hamper, his address book and even his diary, if he kept one.

Worst of all, she was kind of excited at the prospect of snooping around. It wasn't her best trait, she admitted, remembering lonely afternoons as a child when she had peeked into her parents' dresser drawers. She recalled slipping her hand into the pocket of her mother's robe as it hung on the bathroom door and pulling out a strange rubber object and finally figuring out what it was—a diaphragm. Shocking proof that her parents had sex more than the one time it had taken to conceive her, their only child. She smiled at her childhood naivete and shoved the key into the lock.

"Excuse me, miss! What are you doing?"

Startled, Lucy whirled around and saw a man standing outside the back door of the neighboring house. He was in his sixties, rather plump, and wore his pants hitched up high on his suspenders. His plaid flannel shirt was buttoned all the way up to the neck. He hurried across the space between the two houses and was out of breath when he reached her.

"May I ask what your business is?" he demanded, pursing his lips. He had a small mouth to begin with and the gesture made him look like a fish.

"Mr. Cobb's partner, Bob Goodman, asked me to take a look in the house," she said, determined not to say too much. She had every right to be there, and it was none of the neighbor's business. "And who are you?"

"I'm Sidney Snell. I live in the house next door. We had an agreement to watch each other's houses when one of us was away, take in the mail, that sort of thing. I have his keys and he has—er, had, mine."

Lucy held up the keys Bob had given her. "I have a set, also," said Lucy, "so you don't need to stay. I can manage fine on my own."

"Just hold on there, missy," said Snell, pulling himself up to his full five feet and four inches. "You can't go in there."

"I've just explained to you that I can go in," replied Lucy, growing impatient with this nosy neighbor.

"How do I know you're who you say you are?" demanded Snell. "Until I hear otherwise, this house is my responsibility. Sherman Cobb was my neighbor and I'm not going to let him down." He glared at her. "Do you have some identification?"

This was ridiculous, thought Lucy, trying to think of a way to satisfy Snell that she was legitimate. She reached into her purse and handed him her card.

"Lucy Stone, reporter at *The Pennysaver*! I thought so! You're just looking for a story, aren't you?"

Lucy shook her head. "This isn't for the paper. Bob Goodman asked me to check the house. Why don't you call him?" she suggested. "He'll vouch for me."

"And leave you alone? You could be in and out with the silver before I got back. I don't think so."

"Okay," said Lucy, with a big sigh. "Why don't you come in with me? That way you'll be sure that I don't take anything."

Snell considered this for a few minutes. "Okay," he finally said. "But don't try anything funny. My wife is home and she's watching. Don't you forget it."

Lucy saw the curtains at the kitchen window twitch. "I won't forget it."

As it happened, she didn't need the keys. Cobb had left the door unlocked, just as Bob said. She pushed open the door, then reeled back, bumping into Snell.

"Sorry about that. Whew, something smells awful in there."

"Sure does," agreed the neighbor, pulling out a handkerchief and holding it over his nose, preparing to enter the kitchen.

Lucy pulled him back. "Hold on a minute. Maybe we ought to think about this," she said.

"What? First you couldn't wait to get in; now you don't want to because of a bad smell?"

Unfortunately, Lucy was well aware of what bad smells sometimes indicated. Old folks who'd slipped down the cellar stairs and hadn't been missed for days, runaway teenagers who turned up dead in the woods, wives and children killed by abusive fathers who, often as not, turned the weapon on themselves.

"Well, this might be related. Have you ever heard of murder-suicide? Could be a second body in there—I think we should call the police."

Snell made his fish face again. "Let's look first, okay? We don't want to bother the police if it turns out to be the garbage or something." He slapped the handkerchief over his nose and kicked the door open. "Don't touch anything," he added, his voice muffled by the cloth.

Lucy followed, hoping she wasn't walking into a gruesome scene.

"Aha! Here's the offender!" Snell pointed to a plate holding a greenish object covered with plastic wrap that was sitting on the counter. "Looks like a pork chop to me."

Now that she knew what it was, the smell didn't seem so awful. Lucy peered at the plate.

"Yup. Some sort of chop anyway. Probably for his supper."

"I'll just take care of that," said Snell, sliding the chop off the plate and into the garbage. "If you'll wash that, I'll just carry this out to the bin," he said, tying up the plastic liner.

Lucy squirted some soap onto a sponge and scrubbed the plate, setting it in the dish drainer next to a coffee mug, plate, juice glass and a few utensils. Looking around the kitchen, she noticed the coffeemaker's glass carafe still contained a cup or two of coffee. On the last day of his life, Cobb had made coffee, eaten breakfast and washed the dishes.

Glancing out the window, Lucy saw Snell fussing with the bungee cords that secured the lids on the garbage cans so dogs and raccoons couldn't open them. Deciding to take advantage of the situation, she hurried into the next room, a combination living and dining room. It was furnished attractively in what she guessed was Ethan Allen or Thomasville, probably all purchased at the same time. Everything was coordinated. The chair fabric complemented the sofa; the trim on the lampshades matched the welting on the throw pillows. It looked like a display room in a furniture store.

She pulled open the drawers in the end tables, finding coasters, a few decks of cards and a bridge scorecard, some stray pens and pencils. If Cobb had any dirty secrets, there was no sign of them here.

Lucy went down the hall, studying the framed photographs that lined the walls. All were taken at various Civil War reenactments. Some were posed group shots, others were candids of men in Civil War uniforms. There were also action shots of the mock battles, which must have been the work of professional photographers.

Three doors opened off the hallway and all stood open. The bathroom was standard, and the medicine cabinet held only the usual clutter of over-the-counter medications and Band-Aids. It could have been the medicine cabinet in her own home. The only exception was a prescription bottle of painkillers prescribed by Doc Ryder, presumably in response to Cobb's diagnosis. Cancer could be painful, Lucy knew, but the bottle was full even though the prescription had been filled weeks earlier. Lucy thought it was safe to assume that Cobb was most likely not in pain, certainly not enough pain to drive him to suicide.

The smaller bedroom was fitted up as a combination office and guest room with bookcases, a desk and a sleeper couch. Lucy looked longingly at the desk, which no doubt held all sorts of information, but knew she didn't have time to look through it before Snell came back.

In the last room, Cobb's bed was neatly made with his slippers tucked under the side. At the sight of the fleece-lined moccasins, tears sprang to Lucy's eyes. She just knew his pajamas were neatly folded under his pillow, but she didn't look. Instead, she peered into his closet, where she saw a

collection of suits, shirts, pants and jackets hung according
to category. Ties hung from a rack on the inside of the door;
shoes were arranged in a rack on the floor. Unzipping a plastic garment bag, Lucy found several Civil War uniforms
made of heavy blue wool, with gleaming brass buttons.

All of a sudden, Lucy wanted to be someplace else. She
didn't think she could stand another moment in the dead
man's house. She quickly yanked the drawers open and felt
under the piles of underwear, the rolls of socks, the stacks of
sweaters. There was nothing. Turning to leave, her eye was
caught by a framed photo of a man and woman.

"His mother and father," said Snell, looking over her
shoulder.

Lucy picked it up and studied it; she'd seen similar hand-
tinted photos of her grandparents in her parents' house.
Usually taken when a couple were married, they bore little
resemblance to the subjects in later life. A much smaller,
modern color photo, also framed, pictured the same pair standing behind a large cake with the number 50 on top. Their fifti-
eth wedding anniversary? It must be, thought Lucy, peering at
the happy couple.

"They've been dead for some time," he said, shaking his
head sadly. "Probably for the best."

As she studied them, as bright as two buttons in their
matching white hair and blue eyes, Lucy nodded her head in
agreement, thankful that they had gone to their rest ignorant
of the fate that awaited their son.

'Well, if you've seen enough, I'll lock up," said Snell,
placing himself in the doorway to the den.

Lucy looked past him to the desk. He'd never allow her to
look through it.

"I'm done for now," she said, vowing to come back another time, when she could search unhindered.

Lucy could feel Snell's eyes watching her as she walked
down the driveway. The good neighbor was determined to

make sure she didn't sneak back into the house to continue her search without his supervision.

Lucy marched along, venting her frustration by taking long strides and swinging her arms. If only she'd been able to really look around the house at her leisure, she might have come up with something. At least she would have gotten a better sense of the man. All she'd really learned from her search was that he was neat and tidy and conventional.

Maybe a little too conventional, she thought, wishing she'd been able to dig a little deeper. Everybody had some secrets and she wanted to know what Cobb's were. After all, people whose lives were truly open books rarely got themselves killed.

Lucy's steps slowed as she considered the pork chop. It was the strongest evidence she had that Cobb hadn't killed himself, and Snell had thrown it away. She shouldn't have let him do it, she realized; she should have insisted he leave it alone while she called the police.

She stopped, pausing on Main Street in front of *The Pennysaver* office. It was only a little bit farther to the police station. She kept walking.

"Is Barney in?" she asked the receptionist, who was sitting behind a sheet of thick Plexiglass. "I'd like to see him for a minute."

Lucy had been friends with Officer Barney Culpepper ever since they'd served together on the Cub Scout Pack Committee.

"*Officer Culpepper* is out on assignment," replied the receptionist. She had an unfashionable bouffant hairdo and bulging eyes, like a bug's.

Lucy didn't much like her officious attitude. After all, Lucy was hardly a stranger—she came in every week to pick up the police log for the paper. She always made an effort to be pleasant and friendly, and she was always met with the same disapproving stare. Lucy had even suggested dropping the log, but Ted insisted it was one of the paper's most popular features.

"Would you like to see someone else?" The receptionist's tone of voice suggested that Lucy was taking up valuable space in the empty vestibule.

Lucy considered her options. She knew she could count on Barney to take her seriously. The other officers only knew her from her job at *The Pennysaver* and tended to be close-mouthed and guarded with her, unless they saw an opportunity to use her, and the paper, for their own purposes. She'd noticed they were awfully chatty when they'd scored a success, like winning an award from Mothers Against Drunk Driving, but tight-lipped when she questioned them about ongoing investigations, increasing crime rates and the ready availability of illegal drugs at the high school.

"Could I leave a message for Barney?"

The receptionist rolled her eyes and slid a pink memo pad through the opening in the bulletproof barrier. Why on earth the Tinker's Cove Police Department needed such a thing Lucy couldn't guess. Even banks had given them up. Were they expecting an angry populace to attack the station?

She scrawled her name and number on the pad and slid it through the opening, flashing a big smile. It was a personal challenge: no matter how unfriendly the woman was, Lucy refused to respond in kind.

She was turning to go when she heard someone call her name. She sighed, recognizing Lieutenant Horowitz's voice. She'd had plenty of contact with him over the years and, as far as she was concerned, the farther she could stay away from him, the better.

"Hi, Lieutenant."

"What brings you here?" he asked. "Collecting the weekly log?"

"Something like that. Actually, I wanted to see Barney, but he's not here." She started for the door.

"Well, perhaps I can help you."

Lucy wondered what was up. Horowitz had never been particularly eager to help her before.

"What is this?" she asked suspiciously. "Be Nice to Reporters Week?"

The detective chuckled. "Actually, we have a new Elder Abuse Program we're initiating, funded with a community policing grant. The feds are matching the state dollar for dollar. I'd like to explain it to you sometime."

"Well, sure," said Lucy, glancing at her watch. She didn't want to listen to the usual alphabet soup of agencies and official jargon that would have to be translated into English. "I'm kind of in a hurry now."

"Not today." He held up his hand. "One day next week?"

Trapped, Lucy began excavating in her large shoulder bag, looking for her day planner. Finding it, she flipped through the pages.

"If we do it Monday or Tuesday I can get it in Thursday's paper," she suggested.

"Tuesday. Ten o'clock?"

"It's a date." She smiled at him, wondering if she should tell him about the pork chop.

"Something else?" he inquired.

"Sort of," began Lucy, aware that she was probably making a mistake but willing to take the risk. "Bob Goodman asked me to check out Sherman Cobb's house. You know Bob doesn't believe his partner committed suicide?"

"I'm aware of that, yes," said Horowitz, withdrawing into an invisible shell.

"Well, I found something," said Lucy, her spirits sinking but determined to persist.

"What did you find?"

"A pork chop."

"A pork chop?" repeated Horowitz.

"Set out to defrost. For his supper . . ."

"Ahhh . . ." He put his fingers together, making a tent. "You think that if he was planning to cook himself a chop for supper he wasn't planning to kill himself?"

Lucy nodded.

"Well, I'll tell you what I think," he said, sticking his nose in her face. "I think it doesn't mean a thing, because he could've been planning to shoot himself after dinner, but decided he didn't want to wait. Or he could've felt lousy and forgot all about the pork chop. A lot of things can happen in a day."

Horowitz's normally pale face was flushed and his voice had grown louder.

"And you know what else I think? I think you should leave police business to the police."

"So you don't want to see me Tuesday after all?"

Horowitz pulled down his long upper lip and clamped his mouth shut. "You know perfectly well what I mean. See you Tuesday," he snapped, before marching out the door.

Lucy stood for a moment, collecting herself, then dropped her agenda into her purse. Aware of the receptionist's stare on her back, she pulled open the heavy door and stepped outside. She knew she really ought to go straight to *The Pennysaver,* where a mountain of work was waiting for her, but there was something she wanted to do first.

Walking over to Bob Goodman's office took her in the wrong direction, and her guilt goaded her into hurrying. She was out of breath when Anne Shaw greeted her.

"Lucy! What is it? You look as if you ran the whole way."

"Not quite," gasped Lucy. "I've just been walking—for exercise—and it was farther than I thought."

"Can I get you some water?"

Lucy nodded.

When Anne returned with a flimsy paper cup holding an ounce or two, she downed it in one gulp.

"Thanks," she said, wishing for eight or ten more just like it.

"Well, what can I do for you?" inquired Anne. "I'm afraid Bob isn't in right now. He's making arrangements for the funeral Saturday."

"Two things," began Lucy, holding up two fingers. "First, could you ask him to call Sidney Snell, Sherman's neighbor? He's keeping an eye on the house and didn't want me poking around."

"No problem," said Anne. "I'll make sure Bob gives him a call."

"The other thing—I just wanted to look through those case files again. . . ."

Anne hesitated. "This is very unusual, you know—but Bob said I should help you any way I could. . . ."

"I'm just checking something," said Lucy, hoping to reassure her. "One little fact. It's probably nothing"

"Oh, all right," said Anne, unlocking the door to Cobb's office. She remained in the doorway, however.

Lucy glanced through the file folders on Cobb's desk and the credenza, but didn't find the one she was looking for.

"That's funny," she said. "I'm sure Miss Tilley told me she had some legal matters pending, but I don't see her file here."

"Miss Tilley?" Anne looked blank.

"Maybe her will?" prompted Lucy. "Something like that?"

Anne shook her head. "Nothing I'm aware of. Sherman wasn't doing any work for her. I'm certain of it."

"Maybe I misunderstood," said Lucy. "Sorry to bother you."

"It's no bother," said Anne. "Is there anything else I can do for you?"

"I wish there was," said Lucy.

Chapter Nine

Glancing at her watch, Lucy saw that it was almost noon. She really should have been at work a couple of hours ago. She cursed her decision to walk as a selfish indulgence. If she'd used her car, she could have saved time.

Worst of all was knowing that she had nothing to show for her efforts to get to the bottom of Sherman Cobb's death. She might have convinced herself that he hadn't killed himself, but her attempt to convince Lieutenant Horowitz had backfired. All she'd succeeded in doing on that front was to tick him off. And now she'd have to interview him and write that stupid story he wanted on elder abuse. She shook her head in dismay. It would just be a lot of the same old double-speak and an endless list of cooperating agencies, all of which had to be mentioned if she didn't want to get a spate of angry letters and phone calls.

Stopping at the curb and waiting to cross Main Street, Lucy tapped her foot impatiently.

She watched the cars zipping by, each a tiny little universe of its own. Here a mother with a van full of youngsters and an anxious expression, there a twenty-something with spiked hair bobbing his head and banging his hand on the steering wheel in time to music only he could hear. That was how it was with this investigation, she thought. Sherman's life was like one of those cars—you could see in but you couldn't really tell what had been going on. Why was the mother anxious? What was the fellow with spiked hair really thinking? She didn't have a clue, and she certainly hadn't learned much about Cobb from searching his home and office.

The next step, she realized, taking advantage of a break in traffic to run across the street, would be to interview people who knew him well. Rachel could probably give her some names; she'd call her later. But for now, she vowed, yanking open the door to *The Pennysaver* office and setting the little bell jangling, she had work to do.

"Just in time for lunch," said Ted.

"You know I never take a lunch hour," said Lucy, hanging her coat on the rack. "I always eat at my desk."

"Good thing." Ted was clicking away at his computer as he talked to her. "Otherwise you'd never get any work done."

"That's his idea of a joke," said Phyllis, who was making out a deposit slip. "Pathetic, isn't it? Kind of like my paycheck."

"Don't blame me," said Ted. "Blame the federal government, the state government and the Social Security Administration. And don't forget the HMO."

Phyllis studied her pay stub. "Shocking, I call it. Like I'm ever going to collect a dime from Social Security."

Lucy opened her pay envelope and glanced at the total. "There's always the lottery," she said with a sigh.

Phyllis stood up and got her coat. "I'm going to the bank. Anybody need anything?"

"About a million," said Ted.

"Ha, ha," replied Phyllis, shoving open the door.

"Shall we go over the story budget?" suggested Ted, pushing his chair away from his desk and facing her.

"Now's as good a time as any," said Lucy, unsnapping her day planner.

She was busy polishing up an interview with the new superintendent of schools when the phone rang. It was Sue.

"Well?" she demanded.

"Well, what?"

"The interview! How'd it go?"

"Oh." Lucy took a moment to sort out her thoughts. The interview with Miss Tilley seemed to have receded into the distant mists of time. "Okay. Very well, I'd say."

"So you got the answers to all the questions for the *Norah!* show?"

"Uh, no."

"No! Why not? Sidra's already called me twice and I promised I'd get them to her this afternoon at the latest. What am I going to tell her?"

Lucy stared at the blinking cursor on her computer screen. She really didn't have time for this. "Tell her Miss Tilley is ninety years old, almost, and only has a limited amount of energy. She nodded off, as old people are known to do."

Sue was incredulous. "She fell asleep in the middle of your interview?"

"Well, it was actually the end because I couldn't get much out of her after she fell asleep."

"Did you get anything at all on the changing roles of women?" demanded Sue.

"Papa insisted she go to college so she wouldn't have to depend on a man."

"Well, that's something, I suppose."

"Depends on how you look at it," observed Lucy. "She was hardly a groundbreaking feminist if she only went because Daddy made her."

"Anything else?" pleaded Sue.

"They had one of the first automobiles in the town and it used to scare the horses."

"Cute."

"Yeah," agreed Lucy. "And she got to play Barbara Frietchie in 1965 when the town observed the one-hundredth anniversary of the end of the Civil War."

"Who?"

Lucy glanced uneasily at Ted, who she suspected wasn't quite as absorbed in his account books as he appeared.

"I've got to go," she said. "I'll call you tonight."

"But what am I going to tell Sidra?"

"Make something up," suggested Lucy, hanging up.

"What was that all about?" asked Ted as she turned back to the new superintendent's views on education reform.

"Sue's trying to get the *Norah!* show to do a piece about Miss Tilley's ninetieth birthday."

"And when were you going to tell me about that?" he asked, scowling at her. "It's news, Lucy. News."

"Not yet, it isn't," said Lucy, pounding away on her keyboard. "Right now it's just a rumor. But that reminds me. I forgot to tell you that Lieutenant Horowitz wants me to write up a new elder abuse program. I'm going to talk to him on Tuesday."

"Can you do it for next week's paper?"

"Sure."

"Just watch the officialese. Try to find out what it means to the average senior citizen."

"I will," promised Lucy, as her phone started ringing again.

This time it was Rachel.

"I was going to call you," said Lucy. "You beat me to it."

"I'm sorry about the interview—she just nods off like that. Did you get enough material?"

"Probably not, but it's not my problem. Sue's got to deal with Sidra."

"Well, she is her mother."

There was a pause as they considered the ramifications. Sidra, they both knew, was every bit as bossy as Sue was.

"Listen, the reason I'm calling is because something incredible has happened. Miss T's just heard from a long-lost relative! Her niece telephoned today out of the blue. She'll be here Monday. I thought maybe you could take a photo for the paper."

"Her niece?" Lucy was puzzled. "I thought her sister died as a child or something."

"No." Rachel lowered her voice. "She was disowned. By the judge."

"Wow," breathed Lucy, thinking of her struggles with Sara. "Families must have been a lot different then. He disowned his own daughter but left money to Sherman Cobb? Why would he do that?"

"Beats me," said Rachel. "Old Judge Tilley was a force to be reckoned with. He did whatever he wanted. I think Miss T really lived in fear of him. Anyway, she's awfully happy that this niece is coming to see her."

"She's never seen her before?"

"Never! Didn't even know she existed."

"That's some story," said Lucy, giving Ted a meaningful glance. "You're sure she won't mind if I take a photo for the paper?"

"I think she'd love it," said Rachel. "You know, she's been loosening up a lot lately." She paused, collecting her thoughts. "It's almost as if she's having some sort of delayed adolescence. I never know what to expect anymore. She's been kicking up her heels."

"Good for her. What time should I come?"

"Ten?"

"Ten it is. Hey, before you go, just one other thing. I need to talk to someone who knew Cobb really well. Did he have any close friends?"

"Chap Willis was his best friend, I guess. He'd be the one to talk to."

"Great. Can you give me his number?"

"I don't have it here," said Rachel. "But he'll be at the funeral Saturday. You can talk to him there. You'll be there, won't you?"

"I'll be there."

Chapter Ten

———————

Lucy and Sue were walking along the sidewalk to the Tinker's Cove Community Church when Pam Stillings sailed by in her huge Oldsmobile.

"Why does she drive that rusty old boat?" muttered Sue. "It must be at least twenty years old."

"Probably because it's paid for," replied Lucy. "She and Ted are paying college tuition for Adam, you know."

"Well," sniffed Sue, "I'm sure they could find something affordable that doesn't look quite so—"

"Shhh! Here she comes!"

Pam, having parked the car, was running after them. In deference to the occasion, the funeral service for Sherman Cobb, she had traded her usual orange plaid poncho for a sober gray jacket and had jammed her wild mop of curly red hair into a black crocheted beret. Even so, she didn't quite look what Lucy's mother used to call "respectable." Maybe it was the red cowboy boots that peeked out from beneath her wide-legged sailor pants.

"Cowboy boots?" Sue's eyebrow was raised.

"It was the best I could do. I couldn't find my black pumps. I know I wore them at Christmas, but I don't think

I've seen them since. Maybe they got thrown out with the wrapping paper."

Lucy nodded. It sounded logical enough, if you knew Pam.

"Ted tells me our birthday girl has a long-lost relative! Do you think she'll come for the party?" Pam's eyes grew even bigger than usual. "Wouldn't that be great?"

"I wonder what she's like," mused Lucy. "Do you think she looks like Miss T?"

"I hope she doesn't look like the judge," said Sue.

"Well, I think it's nice that she's not all alone anymore." Pam nodded and a few curls bounced loose from her beret.

"Maybe she'll help out with the birthday party," suggested Sue, who had a one-track mind. "I've signed up for the hall at the community center, I've got Bonnie's Bakery to donate a cake, the bottling plant is donating sodas, and the paper company is giving us cups and napkins and plates—"

Sue was interrupted by the chiming of the church bell.

"We'll have to continue this after the service," said Lucy. "We don't want to be late."

The three adopted solemn expressions as they mounted the steps and entered the flower-filled church. They had just taken their seats when the organist pounded out the familiar notes of "O God Our Help in Ages Past."

As they got to their feet, Lucy scanned the crowd looking for familiar faces. Rachel was up front, sitting with Bob and Anne Shaw. She recognized Officer Barney Culpepper and a number of others from the Tinker's Cove police force, as well as a contingent from the fire department. Ted Stillings was there, of course, busily scribbling notes for the story he would write on Monday. Phyllis, she knew, had opted not to go and was spending the weekend visiting friends in Boston. The whole board of selectmen had showed up, as well as people Lucy recognized as members of the planning board and the board of appeals. Cobb had frequently appeared before them, representing clients who needed variances or site plan approvals.

Surprisingly, however, there were a lot of people Lucy

didn't recognize. Perhaps members of the Civil War reenactment group, she guessed, as she opened her hymnal.

When the congregation had warbled a final *amen*, the Reverend Mr. Macintosh led the opening prayer. When she raised her head, Lucy's eyes fell on the flag-draped coffin in front of the church. It was closed, topped with a large color photograph of Sherman Cobb.

Lucy listened to the eulogies with one ear as speaker after speaker mounted the podium; she didn't really expect to discover a motive for murder in the uniformly flattering accounts. As the words droned on she found herself staring at the photograph. A middle-aged man in a brown suit. A smooth, somewhat fleshy face. Brown hair. Brown eyes.

Brown eyes? Lucy remembered the photos of Cobb's parents. Two pair of bright blue eyes. She was certain. Blue eyes. And although she hadn't exactly been the star of her high school biology class, she did remember that blue eyes were produced by a recessive gene. Two blue-eyed parents could not have a brown-eyed child.

She was still pondering the implications of this discovery when the organist struck a chord and everyone got to their feet for the final hymn: "The Battle Hymn of the Republic." Then there was silence, and six men dressed in Union blue marched forward in formation and aligned themselves alongside the coffin. A seventh barked an order and the coffin was lifted onto their shoulders and carried down the aisle and out of the church. As it passed, Lucy felt a lump forming in her throat and tears stinging her eyes.

A nudge from behind reminded her that Sue was anxious to leave; she never liked to linger after an event.

"Are you going to the cemetery?" Lucy asked her as they slipped into the aisle.

"No. I promised Rachel I'd make sure everything was ready at the house. What are you doing?"

"I guess I'd like to go the cemetery, but I don't want to go alone. What are you going to do, Pam?"

"I'll go to the cemetery with you. I'm kind of in the funeral groove here. Might as well go whole hog." She paused at the door and took the minister's hand. "Lovely service, Reverend."

Lucy was still wondering how Pam had managed to shift gears so smoothly when it was her turn to shake hands with the minister. A quick hand clasp and she was out in the sunlight, blinking.

"I'll see you guys later," said Sue, hurrying down the sidewalk to her car, leaving Lucy and Pam standing together.

"I want that at my funeral," said Pam. "I want to be carried out on the shoulders of six stalwart young men. Preferably in loincloths."

Lucy punched her in the arm. "You're awful."

Pam shrugged. "Come on. What do you want at your funeral?"

"Doesn't matter. I'm not going to die," said Lucy.

The mournful sound of taps was still ringing in Lucy's ears as she and Pam drove up to Rachel and Bob's for the reception. As soon as they entered the house, however, she was caught up in the overfriendly exuberance that always seems to follow a burial.

"Thanks for coming," said Bob, clasping her hand. "There's food in the dining room and the bar's out in the sunroom."

"Looks like a heck of a party," observed Pam, approvingly. "There's a full bar. Want to have martinis?"

Lucy's eyes widened. "It's eleven o'clock in the morning."

"Trust me, Lucy. You look like you need a little something stronger than Poland Spring. How about some wine to go with those pigs-in-blankets?"

"Let's call it an early lunch," said Lucy, accepting a glass of wine from a waiter who was passing a tray. "Did you say pigs-in-blankets?"

"And scallops wrapped in bacon. Come on, before they're all gone."

After filling their plates, Lucy and Pam found a pair of

chairs in a corner of the sunroom and sat down. Pam's beret had disappeared and her hair blazed in the sunlight.

"Do you color your hair?" The words had flown from Lucy's mouth. "I'm sorry. I didn't mean to be rude."

Pam shrugged. "Of course I color my hair. Doesn't everybody?"

"I just did mine. Do you think it looks okay?"

"I hadn't actually noticed. Next time, why don't you try something a little brighter?"

"Brighter?"

"Sure. If you're coloring it anyway, you might as well get some bang for your buck."

Lucy was thinking about this when Rachel joined them, pulling up a hassock and perching on it.

"I think I can take a break for a few minutes," she said. "Things seem to be going pretty well."

"It's a great party," said Pam. "But Lucy wouldn't let me have a martini."

"Isn't it kind of early for a martini?" asked Rachel.

"It's never too early for a martini," said Pam, fishing out the olive with her fingers and popping it in her mouth.

"Martinis give me a headache," confessed Lucy. "Hey, while I've got you, there's something I've been meaning to ask you. Do you know why Sherman wanted to see Miss T?"

"Some sort of legal business, I think," said Rachel. "Is it important?"

"I don't know," admitted Lucy. "But I think it was something personal." She took a sip of wine. "I don't know. The more I find out about this guy, the less I seem to know. Was he adopted, by any chance?"

"Yeah, he was. How'd you know?"

"He had brown eyes; his parents had blue eyes."

"I never noticed. But he was adopted as a baby by an older couple. They had always wanted a child but couldn't have one of their own. From what he said they were very loving parents. His father was a court officer or something and he was terrifically proud when Sherman became a lawyer."

Rachel furrowed her brow. "Do you think the fact he was adopted has something to do with his death?"

"I don't know," admitted Lucy. "But instead of sitting here swilling booze with Pam, I really ought to be talking to Chap Willis. Who is he? Just point me in the right direction."

Rachel scanned the crowded rooms.

"See that guy in the uniform, the officer with the gold sash and all the brass buttons?"

Lucy spotted him, a middle-aged man in a knee-length blue coat. He was the man who had led the pallbearers.

"With the sword?"

Rachel nodded. "That's Chap Willis. They were best friends."

As Lucy crossed the room to talk to Chap Willis, she realized she had seen his muttonchop whiskers and big grin in several of the photographs in Cobb's house and office.

"Excuse me," she said, introducing herself. "The Goodmans have asked me to investigate Sherman Cobb's death and they said you might be able to help me."

"I wish I could," said Willis, smiling genially. "But I don't know what I can tell you."

"I understand you were good friends," prompted Lucy.

"The colonel and I go way back, let me tell you. I joined the Fifth Maine Brigade about the same time he did. Longer now than I'd care to admit, that's for sure."

"The brigade was a big part of his life," said Lucy.

"I'll say. He was voted colonel ten years ago. He really put a lot of himself into the brigade, and the fellows all recognized it. There was no question he deserved it."

"I'm sure," said Lucy. "Can you tell me anything about his personal life? Did you suspect he might be considering suicide?"

"Not a clue." Willis shook his grizzled head. "Especially not with the Invasion of Portland reenactment coming up in just a few weeks. It's the biggest thing we've ever attempted. Reenectment groups are coming from as far away as South Carolina." He scratched his chin. "His death has left us in a very awkward situation, you know."

"Invasion of Portland, *Maine?*" Lucy wasn't sure she'd heard right.

"That's right. Not many people know about it. Truth is, the Confederates tried to take the harbor. They penetrated St. Albans, Vermont, too."

Lucy was suspicious. "I never heard that."

"There's a whole lot about the Civil War that they don't teach in school. Don't have time, I guess. But you've got to remember, it didn't take five years to fight the Battle of Gettysburg. It was a big war, over half a million men died. It changed the country."

Lucy wanted to steer the conversation in a different direction; she wanted to learn more about Sherman Cobb. But whenever she brought up his name, Chap Willis would reply with a Civil War history lesson.

"You know what really caught the colonel's fancy?"

Lucy jumped at the bait.

"Them bringing up that Confederate submarine, the *Hunley*. He was just amazed that they had the technology to build a submarine back then. And the courage of those men. It was a suicide mission, you know."

"What did he think about that? About suicide in general, I mean."

"I don't know that he actually said." Chap stroked his beard thoughtfully and returned to his favorite subject. "The mission succeeded. They blew up a Union frigate. The U.S.S. *Housatonic.*"

Lucy felt her eyes glazing over as her brain filled with trivia. She had a feeling the *Hunley* and the *Housatonic* had displaced some vital information in her brain.

"Thanks for your help," she said, wishing he'd actually been helpful. Then she had a second thought. "You know, I write for the local newspaper and I think the reenactment would make a good feature story."

Chap's expression brightened up. "That's a great idea. It's next Saturday, in Granby."

Lucy jotted it down in her day planner. Checking the time, she decided to peek in the kitchen and see if Sue was ready to leave. Pushing open the swinging door, she found her deep in conversation with the caterer, Corney Clark.

"That was a great spread, Corney," she said, joining them. "Too bad it was for such a sad occasion."

"I absolutely hate funerals," admitted Corney. "Give me a wedding, a bar mitzvah, a christening, anything but a funeral." Her eyes locked on Lucy's, indicating she was very sincere about what she was about to say. "You wouldn't believe how much food people eat at funerals."

"I believe it," said Lucy, uncomfortably aware of her tight waistband. "I'm going to work out with my exercise video as soon as I get home. What do you say, Sue? Are you ready to go?"

"In a minute. Corney and I were just talking about the birthday party. She's offered to give us some cookies and finger sandwiches for half price."

Corney smiled graciously. "And I'll throw in some nice pink tablecloths, too."

"That's great," exclaimed Lucy. "Much nicer than the paper ones."

The very thought of paper tablecloths seemed to trouble Corney.

"Have you given any thought to music?" she asked. "It makes a big difference, you know."

"We thought of that," said Lucy, rather proudly. "The high school and middle school bands are going to play."

A cloud passed across Corney's face. "That's nice," she said, without enthusiasm. "I was thinking more along the lines of a string quartet, or a harpist. If the budget won't run to that, you might consider playing some recorded background music, too. When the band's not playing."

"That's a good idea," said Sue. "Thanks for mentioning it."

"I'm full of good ideas—call me anytime," said Corney.

"How much are those 'half-price' cookies and sandwiches going to cost?" muttered Lucy, as they made their way through the living room to say their farewells to Rachel and Bob.

"Plenty—but it's worth it," replied Sue. "She has a lot of experience with big parties and now I can pump her brain. You heard her, she said 'call me anytime' and I plan to. Besides, I have some ideas for fund-raising."

"Fund-raising? How are you going to do that?"

"I'm going to ask some local businesses to be sponsors, like the banks and insurance agencies."

"What? You're going to call it the Tinker's Cove Five Cents Savings Bank Birthday Party for Miss Tilley?"

"If they'll give me enough money, I will," said Sue. Seeing Lucy's shocked expression, she continued. "Calm down. I'll take care of the businesses. I was hoping you could get some donations from local groups, like the Women's Club."

Lucy didn't even pause. The words just came out. "Don't even think about it. You're on your own with that one, kiddo. I've got enough on my plate right now."

For a moment, Sue stared at her in shocked silence.

"Be like that," she sniffed, obviously displeased.

For a fleeting moment Lucy was tempted to change her mind. She was saved by Pam, who was waving at her from across the room.

"I've got to go," she told Sue. "Pam's giving me a ride home."

"I hope you make it home in one piece," said Sue.

But Lucy wasn't worried about the safety of her ride as she seated herself on Pam's zebra-striped front seat. Instead, she was beginning to feel uneasy about Miss Tilley. Why had Sherman wanted to see her? What would he have told her if he hadn't died? And why were relatives popping up now, when she was nearing the end of her long life? Family reunions were all very well and good, but she had a few pointed questions she planned to ask this particular long-lost relative.

Chapter Eleven

"I'm sorry I'm late," said Lucy, when she arrived at Miss Tilley's on Monday morning to photograph the reunion. "I just couldn't get out of the house. . . ."

Rachel waved away her excuses. "Have you got your camera?"

"Right here."

Lucy pulled her little instant-focus camera out of her bag and went into the living room to greet Miss Tilley.

"Are you ready for the big day?" she asked, taking her usual chair.

"Oh, yes."

The old woman's cheeks were pink with excitement and her white hair was freshly curled. She was wearing her best outfit, a periwinkle-blue dress topped with a string of pearls. Despite her age she reminded Lucy of a little girl all dressed up and waiting for her birthday party to begin. Maybe it was the twinkly, silver sneakers.

"You look very nice."

"Thank you, Lucy." Miss Tilley wasn't really paying attention; her eyes kept straying to the window.

Knowing Miss Tilley as she did, Lucy hadn't expected her to be this excited about the reunion. She had lived a de-

terminedly single, solitary life for so many years, often declaring that she always expected the worst of people and was
rarely disappointed.

Lucy was pulling out her notebook, intending to ask how
the meeting with her niece had come about, when a compact
car with a rental agency plate drew up outside. Miss Tilley
clapped her hands together and sat up very straight. She
seemed to be holding her breath as she watched the door
open and a figure emerge. A trim little woman in a neat blue
coat trotted up the path and Miss Tilley exhaled.

"Welcome," exclaimed Rachel, opening the door.

"Come in, come in," called Miss Tilley, from her chair.

The woman rushed in, a small whirlwind of blue topped
with a head of curly white hair, and clasped Miss Tilley's
hands.

"We meet at last!" she exclaimed. "It's like a dream come
true."

"Shirley," cooed Miss Tilley, her face radiant with joy.
She reached up and stroked the younger woman's cheek.
"Harriet's daughter. You look just like her."

"I would know you anywhere," affirmed Shirley. "You
look just like Mother, before she . . ." Unable to finish, she
fumbled in her purse for a tissue.

Despite her doubts, Lucy felt tears springing to her eyes
and noticed Rachel was also blinking furiously. It was an in-
credibly touching moment.

"Here, here. Let me give you a big hug," demanded
Shirley, pressing her cheek against Miss Tilley's.

They clung together for several minutes before Shirley
released the old woman and stepped back, obviously looking
for something to sit on.

"Sit here," said Lucy, springing out of the rocker.

"I want her to sit right here by me," said Miss Tilley.
"Rachel, get a chair."

"It's right here," said Rachel, setting one of the Windsor
chairs from the dining room next to Miss Tilley's rocker.

Noticing Miss Tilley's flushed complexion, Rachel raised
an eyebrow at Lucy.

"How about a little glass of sherry?" suggested Lucy. "In honor of the occasion."

"Oh, yes, I should have thought of that," fretted Miss Tilley. "Is sherry all right? Is there something else you would prefer?"

"Sherry would be lovely," said Shirley, taking the chair and slipping her coat off her shoulders.

Except for the thirty-year difference in age, Shirley could have been Miss Tilley's twin, thought Lucy. She was dressed in a gray tweed skirt topped with a blue twinset; her legs were encased in support hose and sturdy black pumps. A cameo brooch was perched on one shoulder and abundant white curls framed her round face. Like Miss Tilley, her cheeks were plump little red apples.

"I'm Lucy Stone," said Lucy, extending her hand.

"I'm just delighted to meet you," gushed Shirley, clasping Lucy's hand in both of hers.

"And I'm Rachel Goodman, Miss T's helper," said Rachel, holding out a tray with four sherry glasses.

"Lovely to meet you," said Shirley, taking a glass and holding it up to admire the amber liquid.

Her nails, Lucy saw with a bit of a shock, were painted purple. Not quite what she expected, knowing how Miss Tilley loathed nail polish. But lots of women did wear nail polish, Lucy reminded herself. Some women considered it a necessary part of grooming.

"Shall we have a toast?" inquired Miss Tilley, raising her glass. "To long-lost relatives!"

"To long-lost relatives!" they all chorused.

Rachel kept a watchful eye on Miss Tilley as she drank her wine. When her high color began to subside and her breathing became more relaxed, Rachel slipped away to the kitchen to fix lunch.

Miss Tilley didn't notice her absence; she couldn't keep her eyes off Shirley.

"Do you mind if I take a picture? For the local newspaper?" asked Lucy, producing her camera.

"The newspaper?" Shirley seemed taken aback.

"This is big news in Tinker's Cove, you know. And I'll make sure you both get copies."

"Wouldn't that be nice?" urged Miss Tilley.

"Okay, then," said Shirley, "but the flash bothers my eyes. Cataracts, you know. Just let me put on my sunglasses."

Lucy waited while she slipped on a pair of very dark, oversize sunglasses.

"Say cheese."

Lucy snapped several photos, then took out her notebook.

"Now, I need your full name, Shirley," she said, waiting with her pen poised. "For the caption."

"Why, it's Henderson. Shirley Henderson."

"Can you tell me how you found each other?" she asked.

"There was really nothing to it," said Shirley, smoothing her skirt. "I knew that Mama had been born in Tinker's Cove, of course. I just called nationwide directory assistance and they gave me Auntie's number."

Miss Tilley beamed at Shirley, as if she'd done something remarkably clever.

Lucy was scribbling it all down in her notebook. "And if this isn't too personal, what prompted you to contact your aunt after all these years?"

"Well," said Shirley, adopting a mournful expression, "after Mother died, I found myself pretty much alone. It just seemed natural to try and find family, if I could."

Miss T beamed her approval.

"The best part was when I dialed her number and she actually answered the phone." Shirley clasped Miss T's hand in her own and gazed into the old woman's eyes. "I can't tell you how exciting it was for me to hear your voice at last. Mama always talked about you and how much she missed her family."

At this, Miss Tilley pulled a handkerchief out of her sleeve and dabbed at her eyes.

"I don't know why I didn't try to get in touch myself," she said, sniffling. "I had a dream, you know, that Harriet was angry with Papa for disowning her. I've had it many times through the years, but I never did anything. I should have, when Harriet was still alive."

"Well, better late than never, that's what I say," said Shirley, nodding so hard that her curls bounced.

"She's right," agreed Lucy. "Would you mind telling me what it was all about originally? Why did your father disown Harriet?"

"Because she married a Democrat, of course." Miss Tilley made it sound as if this were normal behavior.

Lucy's eyebrows shot up, but Miss Tilley didn't notice her surprise. She was gazing at the bronze bust of Lincoln that sat on the mantel.

"He never forgave her for deserting the party of Lincoln."

"Well, don't you worry," said Shirley. "I always vote Republican myself."

"You don't say?" Miss Tilley was beaming at her.

"I do say. Didn't Florida vote for George W. Bush in the last election?"

Lucy was tempted to say something, but held her tongue as the two women sat together, holding hands, enjoying their reunion. This was no time to talk politics. In fact, Lucy was perfectly willing to bask in the sentimental glow the two long-lost relatives were generating. Reluctantly, she pulled herself away.

She was still floating on a happy little cloud of family feeling when she finally got to the office straight from the while-you-wait film-developing machine at the drugstore.

"Ted told me to tell you not to bother getting the police log today. He's over there anyway and he'll pick it up," announced Phyllis, peering over her half glasses.

"What did I do to deserve this?" asked Lucy, stunned by her good fortune. To tell the truth, she'd forgotten all about the darn thing. She'd goofed up, and been spared the consequences. She handed Phyllis the packet of photographs. "Take a look at these, will you?"

"Good God! As if one Miss Julia Ward Howe Tilley isn't enough. Where'd you find the other one?"

"She's her niece. Never met her, never even knew she existed until she called up one day, out of the blue."

"Kind of scary, if you ask me." Phyllis frowned at the photo. "I hope none of my long-lost relatives start crawling out of their trailer parks to come a-calling."

"I don't think Miss Tilley's niece comes from a trailer park. Look how nicely she's dressed. And I've got to tell you, I've never seen Miss T look so happy. We had to give her some sherry just to calm her down."

Phyllis wasn't impressed. "What's with the sunglasses? Is she in the witness protection program or something?"

"They're the kind people wear after cataract surgery," replied Lucy.

The bell on the door jangled and they both looked up as Ted came sailing in, clutching a handful of papers.

"Clear the way. I've got the ME's report."

"On Monday morning? They're really getting careless over there," observed Lucy. "Don't they usually schedule press conferences for Wednesday afternoon, about an hour after deadline?"

"It was a rare slipup." Ted's tone became sarcastic. "Darn! Now I won't have all week to work on the story."

Lucy chuckled. "I've got breaking news, too. A touching family reunion. Miss Tilley reunited with her long-lost niece. And I've got photographs."

Ted grabbed the packet and flipped through the pictures.

"Good work. Can you give me ten inches?"

"I'll give you ten inches if you tell me what the ME's report says about Cobb's death."

"You've got a deal. 'Not inconsistent with suicide.'"

Lucy's spirits sank. "That's it?"

Ted shrugged. "Pretty much."

"You know, I don't buy it," said Lucy, sitting down at her desk and waiting for her computer to boot up. "I was over at his house. Bob Goodman asked me to take a look around, you know?" Lucy paused for emphasis. "I found a pork chop."

"A pork chop?"

"Yup. Sitting on the counter, like it had been put out to defrost. Cobb wasn't planning to kill himself; he was planning to eat a pork chop for dinner. A nice thick one."

"Probably got it at Dunne's," suggested Phyllis, naming a specialty butcher in the neighboring town of Gilead.

"He might have," agreed Lucy.

Ted was already clicking away on the keyboard. "Maybe he changed his mind."

"No way," said Phyllis. "He'd never waste a Dunne's pork chop!"

"My thoughts exactly," said Lucy, opening a file and starting to type. "'Papa never forgave her for deserting the party of Lincoln. . . .'"

It was a couple of hours later and Lucy was eating a nonfat yogurt for lunch when Ted looked up from his Chinese takeout and said, "Tell me about the pork chop."

Lucy looked longingly at his egg roll, as yet untouched, and licked the last drop of strawberry custard off her plastic spoon. "It was on his counter, like people do, you know. He probably took it out of the freezer in the morning, planning to cook it up that night for supper."

"You're not supposed to do that, you know," said Phyllis, peering suspiciously into her container of wonton soup. "You're supposed to defrost meat in the refrigerator. It's safer."

"Do you do that?" challenged Lucy.

"Naw. It takes too long. I can't think that far ahead."

"Me either," said Lucy. "And if you defrost meat in the microwave, it gets half cooked."

"'Not inconsistent with suicide' isn't very definitive," said Ted, taking a big bite of egg roll.

Lucy's stomach gave a painful twist.

"I mean, it could just as easily mean 'not inconsistent with homicide,' " continued Ted.

"Except that if he said that, then they'd have to investigate," said Lucy. She knew that the bottom line tended to drive a lot of decisions.

"Horowitz said they're leaving the case open, but that there wasn't enough evidence to warrant an investigation at this time."

"So they're waiting for something to come up?" asked Lucy, aware that she was salivating like one of Pavlov's dogs.

"That's the impression I got." Ted chewed the last of his egg roll.

Lucy got up and walked over to the water cooler and filled her mug.

"Who inherits his money?" asked Phyllis, chasing down a dumpling.

"Did he have much money?" asked Ted.

Lucy remembered Cobb's desk, which she hadn't been able to search.

"He was a lawyer. Of course he had money," said Phyllis. "It was on *Matlock* last night. Cooey-boney or something like that. It means 'who benefits.' "

"Cui bono," said Ted. "It's Latin."

"I know what it is," muttered Lucy. "It's a really good idea. I'm going to call Bob up right now and find out who gets the dough."

Bob answered himself; Anne Shaw was probably taking her lunch hour.

"Hi, Lucy. How's it going? I've got the medical examiner's report, if you want it."

"Thanks, but I know all about it. Ted and I don't think it means much."

"That's what I thought," agreed Bob.

"I've got a question for you. Can you tell me about Cobb's will? Who'd he leave his money to?"

Bob groaned. "This is embarrassing. I'm actually one of the beneficiaries, along with the hospital and a bunch of other worthy causes. There's an adoption agency, the Legal Aid Society and, of course, his Civil War group." He paused. "Some people are in for a nice surprise. I found some stock certificates with his stuff, and when I checked them out, I discovered they were much more valuable than I would have guessed."

"You know what this means, don't you?" asked Lucy, adopting a teasing tone. "Now I'm going to have to consider you a suspect."

"Ah," said Bob, slowly. *"Cui bono.* That's not a bad idea, Lucy. I'll fax the will right over. Add me to the list of suspects, if it helps. Do whatever you need to. Just find out who killed my partner."

"You've got a deal. You're on the list," said Lucy. But as she replaced the receiver, she realized she didn't have a list of suspects. Not yet anyway. She looked at Phyllis. Maybe it was time to call for reinforcements.

"Phyllis? How about taking a lunch hour today?"

"Lucy, I hate to point out the obvious, but I've already eaten."

"Actually, I was thinking of checking out Sherman Cobb's place. Want to come?"

Phyllis was on her feet in a flash. "You bet."

"Let's park around the corner and cut through the backyard," suggested Lucy. "He's got some nosy neighbors."

"Tell me about it." Phyllis sighed. "We'd just be getting a little romantic, if you know what I mean, when Snell would come knocking at the door."

Lucy smiled. "So Cobb was a passionate sort of guy?"

"He had potential," said Phyllis, stepping out of the Subaru.

Lucy led the way through a patch of woods, pausing at the edge and studying the back of Sherman Cobb's house and the adjacent Snell home. Both appeared to be deserted.

"I think we're in luck," she said. "There's no car in the Snells' driveway."

"Let's hurry," urged Phyllis. "Before they get back."

In a matter of seconds they were on the back porch, and Lucy was unlocking the door. She turned to look over her back as they entered the house and saw the curtain at the Snells' kitchen window twitch. Or was it her imagination?

"We better make this fast," she told Phyllis.

Phyllis was standing in the kitchen, a sad expression on her face. "It hasn't changed a bit," she said. "I used to think, back in the days when I thought we had a future, that I would paint the kitchen yellow and put up gingham café curtains."

"I like gingham in a kitchen," agreed Lucy, wondering if it had been a mistake to bring Phyllis. "Listen, you stand by the front window there and be the lookout, okay?"

Phyllis's hand fluttered to her chest. "Who am I watching out for? We're not doing anything wrong, are we?"

"Technically, no," said Lucy, "but I'd prefer not to have to explain that to the police."

Phyllis swallowed hard. "Got it."

Lucy went straight to Cobb's home office and began going through his desk. The wide center drawer contained only stationery, with pens and pencils neatly lined up in the wooden tray provided for them. There was also a small cardboard envelope with a number written on it that contained a key, probably the key to a safe deposit box. Lucy pocketed it and pulled open the tall file drawer. It was neatly organized with hanging folders. She pulled out the one labeled "mutual funds" and flipped through the statements. Phyllis was right; Cobb had been a wealthy man with nearly a half million dollars worth of mutual funds. She was reaching for the "bonds" folder when Phyllis called her name.

"We've got company," she said.

Lucy ran to the front window, where she saw a police cruiser pulling up.

"Out the back!" she hissed, watching as a heavy woman in a housecoat came out of the Snells' house and waddled slowly down the front path in her bedroom slippers, waving her arm at the officer.

"Thank goodness she's not in better shape," said Lucy, pausing to lock the door while Phyllis headed for the woods.

She soon caught up to her at the Subaru. The cops were just entering the house, they saw, as they drove by.

"That was close," said Lucy.

"That was a hoot," said Phyllis, fanning herself with her gloves. "Better than hormone replacement therapy."

Chapter Twelve

Ted was definitely not amused when Phyllis and Lucy returned to the office, giggling like two high school girls cutting a class.

"This is a place of business," he admonished them. "The public expects us to behave in a professional manner."

Lucy didn't dare look at Phyllis for fear of setting off another laughing fit. Chastened, she went straight to her desk and was just sitting down when Phyllis let out an explosive snort of laughter. Lucy was soon roaring with laughter and clutching her stomach.

"What exactly is so funny?" demanded Ted.

"Nothing—it's just nervous tension," sputtered Lucy. This didn't seem the time to explain their escapade, especially their close shave with the police.

"Overwork," offered Phyllis, who believed a strong offense was the best defense. "Just letting off steam."

"Uh, well, that's all right then," said Ted, withdrawing to the safety of his desk. He was never quite comfortable with the role of boss.

"Aw, gee," moaned Lucy, studying her calendar desk pad. "I've got a finance committee meeting tonight." Lucy adopted a pleading tone. "I don't suppose you'd let me skip the meeting and listen to the secretary's tape recording tomorrow?"

Ted shifted his weight in his grandfather's chair, making it creak.

"Will you have time tomorrow?" he asked. "I thought you had an interview. That new elder abuse program."

"Oh, right." Lucy sighed, looking ahead at her calendar. "That means I'll have two stories to write tomorrow." She reached for the ever-present stack of announcements. "I guess I'd better get busy."

"That's what I like to hear," said Ted, beaming at her.

Lucy and Phyllis groaned.

Lucy was running late when she finally left the office. She had to stop and pick up some milk, get home, make dinner and be back in town by seven for the finance committee meeting. Intent on her agenda, she was driving too fast.

Exactly how fast she didn't realize until a police cruiser drew up behind her with lights flashing. She immediately slowed the car, but a quick glance at the speedometer showed she was going at least ten miles an hour above the speed limit. And that was after she hit the brakes.

Much to her relief, the officer who got out of the cruiser was Barney Culpepper.

"Hi, Barney," she said brightly, giving him a big smile as she rolled down the window. "How ya doin'?"

Barney didn't return her smile. "Aw, Lucy," he said. "I was afraid it was you. I thought I recognized the car." He sighed. "License and registration."

"You're kidding, right?"

Barney's expression was serious. Lucy stopped smiling and got her license out of her wallet and fished around in the glove compartment until she found the registration, crumpled but readable. Maybe, she hoped, he'd let her off with a warning.

Then again, maybe he wouldn't, she decided, watching him take the documents back to his cruiser.

When he returned, he was shaking his head mournfully. "Your license expired three months ago."

"That's impossible!" Lucy snatched it back and checked the date.

"I guess I never got a renewal notice," she suggested. Barney raised a skeptical eyebrow.

A search through the dim recesses of her memory produced a vague recollection. She had planned to renew the license, but there had been a bad snowstorm and she'd postponed the trip until the roads were cleared. And by then, she'd forgotten.

"Look," said Barney, leaning on the car, "I can't let you go with a warning because of this here." He gave the license a nod. "I've got to cite you for that and I've got to have a reason for pulling you over in the first place, so I'm gonna ignore the speeding and just put down your defective headlight."

"I've got a bad headlight?"

Barney nodded, signed the ticket with a flourish and handed it over. "You better get these things attended to," he advised, his jowls quivering. "And watch your speed!"

"I will," she promised, feeling like a naughty child as she stuffed the flimsy piece of paper in her purse.

Barney didn't go back to his cruiser but lingered, giving his heavy utility belt a hitch.

"I heard you were in the station looking for me the other day," he said, leaning down and peering at her through the window. "I don't suppose that had anything to do with a call we got about two women breaking into Sherman Cobb's house?"

Lucy's face went red. "It wasn't a break-in," she sputtered. "I had Bob Goodman's permission to look around the house. I even had the keys!"

Barney furrrowed his face, looking like a worried bassett hound. "The investigating officer found it kinda suspicious that nobody was there. It kinda looked like the intruders had made a hasty exit. Like they were up to no good, if you know what I mean."

Lucy shook her head. "I didn't want to have to explain, that's all."

Barney nodded, making his jowls quiver. "Did you find anything?"

"Not really," said Lucy. "Why do you ask?"

He shrugged. "I dunno." He studied his shoes, which were polished to a high gleam. "The whole thing's kinda fishy to me. What was a guy like Cobb doing with a Saturday night special? It wasn't even registered."

Lucy hadn't thought about the gun. Guns were common in Maine; lots of people had them. She had just assumed Cobb had owned the gun legally.

"I guess if he wanted to shoot himself, he wouldn't have wanted to wait for the paperwork," surmised Lucy. "Wouldn't a Saturday night special be the quickest, easiest way to get a gun?"

But even as she spoke she thought it was an atypical choice for Cobb. From what she'd learned about the man— his obsessive love of order, his preference for quality clothing and furnishings, his fondness for Civil War trappings—the choice of a cheap, even risky, weapon seemed incongruous. A ritual suicide, a shot from an antique Colt revolver following a toast to the regiment, seemed more in character.

"I guess we'll never know," said Barney, running his hand through his brush cut and replacing his cap squarely on his head. "You take care now," he said.

He went back to his cruiser and waited, lights flashing, while she pulled back onto the road, but there was no need. It was close to six and the brief increase of traffic that constituted rush hour in Tinker's Cove was over.

Lucy was tempted to step on the accelerator and roar off in a cloud of dust, but she knew that wouldn't be wise. It would be stupid and immature, which happened to be exactly how she felt. And betrayed. What kind of friend was Barney? He should have let her go. Now she'd have to tell Bill why she was late and he'd be furious with her. She could just hear him: "Two kids in college and you're getting traffic tickets—like we've got a lot of extra money to waste on fines!"

Reluctantly, she flipped on her signal for the turn onto Red Top Road, the last leg of her drive home. She didn't want to go home. She didn't want to deal with the girls' squabbles; she didn't want to cook a dinner that she wouldn't have time to eat; she didn't want to listen to Bill's reproaches.

Lucy found she had braked and was turning the car around. She didn't have to go home—she could call and tell them to go ahead without her because she'd been held up at the office. Between them, Bill and the girls could certainly cook themselves some supper. She'd get herself a slice of pizza at Joe's, where it was usually nice and quiet on Monday night. People took personal days off from work all the time—she was going to take a personal supper.

Lucy felt rather uneasy when she arrived at the police station on Tuesday morning for her interview with Horowitz. As a state police officer it was unlikely he would concern himself with routine traffic stops, but living in a small town had taught her that gossip traveled fast. She felt as if she were wearing a scarlet S for Speeding when the bug-eyed receptionist nodded at her.

"They're in the conference room," she said, hitting a button that produced a very loud buzz signaling that the triple-plated door was unlocked.

Lucy grabbed the knob and dashed through, resisting the impulse to cover her ears.

Horowitz was standing in the hallway, where the floor was covered with thick, gray vinyl tile and the cement block walls were painted battleship gray. He was dressed as usual in a neat gray suit, white shirt and sober tie. "We're in here," he said, indicating a doorway. "I hope you don't mind, but I asked Liz Kelly from Senior Services to join us."

Lucy's previous experiences with Liz hadn't given her a very high opinion of the woman, but she greeted her with a polite smile when she entered the conference room. Liz had already seated herself at the table, where she had staked her claim to most of the territory with an assortment of papers, brightly colored tote bags and a hand-knitted scarf that appeared to be at least eight feet long.

"Lucy, I'm so glad you're doing this story," gushed Liz. "This is a program that's really going to make a difference for a lot of our elders."

"Well, thank you very much for meeting with me," said Lucy, taking a seat and trying not to look at Horowitz.

She'd noticed an uncharacteristic twinkle in his eye and had a paranoid conviction that he knew all about the citation that was buried in her purse. Maybe he even knew about her visit to Cobb's house. She focused instead on a pamphlet Liz had slid across the table to her. The cover featured a photo of a frail old woman clutching a walker and cringing as a hulking shadow loomed over her.

"Can you start by giving me some idea of the extent of the problem?" suggested Lucy, who found herself fascinated by the photograph.

"It's enormous," said Liz, extending her arms and spreading out the folds of the Guatemalan wrap she was wearing. It made her look eerily like the shadow in the photo, thought Lucy.

"It ranges from unscrupulous contractors who frighten elders into unnecessary and expensive repairs to home-care aides who pilfer cash and jewelry to relatives who deny Grandma the medicine she needs in an effort to preserve her estate for themselves. And that's just the financial aspect. There's also emotional and physical abuse."

"I have a video we'd like to show you," said Horowitz. "It will only take a few minutes."

He picked up a remote that was on the table and clicked on a TV set that was standing nearby on a wheeled trolley.

"This was taken on a surveillance camera we installed in a nursing home, after relatives complained their loved one had a lot of unexplained bruises," he said.

Lucy stared at the grainy footage, eventually picking out the shape of an elderly woman lying quietly in bed. Then another figure entered the scene, yanked back the covers and slapped the old woman.

Involuntarily, Lucy flinched. The video continued to roll as the old woman feebly raised an arm to fend off more blows, but the aide swatted it away.

"Why is she hitting her?" demanded Lucy.

"The old woman had wet the bed," said Liz.

Horowitz clicked the remote and the TV screen went black. "I know it's difficult to watch," he said, "but this video got us a conviction. That aide is in jail now."

"So this is a law enforcement program?"

Horowitz nodded. "Actually, it's a hybrid. We have a state community policing grant from MACP, plus matching funds from HHS, and additional grants from ESAM, COA and Senior Services." He narrowed his eyes. "Are you getting that all down?"

"Ah, yes," said Lucy, scribbling away.

"For the first time we're going to be able to work with social workers like Liz and other reporters." He continued, tapping the TV set. "We were only able to make this case because the family members came to us and filed charges. That doesn't happen very often."

"Lots of times it's family members who are actually the abusers," said Liz.

Horowitz nodded. "Now we'll be able to take a referral from Senior Services, or a bank teller or the mailman, and open a case right away."

"And we're also going to be setting up outreach programs in an effort to educate people in the community—like bank tellers and postal workers—about the issue and what they can do. But we also need for everyone in the community to be more aware of the problem—that's where you come in, Lucy." Liz was staring at her.

"Well, I'll do what I can," said Lucy, deciding that Liz wasn't so bad after all. She certainly seemed to have her heart in the right place.

"If you have any questions, don't hesitate to call us, either of us," said Horowitz.

Lucy took the information packet he handed her and tucked it into her notebook, then stood to go.

"One more thing," said Horowitz. "There's no rush about this, the program is just starting. Take your time. There's no need to speed back to the office."

Lucy felt her face burning. So he did know. He'd probably been waiting all morning to deliver that little zinger.

"I'll keep it in mind," snapped Lucy, glaring at him.

She could hear him chuckling as the conference room door closed behind her.

She marched angrily down the hall and had almost reached the triple-plated security door when she was struck with an inspiration. As she knew all too well, the police patrolled the streets all night long. It was definitely worth finding out who had been on duty the night Sherman died. If there had been any strange activity, it would certainly have been noticed.

Instead of proceeding through the secutrity door, she ducked into the dispatch office, where the receptionist was located. It felt odd to approach her from the rear, without a thick layer of Plexiglas separating them.

"Hi!" said Lucy brightly. "I wonder if you could help me with something?"

Startled, the receptionist jumped. She gave Lucy a baleful look.

"I didn't mean to startle you," Lucy said quickly. "I was just wondering if you could tell me who was on duty the night of the seventeenth?"

"Here at the desk? That would be Marge."

"Actually, I wondered who was out on patrol."

"Why do you want to know?"

Lucy knew she had every right to ask for the information, but decided this was not the time to invoke the public's right to know about the use of its tax dollars.

"I'm thinking of doing a story on people who work at night," fibbed Lucy.

"I work at night, you know," said the receptionist, brightening up.

"Do you?" replied Lucy, feigning interest while the receptionist reached for a clipboard with large wire rings and flipped back through the pages.

"Here it is: three to eleven was Howie Kodak and eleven to seven was Bob Wickes." She paused. "Why the seventeenth? Is it special?"

"Not really. I just picked a random date. A night in the life of Tinker's Cove. That's the idea."

"Too bad. I was off that night."

"That is too bad," agreed Lucy sympathetically as she jotted down the names. "Any chance either of these guys is here in the station?"

The receptionist checked the roster again and shook her head. "Bobby's on vacation this week, and Howie's got the eleven o'clock shift."

"Thanks," said Lucy.

"I'm glad to be of help," said the receptionist, patting her hair. "I'm here if you need any more information."

"I'll keep that in mind," said Lucy, dashing for the triple-plated security door. Sometimes three layers wasn't enough.

Chapter Thirteen

From her usual seat in the Boston rocker, Miss Tilley had an unobstructed view of the mailbox and she kept an eye out for the postman.

"The mail's here," she called to Rachel, as soon as the white van came into sight.

"I'll get it," replied Rachel from the kitchen, where she was washing up the lunch dishes.

She grabbed a towel and ran down the front path, drying her hands as she went. She regretted her haste, however, when the chilly breeze hit her damp hands. Quickly tucking the towel under her elbow, she pulled the mail out of the box and ran back to the house.

"Anything interesting?" inquired Miss Tilley eagerly, holding her hand out.

"Just ads," said Rachel, flipping through the envelopes. "What's this? Social Security? It's not the right time of the month."

"Maybe they sent me an extra one," said Miss Tilley, snatching the envelope.

Rachel looked over her shoulder as she opened the familiar envelope and produced a green check.

"It's a fake!" declared Miss T. "The paper's not right."

Rachel took the flimsy check. "Boy, it looks real, though, doesn't it? But if you cash it, you're signing on for a loan. It's really just a credit card offer."

"Didn't fool me," crowed Miss T.

"But I wonder how many people do get fooled," mused Rachel aloud, as she ripped up the offer and dropped it in the wastebasket.

"Can't blame folks for trying," mused Miss T. " 'A fool and his money are soon parted.' That's what Papa used to say. 'Caveat emptor.' "

Rachel was about to protest, but went to answer the doorbell instead. Shirley was standing on the stoop, her hands clasped together and her handbag dangling from her arm.

"I was in the neighborhood and thought I'd just drop in," she simpered, looking over Rachel's shoulder to Miss Tilley. "I hope it's not a bad time."

"There's never a bad time for you, dear."

Miss Tilley was practically singing. Rachel had never heard her sound like this. What had happened to the Miss Tilley she knew? The woman who proudly declared she never hesitated to think the worst of anyone.

"Come right on in and set a spell," continued Miss Tilley.

"Let me take your coat," said Rachel, remembering her manners. "Have you eaten lunch? Can I get you something?"

"Aren't you sweet," declared Shirley. "I could stand a cup of tea."

"Good idea. I'll have one too," chimed in Miss Tilley, dismissing Rachel.

Rachel headed for the kitchen, trying not to feel snubbed. After all, it was only natural that Miss T would want to spend time with her long-lost niece. She set the kettle on the stove and began arranging cookies on a plate. She didn't intend to eavesdrop but couldn't avoid it; the women's voices carried in the small house.

"Guess what!" exclaimed Shirley. "I brought pictures of Mother. I thought you might enjoy looking at them."

"Photographs? What a good idea. And aren't you thoughtful to bring them."

"I just brought a few today. The most recent ones. But if you're interested, I could bring the family albums."

"Family albums! I'd love to see them."

To Rachel, in the kitchen, it sounded as if Miss T was practically salivating.

"Don't say another word. I'll bring them next time I come. Now this is Mother, sitting on the patio outside her condo at the retirement community."

There was silence as Miss Tilley studied the photograph.

Her voice cracked when she finally spoke, commenting on an irrelevant detail. "What is that plant? I've never seen anything like it here."

Rachel knew she was struggling to contain her emotions, using the tried and true technique of transferring her attention away from the subject she found disturbing: her sister.

"Oh, that? That's bougainvillea," replied Shirley.

"Bougainvillea. I've read about it." There was another pause. "She never went gray, I guess. How remarkable."

Getting closer, thought Rachel, but still at a slant.

"Oh, she colored her hair. 'Tangerine' was her favorite color but sometimes she'd vary it a bit. 'Strawberry Fields' was another one she liked. I swear, I never go by that aisle in the drugstore that I don't think of Mom."

In the kitchen, Rachel nearly choked. In the living room, Miss Tilley's jaw dropped.

"My sister dyed her hair?"

"Religiously. Every month."

"Goodness. I must say she didn't look her age. Is she wearing shorts?"

"That was her golfing outfit. Cute, isn't it? I like the way the color on the shirt matches the shorts."

"Harriet played golf?"

"Oh, yes. She loved it. She played regularly with three friends. They were even in a league. I believe they won a few tournaments. Of course, that was quite a few years ago, now. She didn't play really in the last few years of her life. Her health wasn't that good."

"No?"

"Pretty typical, I guess. High blood pressure, of course. And then she had to have that cataract operation. It was after that the osteoporosis began to be a concern. Considering she smoked all her life it was a mercy she only had emphysema, not lung cancer. It was the leukemia that did her in, however."

"Harriet smoked?"

"Like a chimney. I used to tell her she ought to stop but she'd never listen to me. Wouldn't listen to her doctor, either. Of course, I think she was right there. He had her on so many medications that you had to wonder what happened inside, after she'd swallowed all those pills. Expensive, too. She generally took about half of what he prescribed, but it still took her a good quarter hour or more every morning to take her medicines."

"I do occasionally take an aspirin," admitted Miss Tilley. "I have a touch of arthritis."

Rachel smiled, hearing the waspish tone of Miss T's voice.

"Well, good for you. It must be this good, clean air you have up here."

"Is this a tricycle?"

"Mom loved that trike. She rode it all around the retirement community. Over to the pool and the community center, you know. Mah-jongg every afternoon. She wouldn't have missed it for the world."

"Tricycles are for children."

That's my girl, thought Rachel. The uncharacteristic fit of sentimentality was apparently over.

"And adults. In Florida they're very popular with older folks. Because of the stability, you know. They're not as tippy as a bicycle. You see a lot of them there, believe me."

"I'm sure I would feel ridiculous on a tricycle."

"You should try it! You might like it."

When Rachel brought in the tea, she found the two women sitting side by side, studying the photographs.

"Look at this, Rachel," said Miss Tilley. "It's my sister Harriet on a tricycle. Did you ever hear of such a thing?"

"I have. My father rides one." She turned to Shirley. "My folks live in Naples."

"That's not far from Fort Myers, where my mother lived."

"It seems like another world," said Miss Tilley, taking a restorative sip of tea.

"It's very different from Maine," said Rachel. "My folks say they like it there, but even they say they miss the changing seasons. My mother says she can't get used to Christmas without any snow."

"Not my folks," said Shirley. "Pop said he hoped he never saw another snowflake. Mom used to love to listen to the weather reports; the colder it got up north, the happier she was."

"She used to love snow when she was a little girl." Miss Tilley's tone was wistful.

"People change as they grow older," observed Shirley. "Don't you think so?"

"I don't know," said Miss Tilley, a note of doubt in her voice. "I don't think I've changed." She looked up at the portrait of her father on the wall.

"Well, I say life's an ever-flowing river. It's never too late to jump in and go along for the ride."

"I suppose you're right," said Miss Tilley, beaming at her. "So tell me more about this amazing sister of mine."

Back in the kitchen, Rachel put the last dish away and hung the damp dish towel on the ancient wooden rack that hung above the sink. She looked around the room, basically unchanged since the old wood stove gave way to a newfangled propane model, and wondered why New Englanders were so attached to their old-fashioned things. It was pure cheapness, she decided. As long as something worked, a New Englander would hang on to it.

It was time for her to leave, but she hesitated. She didn't want to barge into the living room and disturb the two women. Miss Tilley was obviously enjoying hearing the titillating details of her sister's racy lifestyle.

Hearing a lapse in the conversation, Rachel stuck her head in the room.

"I'm leaving now, Miss T. Just wanted to say good-bye."

"Is it time for you to go already?"

"Yup. Two o'clock. Oh, one thing before I go. Do you want me to pick up anything at the store for you?"

"No need for you to bother," said Shirley. "I can get Auntie anything she needs."

Rachel knew it was ridiculous, but she felt as if Shirley was taking over and pushing her out.

"Okay. Well, I'll see you tomorrow."

"Don't you worry about a thing," said Shirley. "I'll take good care of my favorite aunt."

"I know you will," agreed Rachel, as Shirley closed the door behind her.

She turned back as she walked to the car and saw Shirley watching her from the window. She raised her hand in a wave and Shirley waved back.

From inside the house, Shirley waited until Rachel had driven away. Then she turned her attention to her aunt.

"Aunt Julia, would you like to watch a little TV? Norah's on in a few minutes and, well, I don't watch much TV, but I do enjoy *Norah!*"

There was no answer, and when she looked closer she saw that the old woman's eyes were closed. She had nodded off.

Because she lived so close to the school, Julia always went home for lunch. She didn't have to bother to carry a lunch pail like the children who lived outside town, and she didn't have to eat at her desk or put up with the antics of the rowdy boys during recess. Instead, she walked the block or two home, her mind lost in daydreams inspired by the morning reading lesson. Today, she was imagining herself as the beautiful Rowena in Sir Walter Scott's *Ivanhoe*.

Rowena's eyes widened as she heard sounds of battle coming from inside the castle. . . . No, it wasn't sounds of battle. It was Father, roaring, and Mother, crying, inside the big white house on Main Street.

Julia pushed open the kitchen door and saw her mother, hunched over the kitchen table with her head in her arms. Mother was sobbing.

"What's the matter?"

Mother sat up and wiped her eyes on her apron. "It's your sister . . ."

"Has something happened to Harriet?"

"It hasn't happened to her! It's what she's done!"

Julia tried to swallow the lump in her throat. "What has she done?"

"She's cut her hair!"

Julia's mouth made a little o. She couldn't believe it. Harriet had been threatening to bob her hair for months, but Father had absolutely forbidden it.

"Her beautiful, long hair. Her best feature. Gone." Mother threw up her hands in a gesture of defeat.

From upstairs, Julia heard the drone of Father's voice, followed by shrieks from Harriet. She knew that Father had found a use for the hairbrush Harriet would not be needing anymore.

"Mother, what's that smell? I think something's burning."

Mother jumped to her feet. "The cream puffs! Oh, no!" She pulled a pan from the oven.

"They don't look too bad to me," said Julia, brightly.

After all, they only had patches of black. For the most part they were just very, very brown.

"I was making them for the bridge club. They're coming this afternoon."

Even Julia, who was only ten, knew that her mother could not serve anything that was less than perfect to the bridge club. If she did, soon everyone would be saying what a shame it was that Mrs. Tilley was having *difficulties*. No, her mother would not serve scorched cream puffs to the bridge club.

"What am I going to do?" wailed Mama.

Julia heard her father coming down the stairs. "Ask Papa to get something at the bakery," she suggested.

"I will!"

Mother jumped to her feet and ran down the hall, but she was too late. The front door had closed and Papa was proceeding down the front walk. Mama would never call to him from the porch; she couldn't run after him. Such conduct was unthinkable in public.

Mama's steps were slow as she returned to the kitchen.

"I'll just make some cookies," she said, reaching for the bread knife and slicing the homemade loaf so she could make sandwiches.

"I wish I'd been born a man," she declared, waving the knife. "Then I could put my hat on and walk out the door!"

"I hope Harriet stops crying before the ladies get here," said Julia.

"I'd like to wring that girl's neck," said Mother.

Miss Tilley's eyes flew open. She wasn't ten years old, she was close to ninety. She wasn't sitting in her mother's kitchen in the big white house on Main Street, she was sitting in the Boston rocker by the fireplace in the little gray-shingled house she had bought after her parents had both died.

"You had a nice little rest, didn't you?" It was Shirley, smiling at her from the couch. In the corner, the TV was on.

Miss Tilley looked at the TV as if it were an ugly spider that had come crawling out of a crack.

"I was just watching *Norah!*" said Shirley, turning it off. "I hope you don't mind."

"Not at all." Her tone indicated that while she didn't mind, she didn't quite approve, either.

"Would you like something? Can I get you some of that sherry?"

"That would be very nice," admitted Miss Tilley.

"I'll just be a jif," said Shirley, scooting into the kitchen.

"A lot of people have color, now, you know," she called from the other room. "I'm surprised you still have black and white."

Miss Tilley waited for her to return to the living room before she answered.

"I only watch the evening news," she said.

"But you don't know what you're missing," insisted Shirley. "Why, take Norah, for example. She looks different in color. That skin. That hair. She's a gorgeous woman."

"I don't need a TV to see Norah in living color. She has a summer home right here in Tinker's Cove."

"She does?" exclaimed Shirley, obviously starstruck.

Miss Tilley was enjoying Shirley's reaction so much that she went even further. "Stick around," she said, casually. "I'll introduce you sometime."

"Actually," said Shirley, seizing the moment, "it's getting rather late for me to drive all the way back to Auburn—that's where I've been staying with some friends. I didn't want to leave while you were asleep and I didn't want to wake you up, so I stayed. But I don't think I'd get back before dark if I leave now." Shirley paused for breath. "Aunt Julia, would you mind very much if I stayed the night?" she finally asked.

"That would be just fine."

Shirley gave the old woman a quick hug, concealing her satisfied smirk.

Chapter Fourteen

It was a slim lead, but it was all she had, so Lucy decided she would call Officers Kodak and Wickes as soon as she got to the office. There was no answer at the vacationing Wickeses' house, however, so she left a message. She'd already started dialing Howie Kodak when she remembered he would probably be sleeping since he was working the night shift. Waking him up would be a bad way to start an interview, so she jotted his name and number down on a yellow sticky and slapped it onto her computer so she wouldn't forget.

"What did we do before stickies?" she asked Phyllis.

"I believe people tied a string on their finger, but I'm not exactly sure how it worked," said Phyllis, greeting Ted with a smile.

He didn't smile back. "Have you got that story you promised me?" he asked Lucy.

"You'll have it in half an hour," promised Lucy, waiting for her computer to boot up.

She quickly polished off the elder abuse story and began working on a summary of last night's finance committee meeting. Phyllis was busy putting the classified ads together, so when the phone rang Ted answered it. It was a reader who took great exception to a letter to the editor that ran the previous week.

"Ma'am, that letter does *not* represent my viewpoint or the viewpoint of the paper—only the views of the person who wrote it."

Lucy's and Phyllis's eyes met and they shared a chuckle as Ted's tone became more exasperated.

"Well, if the letter upsets you so much, why don't you write a response? I'd be happy to print it."

Lucy's phone rang and she picked it up, hoping it wasn't another angry reader. It wasn't.

"Listen, Lucy," said Sue, by way of a greeting, "Sidra called again and they've absolutely got to have more info if they're going to put Miss T on the *Norah!* show. You've got to get over there today and get some more material."

"Whoa," said Lucy, fingering the stack of papers on her desk. "No can do. I have a job, you know."

There was a pause while Sue considered this. "There must be some way."

"Tomorrow afternoon," suggested Lucy. "After deadline."

"Sidra wants it today."

"Well, Sidra will just have to wait," said Lucy.

"I'll call her back and tell her we can absolutely, definitely have great, fantastic material for her tomorrow."

"You tell her that," agreed Lucy, wondering how she could possibly deliver on such a promise. "I've got to go."

She hung up the phone and it immediately rang again.

"How am I supposed to get anything done?" she asked Phyllis, as she picked it up.

"Mom?"

"Toby?" Lucy's heart skipped a beat. Toby hardly ever called home from college, unlike his younger sister, Elizabeth, who checked in every Sunday evening, and he never called her at work. She knew something must be wrong. "Is everything okay?"

"Sure, Mom. I just called to see how you're all doing."

"We're fine," said Lucy, seriously doubting he was telling the truth. "Sara's birthday is coming up next Saturday."

"Uh, really? Thanks for reminding me."

"Maybe you could send her a present. Maybe a Coburn U T-shirt or something?"

"I'm kind of low on cash, Mom."

"A card?" persisted Lucy, rolling her eyes for Phyllis's benefit.

Phyllis was enjoying the conversation; her shoulders were heaving with laughter.

"Sure. I could do that." He paused. "It would need a stamp, wouldn't it? Uh, where do you get those?"

Lucy shook her head in disbelief. "The post office!"

Phyllis was now laughing so hard she was clutching her stomach.

Lucy wasn't seeing the humor in the situation. "You know, Toby, I have work to do. Maybe I could call you tonight?"

"Actually, I kinda wanted to ask your advice."

Lucy braced herself.

"See, I'm kinda worried my grades aren't going to be very good this term."

"What's the problem? You're a smart kid—you got 1400 on your SATs. Are you going to classes?"

"Pretty much."

Lucy's temper flared. "Well, that's not good enough. That's what you're there for. There's really no excuse for skipping classes."

"I know," admitted Toby. "It's just that economics is at eight o'clock, and even though I set my alarm I sometimes sleep through it."

"Get a louder alarm, or get a friend to wake you up."

"I'm going to do that, Mom. I really am. But I don't know if it will be enough. I got some pretty bad midterm grades."

"In economics? Maybe you can talk to the professor about getting some extra help."

"In all my courses actually."

Lucy's ears were beginning to ring. Phyllis, she noticed, was no longer laughing but looked serious.

"Toby, this is unacceptable. You know how expensive college is. We really expect you to take it seriously and do your best. It sounds to me like there's too much beer and partying and not enough studying going on."

"You're right, Mom. I'll try harder."

Lucy was out of patience. "Don't say you'll try harder. Do it. Right now. Grab your books and go over to the library. It's open. Go."

She slammed down the receiver.

Both Ted and Phyllis were staring at her.

"I can't believe it," she exclaimed. "He's a smart kid—what's he been doing all term?"

"Drugs," suggested Phyllis.

"Girls," offered Ted.

"Not on my dime. I'm not sending him to college to waste his time."

They nodded in agreement.

"Bring him home and put him to work," said Phyllis.

"There's always the army," added Ted.

Lucy rubbed her temples. She was getting a headache.

"Here. Take these," said Phyllis, handing her two aspirins and a paper cup full of water.

"Thanks."

Lucy swallowed the tablets and tried to relax her tense muscles by picturing a quiet mountain lake. Instead, she saw a clutter of yellow reminders stuck to her computer screen. She decided she'd better call Officer Kodak before his sticky became as old as the others. A woman answered.

"Mrs. Kodak? Lucy Stone at *The Pennysaver*. Could I have a quick word with your husband?"

"He's asleep right now and I don't like to wake him. He's working the night shift this week, you know."

"Oh, no, don't wake him. Could you just ask him to call me at his convenience? It's kind of important."

"Why don't you just stop by at the house around five or so? He'll be up by then."

* * *

It was a little after five when Lucy pulled into the Kodaks' driveway, carefully avoiding an asortment of bikes and Big Wheels.

"Come on in," invited Mrs. Kodak, who turned out to be every bit as blond and perky as Doris Day. "My name's Bonnie and this is Trevor," she said, pointing to a chubby five-year-old, "and his little brother, Hunter."

"I'm three," said Hunter, holding up four fingers.

"That's four, this is three." His older brother was quick to correct him.

Lucy smiled. They reminded her of Toby and Elizabeth, when they were younger and the problems were simpler.

"What can I do for you?" Howie Kodak was seating himself at the table, giving each boy a high five. With his crew cut, he looked like an overgrown kid himself.

"Lucy, sit down," invited Bonnie. "Can I give you something to eat? A Coke?"

"No, no. I'll only be a minute. I don't want to hold up your dinner. It's just that I've been asked to look into Sherman Cobb's death—Bob Goodman doesn't believe it was suicide, you know."

"I know," said Howie. He didn't bother to hide his disapproval.

Lucy plunged ahead. "Anyway, I know you were on patrol the night he died and I wondered if you saw anything unusual."

"You could say that," replied Howie, and Lucy's hopes rose. "I won't forget that night any time soon."

This was much better than she had expected. "What happened?" she asked eagerly.

"That's the night that tractor trailer slid off the exit ramp out on the interstate. What a mess. Eggs everywhere. I was called out there to help direct traffic."

Lucy tried not to show her disappointment.

"So you weren't even here in town?"

"No, ma'am. I was out there all night while they cleaned up the mess. It was one hell of a night."

Lucy rose to go. "What about Bob Wickes? He started at eleven. Do you think he might've seen anything?"

Howie shrugged. "You'd have to ask him, but you can't talk to him until Monday. He's in Orlando with the whole family."

"Thanks for your help." She smiled at Trevor and Hunter. "Bye, boys."

"Now, what do you say?" prompted Howie.

"Good-bye. Thanks for coming," they chorused.

Lucy's smile vanished as soon as she was out the door. Another lead fizzled, another dead end in this investigation that was going absolutely nowhere. No wonder the police were calling it a suicide.

And even worse, she was going to have to tell Bill about Toby's difficulties at college. What she wouldn't give, she thought as she started the car, to go back in time about fifteen years. Back when Toby and Elizabeth were five and three—and she was every bit as pretty and perky as Bonnie Kodak.

Chapter Fifteen

Taking her cue from an article she'd read in a women's magazine, Lucy chose her moment to deliver the bad news about Toby. She was on her way out the door on Wednesday, deadline day, and had little time to spare.

"Oh, by the way," she said, as she buttoned her coat, "Toby called me at work yesterday."

Bill's eyebrows shot up. "He did? That's kind of unusual, isn't it? Is something the matter?"

"He said he's worried about his grades." Lucy was pulling on her gloves. "He doesn't think they're going to be very good. Sounded pretty bad, actually."

"What did you tell him?" asked Bill, as Lucy opened the door.

She was on the porch. "I told him to stop partying and get his ass to class," she said, giving him a little wave. She was halfway down the driveway when she caught sight of Bill in the rearview mirror, still standing in the doorway.

Arriving at *The Pennysaver,* Lucy was soon caught up in the rush to beat deadline. She was surprised when she looked up from the page she was proofreading and saw Sue.

"What are you doing here?" she asked.

"We have a date, remember? We're going to see Miss Tilley."

"Right, right. I'm almost done."

"I'll wait," said Sue, taking a seat and giving Ted a big smile.

"I saw Pam at the IGA," she told him. "I hope you like chicken. They're on sale and she was buying a lot of them. I guess she must be going to freeze them. I didn't know you have a freezer. When did you get it, Ted?"

Ted gave her a blank look, grunted, and started searching through a stack of papers.

"Is he always this sociable?" asked Sue, turning to Phyllis. "You'll never guess who else I saw at the IGA. Your cousin."

Phyllis was flipping through the phone book, checking on a number.

"You know, Elfrida! She's just back from a week in the Caribbean. She looks great. She got a terrific tan. Says she never burns, lucky girl."

Phyllis closed the book and went back to her computer.

Sue let out a big sigh. "How much longer do you think you're going to be, Lucy?"

Lucy looked at Ted.

"Go," he said.

"Are you sure?"

"We'll get done faster if you get her out of here," he said.

"Am I interrupting you?" Sue's eyes were round. "It didn't look as if you were doing anything important."

"Go, go." Ted shooed them with his hand.

"Well, I must say, that wasn't very nice," fumed Sue, pausing on the sidewalk while Lucy fumbled with her coat.

"It's always a little tense just before deadline," explained Lucy. "We have to make sure there aren't any mistakes."

"Right." Sue laughed. "Like there are never any mistakes in *The Pennysaver.*"

"Well, we try," insisted Lucy, climbing up to perch beside Sue in her big SUV.

When Lucy and Sue knocked on Miss Tilley's door, it

was Shirley who answered. She didn't invite them in, but placed herself squarely in the doorway.

"Where's Rachel?" Lucy blurted out the words, then realized how rude they sounded. "I'm sorry, Shirley. It's lovely to see you again. I was just surprised because Rachel always answers the door."

"Rachel's doing errands, so I said I'd stay home with Auntie."

"Isn't that nice," said Sue, in a brisk, businesslike tone. "We're here to see your aunt. I called yesterday and she's expecting us."

Shirley didn't move. "Actually, it might be better if you came back later. She's resting now."

Sue rose to the challenge. Raising her voice, she said, "She's expecting us, and I'm sure she would be disappointed to miss us."

"Who's there?" It was Miss Tilley. "Is it Lucy and Sue?"

Defeated, Shirley turned aside and Sue sailed past her. Lucy followed, catching a glimpse of the look Shirley gave Sue. It wasn't very nice, she thought.

"How nice to see you both," chortled Miss Tilley, clasping their hands and holding her wrinkled cheek up for the obligatory peck. "Can I offer you some tea?"

"Tea would be lovely," said Sue, settling herself on the sofa.

"We can't stay long," added Lucy, perching beside her. "I just have a few follow-up questions from that interview."

"What interview would that be?" inquired Shirley.

"Just a little profile I'm writing about your aunt," said Lucy. She didn't want to say anything about the party or the *Norah!* show because the birthday celebration was supposed to be a surprise.

"I thought somebody mentioned tea," said Sue.

"Oh, that's right." Miss Tilley turned to Shirley. "Would you mind, dear? Since Rachel isn't here."

Shirley looked as if she did mind, but she went off to the kitchen.

"Well, like I said, when I started writing this little profile

I discovered I needed a bit more information, especially about how life here in Tinker's Cove has changed. For instance, what was the school like when you were a little girl?"

"It was a one-room schoolhouse and Miss Simmons was the teacher. She taught all of us. I don't know how she managed it, really. Then there got to be too many children for one teacher and they hired Mr. Brown. He took the boys and Miss Simmons kept the girls."

Lucy felt Sue poking her in the ribs.

"Did the girls and the boys get the same education? Was it equal?"

"I don't know. I was never in class with the boys!" Miss Tilley cackled and slapped her thigh, as Shirley returned carrying a tray with four mugs. "Did the kettle boil? I didn't hear it whistle. And why aren't you using the teacups?"

Lucy almost felt sorry for Shirley. Miss Tilley could be crotchety at times, and no amount of family feeling and sentiment could overcome the habits of a lifetime.

"I can fix it the way she likes it," said Sue, taking the tray back into the kitchen.

"Was Miss Simmons a good teacher? Were you prepared for college?" asked Lucy, continuing her questions.

"She was a very good teacher, and she encouraged me to go on to college. Most of the girls didn't, you know. Neither did the boys, for that matter. Most of the boys farmed or fished, like their fathers, and the girls got married and kept house for them." She paused when Sue returned with the tray holding the teapot, nestled in its bright chintz cozy, cups and saucers, silver teaspoons and tea strainer, and a plateful of hot, buttery toast. "Now that's more like it."

Lucy glanced at Shirley, but if her nose was out of joint she wasn't showing it.

Sue poured out a steaming cup for Miss Tilley, adding a tiny bit of sugar and a slice of lemon. She perched a couple of toast triangles on the saucer.

"I hope that isn't butter!" exclaimed Shirley.

"I know what they say," agreed Lucy, "but she's been eating it her entire life. . . ."

"With no apparent ill effects," said Sue, passing a cup to Shirley.

"Considering the amount of cholesterol she eats, I don't know how she can be so healthy. It's very puzzling," said Shirley, scratching her head.

From the way her hair moved, Lucy wondered if she might be wearing a wig.

"I do want to take good care of my aunt," continued Shirley, lifting her cup with a raised pinky. "But she's very set in her ways."

"Don't worry," said Lucy. "We know what an old witch she can be. Isn't that right, Miss T? But your bark is worse than your bite."

Lucy had expected the old woman to answer with a sharp retort, but she remained silent, chewing her toast.

"How did you two find each other, after all these years?" asked Sue.

"I think it was meant to be," replied Shirley, smoothing her collar. "Just like Norah says—do you watch *Norah!* on TV? My aunt says she has a home right here in Tinker's Cove. I'd so love to meet her—well, anyway, as Norah says, things happen for a reason. And I didn't feel well that day so I didn't go in to work and I was watching her show and there was a wonderful family reunion. Then they had a TV commercial about this nationwide information service. So I called and gave the operator Auntie's name and state and she came right back with a number. Someone was certainly watching over me that day." She took Miss Tilley's hand.

"Were you surprised when Shirley called?" Lucy asked Miss Tilley.

The old woman didn't seem to hear her, so Lucy raised her voice and asked again. This time, Miss Tilley heard.

"I sure was. I didn't know my sister had even had a child."

"And you never thought of looking for your sister?" asked Sue.

"Not even after your father died?" asked Lucy, glancing up at the portrait of Judge Tilley. Had his influence been so strong, even after his death, that it had prohibited Miss Tilley from finding her sister? When she glanced back at Miss Tilley, she noticed the old woman's eyelids were drooping.

"I guess we'd better go," she said, getting to her feet. "It looks as if it's nap time."

"She does this all the time," said Shirley. "She'll be chatting away one minute and next thing you know she's drifted off."

"One of the perks of old age," said Sue, gathering up her purse.

"Thanks for the tea," said Lucy, making her farewell.

But when they were outside, she grabbed Sue's arm. "What do you think of Shirley?" she demanded.

"I think she's a saint," said Sue. "Imagine putting up with that old bat's demands. It would drive me crazy. Can't have tea in a mug, for goodness' sake. It's ridiculous." She screwed up her perfectly outlined and painted lips. "At this rate, Miss T will be a hundred before I have enough information for Sidra. Maybe I should let Shirley in on the plan for a surprise party—do you think she would help? She's a big Norah fan, after all."

Lucy remembered Shirley's reluctance to admit them.

"She probably could, but I doubt she would," said Lucy. "I think she's up to something. Did you notice she was wearing a wig?"

"Big deal. Lots of women wear wigs."

"They do? I don't know anyone who wears a wig."

"Yes, you do. Marge Culpepper wore one when she was having chemotherapy. So did Andrea Rogers. And Fanny Small has one, too. She says it's easier when she travels on business trips because she doesn't have to worry about doing her hair."

"Well, that may be so, but I still think there's something fishy about Shirley," said Lucy, darkly, as they got into the car.

"Mama! Mama!"

Little Julia woke from her afternoon nap and called for

her mother. When there was no answer, she decided to find her. She sat on the side of the bed with her legs dangling. Far below her, on the flowered carpet, were her shoes. They were black and had buttons that fastened up the side. Eight buttons on each shoe. The buttonhook lay high above her, on top of the chest of drawers.

She would have to go in her stocking feet, decided Julia, jumping off the bed and landing with a thud. She knew she wasn't supposed to walk around without her shoes, but she knew that if she put them on without buttoning them they would be too loose and might trip her. She certainly didn't want to fall down the stairs.

She paused at the top of the long flight. The front hall, with its crystal chandelier and ornate mirrored coat stand, seemed very far away. What if she fell? Papa would be very angry if she hurt herself, and Mama would cry.

"Mama!" she called.

There was no answer. Julia knew she would have to go downstairs, because Mama was most certainly in the kitchen. That's where she almost always was, making bread or basting the roast or shelling peas or rolling out piecrust with her long, heavy rolling pin. Julia gathered up her courage and grasped the carved walnut railing with her hand and lowered her foot to the next step. That wasn't so hard, she told herself, taking the next step. Gaining courage, she was down the stairs in no time and running down the long hall to the kitchen in the back of the house.

She shoved the swinging door open and ran in, but Mama wasn't there. Where could she be?

"Mama!" Julia shrieked, using every bit of lung power she possessed.

The only answer was a thud, from far off. Another thud, louder this time, seemed to come all the way from the top of the house. The attic. Mama must be in the attic.

Julia sat down on the bottom step of the kitchen stairs. It was a long climb up to the attic. Two flights, and the back stairs were much steeper than the fancy front stairs. Julia had never climbed that far and she wasn't sure she could do it.

She looked at the cookie jar. It was full of molasses cookies Mama had baked just yesterday. She wanted a cookie very much, but she knew she must not take a cookie without asking. She could only ask, she realized, if she climbed up to the attic. She stood up and grasped hold of the flimsy railing that wobbled on its bracket.

The steps were steep and she had to lift her knees very high and then haul herself up by pulling on the railing. It was a lot of work, but Julia was determined to get to the top. Mama would be so surprised! Especially when she told her she had climbed up two flights, all the way from the kitchen.

After the first flight, Julia stopped to catch her breath and to stoke up her courage. She didn't like the attic. It was dark and smelled dusty and there were spiderwebs. Julia didn't like spiders—the way they seemed to appear out of nowhere and scuttled across the floor made her hair stand on end and her stomach clench.

"Mama!" she yelled, from the bottom of the attic stairs.

The only answer was a long scraping sound, and a grunt. Mama was definitely in the attic.

Before she knew it, Julia had climbed up the stairs.

"Mama! I woke up and I couldn't find you!"

Mama was on her knees, leaning on a wooden trunk with a rounded lid. Her hair had come loose and there was a streak of dirt on her cheek. Her shirtwaist had come loose from her skirt. Julia had never seen her so disheveled. She stared.

"I was just putting the winter clothes away," she said. "We won't need our heavy woolen coats until next winter."

Julia looked around the shadowy attic nervously. "I'm hungry," she said.

"I suppose you want some cookies," said Mama. "We'll have some just as soon as I get this trunk back where it belongs."

Mama gave a great shove and the trunk slid about six inches.

"It's very heavy," she said, panting.

"Can I help?" offered Julia.

"I think I can do it," said Mama, rising off her knees and throwing her weight against the trunk with a great grunt.

The trunk moved about a foot. Mama slid to the floor, leaning her back against the trunk and blowing at a dangling strand of hair.

"Sometimes I think you need a lot of muscle to be the lady of the house," she said, lifting her arm and bending it, like the weightlifter Julia had seen at the circus. "I wring the laundry and beat the carpets and turn the mattresses. Who do you think is stronger? Me or Papa's secretary, little Miss Kaiser, who sits at a desk and uses a typewriting machine?"

Mama gave a great heave and shoved the chest back under the eaves, then stood up and dusted off her hands.

"You are," said Julia, looking down at her dusty, stockinged feet. She hoped Mama wasn't going to spank her.

"Where are your shoes, little miss?"

"In my room."

"Couldn't do the buttons, could you?"

Julia shook her head. "No."

"Well, let's get those shoes on and then we'll have some cookies. What do you say to that?"

Julia let out a big sigh. "Good."

In the kitchen, Shirley was washing up the tea things. Ridiculous, she fumed, dumping the tea leaves into the garbage. Instead of four mugs she had all this china to wash, just because the old biddy wouldn't use tea bags. As if anybody could taste the difference! And what was the matter with setting a piece of cake or some toast on a paper napkin, instead of a plate, to save on washing? Not that there was a heck of a lot to do in this place, with no color TV and nobody except Her Nibs to talk to. It was enough to make her miss Snake, for goodness' sake.

The phone started to ring and she grabbed it, hoping the old lady wouldn't wake up.

"Ma! What's up?'

The gruff voice was music to her ears.

"Snake! I was just thinking about you."

"I told you you'd miss me, didn't I? So what do you say? Is it time for my big entrance?"

Shirley considered. It was a risk. What if the old bag got uppity? Well, what if she did? She could handle her, as long as those nosy women stayed away. And she was pretty sure they wouldn't come calling once Snake was on the scene.

"Like they say on TV: 'Come on down!'"

"Get ready to rumble, Mama!"

Shirley replaced the receiver and went into the living room just as Miss Tilley was awakening.

"Guess what?" she cooed to the blinking old woman. "Your grand-nephew is coming to visit!"

"How wonderful!" exclaimed Miss Tilley, clapping her hands together. "I can't wait to meet him."

Chapter Sixteen

Lucy was sitting at the kitchen table, nursing a cup of coffee but skipping her usual English muffin because she was going to have breakfast later with the girls, and thinking about Toby. She was so disappointed in him. If he were home, she could shake some sense into him. But he was miles away in New Hampshire. Maybe she should drive out for a visit and see for herself what was going on.

Bill had laughed when she suggested the idea the night before. "Don't be ridiculous," he'd told her. "Toby's a big boy now. If he's got himself in a pickle, he'll just have to get himself out."

"But we can't just let him throw away an opportunity like this," she'd protested.

"You know what they say: 'You can lead a horse to water but you can't make him drink.' We got him to college, but we can't study for him. He's got to do it for himself. It's his life, after all. He's got to take responsibility for it." He paused, studying her expression. "You know I'm right."

"I know," agreed Lucy. "But I don't have to like it."

She was startled out of her reverie by Sara, who thumped in, yanked open the refrigerator door and stared inside.

"There's never anything good to eat in this house," she said.

"There's OJ, V8, bananas, hot chocolate, milk, cereal, oatmeal, toast, English muffins, bagels, yogurt, frozen waffles, eggs, ham and cheese, fresh fruit—what do you mean there's nothing good to eat?"

"It's all way fattening," complained Sara.

"Nothing is fattening, if you eat a sensible portion. Those are light yogurts, by the way. A hundred and ten calories. Definitely not fattening. V8 only has thirty-five calories, and it's full of fiber."

Sara poured herself a glass of V8 and cautiously took a sip. "That's disgusting," she exclaimed, pouring the rest of the glass down the sink.

"Waste not, want not," muttered Lucy as Zoe arrived on the scene.

"Cereal?" asked Lucy.

"Yes, Mommy," said Zoe, taking her usual seat and taking a banana from the fruit bowl in the center of the table. She peeled it and took a bite while she waited for her mother to fix the cereal, then dropped her head to her hands.

"Are you tired this morning, sweetie?"

Zoe nodded. "I couldn't sleep because Sara was on the phone late last night."

"Tattletale," hissed Sara.

Lucy and Bill had reluctantly agreed to let the girls have a phone extension in their room on the condition that it not be used after eight o'clock, which was Zoe's bedtime.

"Is this true?"

Sara's expression was defensive. "She wasn't supposed to tell! It was an emergency, Mom! Honest."

"An emergency?" Lucy was puzzled. There had been no sudden asthma attacks, no falls down the stairs, no fires that she was aware of.

"Davia Didrickson says she might not come to my party," wailed Sara.

"Well, you have plenty of other friends."

"You don't understand, Mom. Davia is the coolest girl in the eighth grade. If she doesn't come, nobody will."

"Nonsense. All your old friends will come."

"Not the boys. The boys won't come without Davia. The party will be ruined. We'll just be a bunch of sad, unpopular girls, getting fat on pizza and doing each other's nails in social Siberia."

"Well, at least you've got a sense of humor about it," observed Lucy. "That's a step in the right direction."

"I wasn't joking, Mom." Sara grabbed her backpack and marched out the door.

Watching from the window, Lucy saw her wiping her eyes with the back of her hand.

"You're going to miss the bus if you don't hurry, Pumpkin," Lucy told Zoe. "You better scoot, and take Sara's jacket. She forgot it."

"Okay, Mom." Zoe held out her cheek for a kiss.

If only they could stay little forever, thought Lucy, watching as Zoe ran down the driveway after her older sister. Arrest growth at second grade. *Why not? Think of the anguish it would save.*

Half an hour later she was parking the Subaru in front of Jake's. Joining her friends at their usual table, she ordered the day's special: Belgian waffles.

"Going a little overboard, aren't we?" asked Sue, nibbling on her wheat toast, no butter.

"I need nourishment. It's been a rough day."

"It's only eight-thirty," said Rachel.

"Tell me about it. Sara's upset because Davia Didrickson is threatening to skip her coed sleep-over birthday party."

"Ah, Davia," said Pam. "The queen of eighth grade."

"You know her?"

"I have not been so fortunate. I know of her. From volunteering at the middle school. Even the teachers are smitten with Davia."

"How does this happen?" demanded Sue. "Why do some kids become popular and others don't?"

"Hormones?" ventured Lucy.

"Did you say coed sleep-over?" inquired Pam. "I don't think I heard right."

"You heard right." Lucy paused while the waitress set the plateful of Belgian waffles in front of her. "But if Davia doesn't come, the boys won't come and then it will just be Sara's regular friends. Which would be fine with me but would break Sara's heart."

"This is what they call a lose-lose situation," said Sue.

"I know all about those," moaned Rachel. "I'm in one now, with Miss Tilley."

Lucy's and Sue's eyes met. "Shirley?" they said in unison.

"I know I should be happy for Miss T that she's got Shirley to take care of her, but I can't help feeling a little resentful about being displaced. Now I don't know whether I should keep going or what. They don't really need me over there anymore since Shirley moved in. She does everything I used to do. And more."

"You could visit," suggested Lucy. "Miss T enjoys your company."

Rachel put down the muffin she was about to bite. "The truth is I don't feel welcome there anymore. Shirley just glares at me. I'm afraid I'm going to go over there and she's not going to let me in."

"That couldn't be true!" exclaimed Pam. "I'm sure you've misunderstood."

"I don't think she's misunderstood anything," said Lucy. "There's something that isn't quite right about Shirley, if you ask me. You know she wears a wig? And she's been hitting Miss T's sherry. I found the empty bottle hidden behind the cleaning supplies."

"She's probably having chemo, poor thing," said Pam.

"That's what I told Nancy Drew here, but she doesn't believe me," said Sue.

"I think Lucy may be on to something," said Rachel.

"That Shirley's sneaky. Why didn't she just put the sherry bottle with the other bottles to be recycled?"

"Who knows?" said Pam, impatiently. "Maybe she's got some hang-up about alcohol. Listen, we've got to talk about the party. I've got the music lined up. Who else has something to report?"

"I've got the food organized," said Sue. "And Lucy's going to send some notes to Sidra. How's that coming?"

"It's coming," said Lucy, uncomfortably aware of how little she'd accomplished. "I'll fax it today," she promised.

"I only hope Shirley will let the birthday girl out of the house," said Rachel.

"Don't be silly," said Pam, dismissing her concern with a wave of the hand. "She can't lock her up!"

"I suppose not," said Rachel.

"I still can't get over it," said Pam, finishing up her oatmeal. The woman is going to be ninety years old. It's amazing."

"Not that amazing these days," said Sue. "There was a report on the evening news last night that said the fastest-growing segment of the population is the extremely old. We could all live to be a hundred."

"I'll never make it," groaned Lucy. "I'm ready to retire now."

"What will we look like?" asked Sue. "I'd rather die young and stay pretty."

"You've got to exercise, of course," advised Rachel. "The news report said exercise was a big part of it."

"Exercise can only do so much," complained Lucy. "I've been exercising, taking vitamins, drinking water, smearing myself with lotions—and I found a new wrinkle this morning."

Sue studied her face. "What moisturizer are you using?"

"Forever Young. I got it at the drugstore. I put it on every time I wash my face."

"You're not using soap, are you?"

"Of course. What else would I use?"

"Cleanser. If I were you, I'd head straight to Markson's, at the new Galleria. Go to the Countess Irene counter and ask for Natalie. She'll fix you up."

"Do you really think I should?"

"If you want your face to last until you're a hundred, you'd better hurry."

Lucy looked at her watch. "Actually, I'd better hurry if I want to keep my job. See you all next week!"

"I've got to go, too," said Rachel. "Bye, guys."

She walked out of the restaurant with Lucy, pausing on the sidewalk to ask her if she'd learned anything about Cobb's death.

"I'm pretty much at a dead end," Lucy admitted. "I spoke to Chap Willis at the funeral, but I didn't get much information from him."

"Really?" Rachel was surprised. "They were best friends."

Lucy shrugged. "He didn't want to talk about it. I think he's grieving." She paused. "I didn't find much at the house, except for a safe deposit box key. I'd love to take a look inside, but I don't know the procedure after someone's dead."

"I'll have Bob give you a call. He'll know."

"Thanks. Oh, and there's one other thing. I've been trying to find out if any of the cops on patrol that night saw anything unusual. I've already spoken to one, but the other is on vacation until Monday."

Rachel nodded excitedly. "You know who else you might try? The cleaning service. They might have seen something."

"That's a good idea," said Lucy, jotting down the phone number Rachel gave her. "Well, it's off to the salt mines for me. What about you?"

"I'd like to go over to Miss T's, just to see if she's all right, but I feel funny about it. Shirley just doesn't seem to like having me around."

Lucy thought for a minute. "You know, I could use some more information for Sidra. Why don't we go together and see what's going on?"

"Great idea."

* * *

When they arrived at Miss Tilley's little gray house, they were surprised to see that the window shades were drawn. It gave the house a blank, unwelcoming look.

"That's weird," said Rachel. "She never draws the shades. Not even at night. Says she likes to wake up to the sun shining through the windows."

"You don't think something's happened? After all, she's very old."

"Don't say that, Lucy."

Together they hurried up the walk and knocked on the door.

After what seemed a long wait, it was opened by Shirley.

"Oh, it's you two," she said, scratching her head.

Definitely a wig, thought Lucy. Shirley was only standing a few feet from her and she had an up-close view.

"We just thought we'd drop by for a little visit," said Rachel. "Can we come in?"

"It's awfully early, isn't it?" countered Shirley. "I haven't got the housework done."

That sounded reasonable enough to Lucy, noting that Shirley was dressed in jeans and a sweatshirt. She glanced down and was shocked to see that Shirley was wearing metallic-gold mules.

"We won't be long," promised Lucy.

"I'd be happy to help," offered Rachel.

"Uh, well, the truth is she's not feeling very well today. She woke up with a headache and decided to stay in, hoping to sleep it off."

"You mean she's still in bed?" Rachel was incredulous.

"Yes, she is." Shirley's eyes were flat and expressionless. "She's sleeping like a baby. You don't want to disturb her, now, do you?"

"Oh, no," said Rachel, stepping back from the door.

"Why don't you try later? Call first, okay?"

Rachel leveled her gaze directly at Shirley. "I'll do that," she promised.

They were getting in the car when they hear a roaring noise approaching.

"What's that?" asked Lucy, as the noise grew louder.

She was about to cover her ears when a huge motorcycle rounded the corner of the street and turned into Miss Tilley's driveway.

Rachel's and Lucy's jaws dropped as the rider, a heavyset man dressed in jeans and a leather jacket, got off the bike. The back of the jacket was embellished with a picture of a coiled snake and the words Mountain Rattlers M.C. Club. The rider removed his helmet, revealing long, greasy hair and an unkempt beard. He set the helmet on the back of the bike and walked up to the house, setting his chains to jingling. When he reached the stoop, the door flew open before he had a chance to knock, and he stepped inside. The door shut.

Stunned, Lucy and Rachel sat in the car for a long time. Finally, Rachel spoke.

"Oh, my God," she said.

Inside the house, Snake gave Miss Tilley's living room the once-over. Spotting the bronze bust of Lincoln on the mantel, he strode over and picked it up, examining the bottom.

"Might be worth something," he decided. He glanced up at the portrait of Judge Tilley. "Who's the old geezer?"

"Your great-grandfather. The judge."

Snake stepped back, shuddering. "Looks like a mean bastard."

"From all accounts, he was."

Snake plopped down onto the sofa and rested his motorcycle boots on the antique sea chest Miss Tilley used for a coffee table. "So what's the deal?" he asked, pulling out a crumpled cigarette pack.

"Don't light up," warned Shirley. "She doesn't like it."

Snake stared at her, then flicked a match against his thumbnail. "We'll see about that," he said.

* * *

"Who was that?" Rachel's eyes were saucers.

"A relative? A boyfriend?"

"I admit I had my differences with Shirley, but I never thought she'd have anything to do with someone like that," said Rachel.

"She let him in the house," said Lucy, who couldn't get the image on the elder abuse pamphlet out of her head. Only this time, the shadow had taken the form of a bearded, helmeted biker. "I don't like to think of Miss T being alone with them."

"You don't think they'd actually do her harm, do you?" Rachel's face had gone white, and she was so tense that her grip on Lucy's hand actually hurt.

"Oh, no," said Lucy, gently prying her hand loose and grasping it. "I only meant that it could be awkward. They don't really seem like her type." Lucy paused and climbed into her car. "I was just thinking that this branch of the family tree seems to have gone off in a different direction."

"Like Bob's cousin Alfred?" Rachel was fastening her seat belt. "The family had such high hopes for him when he got his degree in psychology, but then he went to work for a tobacco company. His job is figuring out ways to get people to smoke."

"No!"

"Yes. Especially people in Third World countries who don't know better."

"That's low."

Rachel nodded. "You can't choose your family."

"It's like those Chevy Chase movies, where the awful brother-in-law keeps turning up."

"Exactly," said Rachel, as they pulled into her driveway. "Just because he's dressed like a Hell's Angel and is kind of scary looking doesn't mean he's a bad person. We shouldn't judge him until we know him better."

Lucy smiled encouragingly at Rachel, waiting while she got out of the car, but she wasn't convinced.

"Right," she muttered to herself as she backed out into the road. "He dresses like that because he wants to win the Miss Congeniality contest."

* * *

On Friday, Lucy made a point of phoning Miss Tilley and was reassured when she heard the old woman's voice.

"How are things going?" she asked.

"Just fine. Shirley's son is here. My grand-nephew. He's a very interesting fellow." She lowered her voice. "He has a tattoo."

This wasn't quite the reaction Lucy was expecting. "Oh, well," she replied. "It takes all kinds to make a world."

"Yes, it does," agreed Miss Tilley.

That thought echoed in Lucy's mind on Saturday, as she watched the Civil War reenactors prepare for their recreation of the Battle of Portland, which was taking place in the nearby town of Granby. Why on earth grown men would dress up in costumes and play soldier was beyond her. Especially on an unseasonably warm spring day when the mercury was threatening to hit seventy or higher. The trees hadn't leafed out yet, so there wasn't a scrap of shade to be found on the grandstand overlooking the harbor, where the audience was seated. Before she could take her seat, however, Lucy had to track down Chap Willis. She found him on his hands and knees, rearranging the flags that decorated the bandstand.

"The country's in a sorry state," he said, as she approached. "The blue is supposed to be on the left. Always. You'd think people would know that."

Lucy shrugged sympathetically. "Those outfits seem pretty warm," she said, noticing that Chap Willis was sweating profusely in his blue wool jacket. "Did they wear them year-round?"

"You just got one set of clothes in those days," replied Chap. "You were hot in summer and cold in winter."

"I guess people were made of sterner stuff then." Lucy fanned herself with her notebook. "You know, I still have some questions I'd like to ask you about Sherman Cobb."

Willis surveyed the pier, where costumed soldiers were gathering and forming ranks, preparing to board the four ships moored alongside. Two were side paddle-wheelers, the third a five-masted fishing schooner named *Archer* and the fourth a sleek black sailboat with three tall masts named the *Caleb Cushing*.

"Sherman would have loved this," said Willis, growing misty-eyed. "He was the one who tracked down the *Caleb Cushing,* you know. A genuine U.S. revenue cutter, circa 1860. Isn't she a beauty?"

"She sure is."

"O' course she isn't the real *Caleb.* The Confederates burned that ship."

"What a shame," said Lucy, scribbling in her notebook.

"Oops, I've got to go. They're running up the Stars and Bars, and it's too early. The Confederates haven't taken her yet!"

Before she could protest, Cobb was gone. She decided to get a seat in the bandstand where she could enjoy the spectacle. She headed for the highest row of seats and sat down, watching the preparations. If she focused on the pier, she could almost imagine herself back in 1863, when Confederates aboard commandeered cruisers were raising havoc among fishing vessels in the Gulf of Maine. Of course, it took a certain amount of willpower to erase the modern buildings around the harbor, not to mention the McDonald's sign.

The two sailing vessels were soon under way. The *Caleb Cushing* anchored out in the harbor under the Stars and Stripes and waited while the *Archer* sailed off to the harbor entrance. There it turned, raised all its canvas and the Confederate flag, and rushed the *Caleb Cushing* at full speed.

Surprised, the crew aboard the revenue cutter put up little resistance, and soon the Confederate crew swarmed aboard and lowered the flag, replacing it with their own. Everyone in the stands booed energetically. All attention now turned to a group of men on the dock, dressed in nineteenth-century garb. One man, sporting a top hat and luxuriant side-whiskers, appeared to be their leader.

Gesturing broadly, he indicated that the men should board the two side-wheelers and attempt to take back the *Caleb Cushing*. Soon the two paddleboats were steaming out into the harbor, neatly cornering the captured ship and forcing the Confederates to surrender.

Lucy joined the applause as the boats returned to the dock and the reenactors took their places on the flag-draped, raised platform. While she waited for the ceremony to begin, Lucy studied the enlarged photograph of Sherman Cobb that had been placed in center stage and draped with red, white and blue bunting.

That face, she thought, reminded her of someone. But who? Brown eyes, square jaw, hooked nose, all arranged in a pleasant and relaxed expression. A slight smile revealed straight, white teeth. Where had she seen that face before?

"First off, I want to thank you all for coming," began Chap Willis, taking the podium. "We are here today to honor those brave men from both the North and South who fought so gallantly for their beliefs, and especially to commemorate those valiant citizens of Portland who, under the leadership of Mayor George Washington Tilley, rallied to defend their fair city from Confederate invaders in 1863."

Everyone applauded, and a few folks even cheered. When the commotion died down, Willis continued.

"We also want to take this occasion to honor one of our own, Colonel Sherman Cobb, who played such a big part in bringing about today's reenactment. It was a project very dear to his heart and it's a shame he couldn't be here with us as he has gone to answer that Final Roll Call. Now, I'd like to call for a moment of silence."

With the others, Lucy lowered her head. The sudden silence was punctuated only by a distant honk from an automobile.

Willis cleared his throat and shook his head sadly. "A fine man. He first became interested in the Civil War, he told me, when he learned he had been named for the great general, William Tecumseh Sherman. He will be missed. And now, I'd like to introduce . . ."

Lucy jotted down the names, remembering Miss Tilley's comment that her grandfather was the "hero of Portland." Putting two and two together, she concluded that George Washington Tilley must indeed have been Miss Tilley's grandfather. She snapped a few photographs of the crowd, then went out on the dock to photograph the boats. It would be an interesting story, she thought, something a little different for *Pennysaver* readers. And, she realized when she checked her watch, it hadn't taken nearly as long as she had thought. She wasn't expected home for at least four hours; she had time to do something for herself before Sara's party.

Lucy could hardly wait for the AC to cool down her car. It had been sitting in bright sunlight, which had turned the interior into a sauna. She opened all the windows and turned the fan on high, enjoying the cool air on her face. She flipped down the sun visor and looked at her reflection in the mirror. These days she was constantly checking the crow's-feet around her eyes and the little lines on her upper lip, as if constant vigilance could stop their progress.

Maybe Sue was right, she thought, spotting a new line at the corner of her mouth. Maybe that cheap drugstore moisturizer wasn't doing enough. Sue had raved about the stuff she got at Markson's, in the new Galleria. Lucy hadn't been there yet, and everybody said it was worth the trip. This was her chance to see it without any distractions, and maybe she'd even get some of that Countess Irene face cream. How expensive could it be?

Chapter Seventeen

Parking, Lucy was delighted to discover, was located underneath the glittering Galleria and was free, with validation. She carefully tucked the ticket in her purse and headed for the elevators, leaving the dank garage behind and emerging into a bright, fragrantly scented fantasyland. Stunned, she stopped in her tracks and gazed at the glass-roofed atrium, where long strands of crystal beads shimmered high above her.

"Watch out, lady!" A gruff voice reminded her that she was blocking the elevator door and she stepped forward, wandering past the tempting store windows. Gourmet cookware, soaps and lotions, imported linens, lacy bras and panties, fine stationery, leather luggage—it was a far cry from the outlet mall that had popped up near the interstate that sold seconds and discontinued merchandise.

Coming to the end of a row of shops, Lucy paused outside the cavernous entrance to Markson's. Inside, tempting display cases were filled with jewelry, purses and shoes. Colorful scarves flowed from racks, baskets of trinkets were set out to tempt the reluctant shopper. In the distance she noticed the glimmering mirrors of the cosmetics department.

Lucy stepped forward, drawn by the promise of youth.

She would find it, she knew, at the Countess Irene counter, where Natalie held the secret.

"Oh, dearie, you do need help," said the heavily made-up woman in the pink smock. Her name tag identified her as Natalie. Her hair color, you didn't have to be her hairdresser to know for sure, came from a bottle. Nobody had lavender hair naturally.

"I'm looking for a good moisturizer," said Lucy.

"I've got just the thing," said Natalie. "It's our Reviva-derm night cream. Heavy duty, but it still feels light on the skin. You won't believe the difference. In just six weeks you'll look ten years younger."

Lucy studied the jar, looking for a price. There was none.

"Try it, dear." In a second, Natalie had twisted off the top and was holding out the sweetly scented cream.

Lucy hesitated, then dipped in her finger.

"Now just smooth it under your eyes. Doesn't that feel fabulous?"

It tingled slightly, and she could imagine her skin tightening and firming. It was fabulous.

"Oh, yes."

"Some of my customers say this is better than, you know, sex."

Lucy studied her face in the mirror. "Is that where these wrinkles come from? Kissing?"

"Kissing is no longer a problem, thanks to our Countess Irene lip moisturizer. It's called 'Smacker.' Isn't that cute?"

Lucy took the tube Natalie was proffering and spread the creamy unguent on her lips. It made them feel so silky.

"Of course, you will want to try our day cream, Preser-vaderm. It battles the effects of pollutants and UV rays, pre-venting skin damage."

"Really? Day cream is different from night cream?"

"Oh, honey, you've gotta have both. Revivaderm replen-ishes and heals your skin while you sleep. Preservaderm protects the skin during the day."

"I see. And they will make my wrinkles disappear? Es-pecially these little ones around my eyes?"

Natalie nodded sagely. "Of course, the skin around the eyes is very delicate. You might want to try our Where'd You Get Those Peepers eye cream. Gets rid of puffiness without drying that fragile under-eye area."

"I sometimes use tea bags," confided Lucy. "I just soak them in cold water and place them on my eyes."

Natalie's widened in horror. "Then you should definitely try Where'd You Get Those Peepers. There's absolutely no tannin. Tea is full of tannin, and you know what they use that for, don't you? Tanning leather."

Lucy took the little jar. It couldn't cost much, she reasoned. It was tiny. And she certainly didn't want her delicate under-eye skin to turn into leather.

"Do you mind if I ask you what cleanser you're using?" inquired Natalie, her voice seemingly full of sincere concern.

"Soap and water."

Natalie seemed ready to burst into tears at this horrifying news.

"No!"

"Actually, yes," confessed Lucy.

"My dear, soap is so drying. It adds years to your face. You must promise me not to use soap anymore. Use anything but soap. Promise?"

"But what can I use?"

"Facial cleanser. Countess Irene Clean as a Whistle not only cleans, and I mean really deep-cleans your skin, but it also nourishes your skin with vitamin E."

"I take vitamin E," said Lucy, nervously eying the collection of products Natalie was setting aside for her. "I don't think I need the cleanser."

"Dearie, I'm going to be frank with you. You can't afford not to take the cleanser."

Lucy reflexively stroked her throat. "Really?"

"Trust me on this. Thorough cleansing is vital. Why, it's practically the first thing our mothers teach us. Never go to bed without washing your face."

Lucy nodded. Her mother had certainly warned her of the perils of sleeping with a dirty face.

"Prevention is worth a pound of cure," continued Natalie. "That's why I want to let you know about Countess Irene Throat Cream. It prevents that saggy, baggy look." She leaned closer, whispering. "I had a woman in here yesterday, I'm telling you, she looked like a turkey. Her neck was that red and wrinkled. And the shame of it is, she could have prevented it by using Countess Irene Throat Cream." She clucked her tongue. "Such a shame."

Lucy didn't want to look like a turkey. "I'll take the throat cream, too. But that's all. How much do I owe you?"

While she rummaged in her shoulder bag for her wallet, Natalie rang up the cosmetics and bagged them. "Two hundred seventy-eight dollars. Shall I put that on your Markson's account?"

Lucy gasped. She had no idea these things were so expensive. How much did Sue spend on her face?

"This is embarrassing," said Lucy. "But I don't have a Markson's charge account, and I don't have that much cash with me."

"No problem." Natalie waved a hand tipped with highly polished lavender talons. "Why don't you just take the basics today? Clean as a Whistle, Revivaderm and Preservaderm. They come packaged together in a special travel-size offer for only sixty dollars."

Lucy felt a huge sense of relief. "That sounds great." She watched as Natalie canceled the sale and rang up the new purchase. "I'm so sorry about causing you trouble."

Natalie dismissed her apology. "It was no trouble at all. And I've given you plenty of free samples to try."

"Thank you so much," said Lucy, handing over three twenty-dollar bills.

"You're welcome, dear."

Lucy was floating as she left the store carrying the little pink bag with the Markson's logo. She could hardly wait for bedtime, when she would wash her face with Clean as a

Whistle and anoint her skin with Revivaderm. But first, she realized as she came down to earth with a thud, she had to get through Sara's birthday party.

Actually, she thought, as she pulled off Red Top Road and into the driveway, now that the kids were older it was easier to throw a party. Bill was going to pick up a couple of videos on the way home, and she had plenty of soda and microwave popcorn on hand. All she had to do this afternoon was bake a cake and order the pizza. She would have plenty of time to experiment with her Countess Irene purchases.

Kudo bounded up to the car as she got out, and escorted her to the door, licking her hand to signal his happiness at her return. She scratched him behind the ears and went inside.

"Mom! You're home!" exclaimed Zoe. "I made Sara's cake for you!"

Lucy stood in the doorway, clutching her little pink Markson's bag. She would have liked to put it down, but there was no place to put it. Zoe had managed to transform the kitchen into a snow scene, covering every surface with sugar and flour. The mixing bowl, with batter dripping down its side, sat in the middle of the table. The floor was covered with baking pans of assorted sizes. The temperature in the room was at least ninety degrees, thanks to the oven, which Zoe had set at five hundred.

Lucy yanked the door open and pulled out the layer pans, not surprised to find the cakes were burned to a crisp on the outside while the middles remained white and wobbly.

"I added lemon juice," Zoe confided proudly. " 'Cause Sara likes lemon cake best."

Lucy didn't have the heart to scold her. The little girl had meant well, after all.

"I wish you'd waited for me," she said. "We could have made the cake together."

Zoe looked down at the burned pans. "Maybe we could scrape off the burned part?"

"Baking a cake is harder than it looks," said Lucy. "There's always next time."

Zoe took the bad news philosophically. "I think I'll go outside and swing awhile."

"You do that," said Lucy, scraping the cake into the garbage. "I'll call Dad and ask him to pick up a cake at the store."

Left alone in the war zone that used to be her kitchen, Lucy didn't know whether to laugh or cry. She was saved from having to choose by the telephone. It was Bob.

"Hi, Lucy. Sue told me you want to see the contents of Sherman's safe deposit box? She said you found the key?"

"I did. It was in his desk."

"That's great. I'd been meaning to look for it, but I've been so busy I haven't had a chance." He sighed, and his voice sounded tired. "Just keeping the practice going is taking everything I've got. I haven't really had time to deal with his estate. Of course, there's no rush. I've got a year before there's any negative tax impact."

"Right." He might as well have been speaking Greek to Lucy. "Will there be any problem getting into the safe deposit box? I know banks can be awfully picky."

"No problem. I have all the necessary documents. So when do you want to do it? It's just the good old Five Cents Savings Bank on Main Street."

"How long do you think it will take?"

"Five, ten minutes, if we get there first thing Monday morning."

That sounded good to her. Monday was already filling up; she knew it would take most of the morning to write up the Battle of Portland reenactment.

"I'll meet you at the bank at eight-thirty."

"Eight-thirty sharp," promised Lucy, hanging up the phone.

Chapter Eighteen

The one bright spot, thought Lucy as she surveyed the scene, was that it was only four o'clock and the kids weren't due to arrive for the party until six. Consoling herself with this thought, she bent to the task of picking up the pans off the floor so she could move around the kitchen without breaking her neck. That accomplished, she set the mixing bowl in the sink and began sweeping up the spilled flour and sugar with a dustpan and brush. A wet sponge, she reasoned, would only make things worse. Occupied with the task at hand, she didn't hear a car pull into the driveway.

"Hi, Mrs. Stone."

Startled, Lucy jumped.

"I didn't mean to scare you," said a young fellow with his blond hair gelled into little points that stood out from his head like porcupine quills.

"You must be one of Sara's friends," said Lucy, hoping her heart would resume its normal beat soon.

"I'm Matt Zumwalt."

"Well, hi, Matt. It's nice to meet you." She paused, neatly depositing a pile of flour and sugar into the dustpan. "You do know the party doesn't begin for a couple of hours?"

"I'm sorry," he said politely. "My mom had an errand on this side of town so she thought she'd drop me off."

Some people have a lot of nerve, thought Lucy. The woman could at least have called to see if Matt's early arrival would cause a problem. She studied the boy. Whatever was she going to do with him?

"Did you notice the dog outside?" she finally asked. "Why don't you play soccer with him for a little while? I'll tell Sara you're here."

"Okay. Where's the ball?"

"It's out there somewhere," said Lucy. "He'll probably bring it to you."

As soon as Matt stepped out, Lucy headed upstairs, where she found Sara blow-drying her hair.

"Matt Zumwalt's here."

"What?" shrieked Sara. "Look at me! I'm a mess!"

"You think you're a mess, you should see the kitchen."

"This is no joke, Mom. What am I supposed to do?"

"Pull yourself together as fast as you can and go entertain him. Listen to some CDs, watch TV, play a game or something. He's outside with the dog now."

"You didn't, Mom! That dog is so disgusting."

When Lucy returned to the kitchen, she peeked out the window and saw that Zoe had joined Matt and the dog. They seemed to be having a fine time together chasing the ball around.

Lucy had just finished wiping the counters off when an enormous black SUV pulled into the driveway and disgorged a remarkably curvaceous girl. Lucy didn't recognize her, so she guessed the girl must be Davia Didrickson. Flicking her long blond hair, Davia approached Matt Zumwalt. Minutes later, Zoe marched into the kitchen.

"That Davia spoils everything," she grumbled.

"Davia's here!" exclaimed Sara, rushing into the kitchen. She paused to pat her hair nervously. "How do I look?"

"Great," said Lucy, automatically.

"Look at me, Mom," demanded Sara.

Lucy looked. Sara seemed taller and thinner, she realized. Her hair was clean and shiny, and the turquoise top she was wearing complemented her complexion.

"You really do look great," she said. "Take these balloons out and ask your friends to help blow them up."

"She stole your hair spray," said Zoe. "And your lipstick, too."

Zoe was obviously jealous at the attention Sara was receiving. Lucy gave her youngest a consolatory hug. "What do you say we make a birthday banner for Sara on the computer?"

"Okay."

Three hours later, the family room resembled the old town dump before it had been replaced with the neat, new transfer station. Every surface was littered with gift wrap, pizza boxes, soda bottles and paper plates. The air was heavy with a mixture of sugar, Italian spices and teen sweat. Bill popped a video in the machine, and Lucy gathered up as much of the mess as she could, then returned with a big bowl of popcorn and some fresh sodas.

Exhausted, she joined Bill in the living room.

"What's going on in there?" he asked her.

"Something with Bruce Willis, I think. You got the video."

"Not the video. The kids. What are they doing?"

"Watching the video."

"Are you sure?"

"What else would they be doing?"

Bill gave her a look.

"Bill! They're just kids."

"Kids mature younger these days," he said, darkly. "You better go check on them."

"Me? Why not you?"

" 'Cause you can look more casual. Ask them if they want more soda or something."

"I just gave them fresh sodas."

"Maybe they'd like popcorn?"

"I gave them a big bowl."

Bill was quiet. Lucy could practically hear the wheels turning.

"I know," he finally said. "Tell them you just want to check the tracking on the VCR. Say it slips."

Lucy groaned and got up. She pushed open the door to the family room. Eight pairs of eyes gleamed at her in the darkness. She flicked on the lights and peered at the VCR.

"Just checking the tracking," she said.

"Mom!" protested Sara. "The tracking is fine."

"Good." Lucy glanced around at the hostile faces. "I'll make you some fresh popcorn," she said, grabbing the bowl.

When she returned with the popcorn, only six pairs of eyes gleamed at her in the darkness. When she set down the bowl, she noticed two pairs of legs extending behind the couch. Taking a closer look, she found Sean Penfield entwined with Davia Didrickson.

"Break it up," she said, prompting a chorus of giggles from the other kids.

Once she had everyone rearranged, she left the room, followed by Sara.

"Mom!" hissed Sara in the kitchen. "You're embarrassing me."

"Well, your friends are embarrassing me and they ought to be embarrassing you, too."

"You are *so* uncool," was Sara's parting zinger.

"I'm *so* uncool," Lucy told Bill.

"Hunh." Bill was absorbed in his *Renovator's Digest.*

"I had to break up a couple who were making out behind the couch!"

"What did you expect?"

"I didn't expect that. Next time you go in and break them up."

"No way."

"What do you mean?"

"This wasn't my idea, you know. I was never in favor of

this shindig." He got up and yawned. "Maybe this will teach you how to just say no." He headed for the stairs. "I'm going to bed. Good night."

Left alone in the living room, the horror of her situation dawned on Lucy. She had eight hormone-crazed adolescents on her hands. How on earth was she going to manage?

Hearing a shriek of protest from the family room, she hurried to investigate. What were they up to now?

In the family room, the kids had spread out sleeping bags on the floor and on the sectional couch. In the corner of the couch, Jennifer Walsh was sniffling.

"What's the matter?"

The other kids were giggling, looking rather guilty.

"Nothing," said Jennifer, wiping her eyes and swallowing hard.

Group pressure, surmised Lucy. It would be fruitless to try to get Jennifer to tell her what really happened. The only thing she could do, she realized with a sinking heart, was to stay in the family room with the kids.

"Okay," she announced, grabbing a pillow off the couch. "This is how it's going to be. Boys on my right, girls on my left."

Predictably, her announcement was met with groans. She persevered, however, and soon had the boys on one side and the girls on the other. She stretched out in the middle. She hadn't intended to sleep, but next thing she knew it was three in the morning, every bone in her body ached and she had to pee. But the kids were all sleeping soundly. She could go upstairs to her own bed.

Morning found a groggy Lucy standing at the stove, cooking bacon and blueberry pancakes.

"My mom never cooks breakfast," confided Matt Zumwalt.

"This is really yummy," said Jennifer, coming back for seconds.

"I guess I'll have just one," said Davia, yielding to temptation. "And bacon doesn't have very many calories, does it?"

"Hardly any," Lucy told her. After all, Davia hardly had to worry about her figure.

"When are these kids supposed to go home?" asked Bill, as the girls disappeared upstairs for showers and the boys went outside to kick the soccer ball around.

"The invitations said ten o'clock," said Lucy.

"That was an hour ago."

"I know, and frankly, I don't think the cavalry's going to show up any time soon. Think about it. If you were their parents, and you'd got a rare morning to yourself, would you hurry over to pick them up?"

"I'd like to think my nobler instincts would win out," said Bill.

"I'll bet you nobody shows up before noon."

Bill considered this. "You know, I'm a little behind on the job. I think I'll go over and bang some nails."

Lucy's jaw dropped. "On Sunday? You never work on Sundays."

"It's a big job and I've got some contractors coming this week."

Lucy knew Bill was converting a huge old barn out by the town line into a summer home. It was a bigger project than he'd tackled in some time, but she didn't believe he was really worried about being ready for some contractors. He just wanted to get away from the kids.

"You'll pay for this. I'll make sure of it."

He looked at her, wide-eyed and innocent. "I'm only trying to be a good provider—"

Bill was interrupted by a shriek from upstairs. He grabbed his jacket and ducked out the door.

"Coward," muttered Lucy.

It was almost two o'clock when the last of the kids finally left and Lucy had some time to herself. She was tempted to settle down with the Sunday papers, but knew she couldn't afford that luxury. Instead, she sat down at the computer with her notebooks and started writing up her interviews with Miss T so she could fax them to Sidra tomorrow.

As her fingers flew over the keyboard, she wondered how the *Norah!* show would use the material. Would they show Miss T telling some of her stories? Maybe they would find old photographs? Or maybe, thought Lucy, chuckling to herself, they could use some old silent film footage. The incident with the motorcar scaring the horses, for example. Or a suitor, coming to call with flowers in hand, only to be sent firmly on his way by an angry father.

Old Judge Tilley, thought Lucy, could have scared off the most ardent suitor. She paused, thinking. That was wrong. Old Judge Tilley, terrifying fellow that he was, hadn't scared off Harriet's boyfriend. He had persisted and, in the end, the judge had only succeeded in ripping his family apart.

His daughters had indeed chosen two very different paths, thought Lucy. Miss T had stayed in New England, preserving the values her father held so dear. Harriet, on the other hand, had stepped boldly into the future alongside her card-carrying Democrat of a husband. What would the old fellow have made of Shirley, wondered Lucy, and her Hell's Angel? Not much at all, she suspected, resolving to keep an eye on that situation.

She finished up her notes and started printing them out. Her printer was old and slow, so she looked out the window while she waited for it to finish spewing out pages, catching sight of Kudo. The dog was throwing up, having helped himself to the dirty paper plates in the trash.

Zoe soon arrived with the official announcement.

"Kudo's sick," she said. "And there are paper plates all over the yard."

"Well, pick 'em up," snapped Lucy.

It was an hour later when, by way of an apology, Lucy asked Zoe if she'd like to go with her to see the barn Bill was renovating. It was almost five, anyway, and Bill would be finishing up. To tell the truth, she was surprised he had worked this long.

Zoe chattered away as they drove along, full of gossip about her older sister.

"I saw Sean Penfield kissing Jennifer," said Zoe. "And you know what? I think Sara likes Billy Hogan."

"I think he likes her back. He gave her a really nice present."

"Sara's too fat to have a boyfriend."

"Zoe! Sara's a very pretty girl. Lots of boys are going to like her, just like lots of boys are going to like you."

"Yuck! I'm not going to like them."

"We'll see," said Lucy, spotting the big red barn in the distance.

It sat on a little rise, surrounded by acres of hay fields. It would make a great summer home, thought Lucy, especially since a creek ran through the property. A perfect spot for kids to hunt for frogs and crayfish and to cool off on a hot summer afternoon.

She was bouncing down the drive that ran along the stone wall when she first sensed that something was wrong. The big window that took up the entire eastern wall wasn't reflecting the light the way it should.

It was broken, she realized, pulling up beside Bill's red pickup truck and braking.

It wasn't until she'd gotten out of the car that she spotted Bill, lying on the ground outside the window, surrounded by bits of glittering glass.

"Stay in the car!" She barked the order to Zoe.

Then she ran to Bill, fumbling in her purse as she went, groping for her cell phone.

It was in her hand and she was punching 911 as she knelt beside him.

So much blood. He seemed to have cuts everywhere. The phone was pressed to her ear and she could hear it ringing. Why was his arm bent at that odd angle?

"Rescue," came the dispatcher's voice.

"My husband's been hurt," screamed Lucy, feeling for his pulse. She found it, but it didn't seem very strong to her.

"Your location, ma'am?"

Where were they? Lucy babbled out the answer. "That old red barn on Slocum Road, out by the town line."

"Is your husband breathing?"

"Yes, but he's unconscious." She knew she was yelling, but she couldn't stop. "You've got to get somebody out here—he's got cuts all over. He fell through a window. There's a lot of blood."

"I'm sending an ambulance. They're on their way. Don't try to move him."

"Thank you," sobbed Lucy. She clicked off the phone and set it on the ground. Then she slipped off her jacket and laid it across Bill's shoulders, listening for the sirens that meant help was coming.

Hours later, Lucy was sitting in the ER waiting room at Tinker's Cove Cottage Hospital with Zoe sound asleep on the couch beside her. The waiting room was deserted. It was apparently a quiet night in Tinker's Cove. So why, wondered Lucy, were they taking so long with Bill? Why wasn't someone telling her what was going on?

She stroked Zoe's soft hair and told herself Bill was a big, strong man. He would be fine. She refused to think about the possibility of spinal cord damage and paralysis; she would not even acknowledge the possibility that the fall had occurred because of a heart attack or stroke. Bill had always been healthy, he never took a day off from work and she didn't doubt for a minute that he would walk out with nothing more than a Band-Aid on his forehead and a prescription for a muscle relaxant.

But when the ER doctor appeared in the doorway dressed in those green hospital scrubs, it was all she could do to keep herself from leaping to her feet and knocking Zoe off the couch. He motioned for her to stay seated, however, and took the closest chair.

"It looks like he'll be fine," he began, keeping his voice low. "Most of the cuts were superficial, though I'm a little concerned about one in his thigh. I had to remove a good-sized piece of glass. Luckily, it missed the artery."

The room began to suddenly darken, which Lucy found puzzling. Even more puzzling was the fact that she found herself with her head between her knees.

"Have you eaten anything?" asked the doctor.

"I had something from the machine," said Lucy, realizing the soda and peanut butter crackers she'd bought were untouched on the table beside her.

"Eat this," he said, unwrapping the crackers and handing her one.

"Well, as I said, the wound in his thigh will need watching and he has a broken leg, but it's a nice, simple fracture. Nothing complicated there. He'll have to stay off his feet for a couple of weeks. As for the contusion on his forehead, I'd really like to keep him overnight just to make sure there's no concussion."

Lucy nodded, her mouth full of crackers that were as dry as dust.

"You can see him if you like. He's still in the ER while we get a room ready."

She gave Zoe a little shake and helped the sleepy little girl to her feet. Together they followed the doctor to Bill's curtained bed.

Bill was propped up on pillows with a bandage on his forehead and an enormous plaster cast that extended from midthigh to his ankle. An IV tube was attached to his left hand, and his left leg, the one with the cut, was elevated.

"Oh, my God," exclaimed Lucy.

"It's not as bad as it looks," said Bill. "They say I'm going to be fine."

"Do you know what happened?"

Bill grimaced. "I was painting the casing around that window and reached a little too far. It was as simple as that. I lost my balance and fell right through the window."

"Ouch," said Zoe.

"You can say that again," said Bill, grinning.

Lucy suspected he was well medicated. "They want to keep you tonight," she said, yawning.

Bill nodded. "You go on home and get some sleep."

"You, too," said Lucy, brushing her lips against his. "I'll see you in the morning."

Lucy felt a little surge of energy as she left the hospital. Bill was going to be okay, and hopefully it wouldn't be too long before he was back at work. They had some disability insurance and that would help. It didn't look as if he'd require any complicated nursing, and she was sure Ted would let her rearrange her schedule so she could take care of him. All in all, he'd been pretty lucky considering what could have happened.

She felt a sudden chill and shivered, hurrying across the parking lot to the car.

Only Sara was home, but every light in the house on Red Top Hill Road was burning. The TV was blaring, as was the stereo, but Sara wasn't listening to either of them because she was on the phone.

Lucy sent Zoe up to take a bath and went around the house, turning things off. Then she stood in front of Sara, giving her the evil eye.

"I've got to go," said Sara, putting the receiver down. "How's Dad?"

"He's going to be fine, but he's got a broken leg. You're going to have to pitch in for a while, help with dinner and that sort of thing."

"Sure, Mom." Sara was halfway up the stairs.

Lucy opened the refrigerator and took out the milk, pouring herself a glass. Then she cut herself a piece of leftover birthday cake and sat down at the table, wishing that Monday morning wasn't looming like a black cloud on her horizon. How was she going to manage taking care of Bill and working and keeping track of the girls and making meals, not to mention her other commitments? She had an appointment with Bob to go through Sherman's safe deposit box, Sue would no doubt be calling to find out if she'd sent the promised fax to Sidra, she had promised Ted she would have the feature story about the Battle of Portland reenactment for him, and she was willing to bet that Rachel would be calling with some new and horrifying development at Miss Tilley's.

Hearing a commotion upstairs, she popped the last bit of cake into her mouth and ran the fork around the plate, getting the last of the icing. She rinsed the plate, set it in the sink and went to investigate.

She found an irate Sara banging on the closed bathroom door.

"Mom! Zoe's taking forever in there and she won't come out."

"Zoe! You know we have a rule. Unlock the door."

"Mom! I'm not done. Sara keeps distracting me."

"Out! Out! It's past your bedtime."

"See? I told you Mom would be on my side," crowed Sara.

"I'm really getting tired of this endless bickering, Sara. If you don't watch it, you're going to find yourself grounded for life."

"See? I told you Mom was gonna ground you!" Zoe exclaimed.

"If I can ground Sara, I can ground you, too," Lucy warned.

An hour later, Lucy was lying in the bathtub beneath a cloud of billowy bubbles. She leaned her head back on her inflatable bath pillow and inhaled the delicious scent of lavender. It was supposed to be relaxing, and it seemed to be working. Lucy felt as if she could lie there forever, soaking away all her aches and pains, all her cares and worries.

When her fingers began to pucker and the water began to cool, she summoned her energy and heaved herself out. She slipped on her terry robe and brushed her hair, looking at her reflection in the mirror and studying her wrinkles. It was definitely time for Countess Irene.

She unscrewed the jar and smoothed on the lovely pink

lotion, taking extra care with the tender area around her eyes. She ripped open the little sample packets of eye cream and throat cream and applied them. Amazing, she thought, taking a final look in the mirror—she looked better already. By tomorrow morning, when the creams had been able to work all night, she would certainly awake looking exactly like Isabella Rossellini.

Chapter Nineteen

Something was wrong. Lucy knew it the minute she opened her eyes. Then, sensing the emptiness in the bed, she remembered. Bill was in the hospital. Brushing an annoying stand of hair away from her face, she looked at the clock. It took a second or two for her eyes to focus. Eight-twenty-five.

Damn! She'd overslept. She'd overslept by two hours. She jumped out of bed, brushing furiously at her face. What was that itchy, tickling feeling? She looked in the mirror. Cripes! Her face was covered with pink bumps. Hives. She must be allergic to all those herbal extracts Countess Irene put in her Revivaderm cream. Knocking on the girls' door as she passed, she headed for the bathroom.

She looked even worse there, thanks to the bright light. Afraid of aggravating the eruption even more, she simply splashed some cold water on her face. She brushed her teeth and ran a comb through her hair, then headed back to her room to throw some clothes on.

"Wake up, girls! We're late!" she yelled.

* * *

She was nursing a cup of coffee at the kitchen table when the girls came downstairs.

"I can't believe you didn't wake me up, Mom," complained Sara. "I had an algebra test first period."

This was a change, thought Lucy. Sara complaining about being allowed to sleep in.

"These things happen," said Lucy, yawning.

"I missed the field trip," said Zoe, in an accusing tone. "Now I'll have to stay in the library with Mrs. Growley the Barbarian."

"It's Mrs. Crowley the librarian," said Lucy, automatically correcting her. This had been going on for years, ever since Toby had been reprimanded—unfairly, he claimed—by the school librarian.

"I bet I can get you there in time, if we hurry," said Lucy, turning her face toward the girls.

The sight was too much for Sara, who let out an ear-splitting shriek and pointed.

"What happened to your face, Mom?" asked Zoe.

"It's just an allergy, I think." Lucy reached for a sponge and began mopping up her spilled coffee.

"You're not going to go out looking like that, are you?" challenged Sara.

"I have to. I have a lot to do today. I've got to get you guys to school, I've got to go to work and I have to pick up your father at the hospital."

Sara grimaced. "Can't you put a scarf over it or something?"

"What are you? The Taliban?"

"Mom, Sara's right. You look *awful*," agreed Zoe.

"I'll wear a hat and sunglasses. Now hurry up. We're leaving in ten, nine, eight . . ."

The girls scurried to get their bags and she popped into the downstairs powder room to look in the mirror. The girls were right, she admitted. She looked gruesome. Even jamming a long-brimmed cap on her head didn't help.

* * *

"You can drop us off here," said Sara, when they were about a block from the school complex.

Lucy was driving the Subaru, disguised with hat and sunglasses. She'd wrapped a scarf around her chin. She felt ridiculous, like a bad imitation of Greta Garbo, but only a few inches of her blotchy cheeks were visible.

"That's right, Mom," added Zoe. "It's really faster than if you go all the way up the drive to the door."

"Don't be silly," said Lucy. "It's faster if I drop you off at the door."

"No, Mom. We can run really fast. You'll see."

"Please, Mom."

Lucy finally got it. The girls were afraid someone—one of their friends, for example—would see her swollen face.

"Okay," she said, pulling over to the curb and braking.

"Thanks," they chorused, clambering out.

"Poison ivy?" inquired Phyllis, when Lucy arrived at *The Pennysaver* office. "You can get in real trouble if you try to clean your yard this early, before things have leafed out."

"Not poison ivy. Poison Irene."

Phyllis smoothed her cardigan over her size-44 bust. "Never heard of it."

"It was a new face cream I tried. Countess Irene. Very expensive. I must be allergic to the herbal extracts."

"Stick with Vaseline. That's what I do." Phyllis patted her heavily powdered and rouged cheeks. "You should take that stuff back for a refund, you know."

"That's a good idea. I think I will. When I get a chance." She yawned and collapsed into her chair. Summoning her last reserve of energy, she switched the computer on. It groaned in protest.

Phyllis furrowed her brow, watching the performance. "Honey, you look like something the cat dragged in! You have a rough weekend or something?"

Lucy told her about the coed sleep-over party and Bill's accident. She told her about oversleeping and waking up looking as if she'd slept in a beehive and how the girls hadn't wanted to be seen with her. Phyllis clucked her tongue sympathetically.

"Here's some coffee," said Phyllis, setting a mug down in front of her. She narrowed her eyes, staring at Lucy's face through her rhinestone-trimmed glasses. "Have you tried cortisone cream?"

"No."

"I'll get you some. You hold the fort here and I'll be back in a mo."

Bob came in just as she was leaving.

"Hi," said Lucy, hoping he wouldn't notice her face. "What brings you here?"

"Poison ivy?" he asked, leaning closer for a better look. "I figured something had come up when you didn't show up at the bank."

Lucy slapped her hand against her head. "Aw, gee. I'm sorry. I forgot all about it."

"No problem. I've got everything from the safe deposit box in here." He held up a shopping bag.

"Didn't you need the key?" asked Lucy, leading the way into the tiny morgue, where a table was kept free of clutter for consulting the fragile old bound newspapers that were arranged in chronological order on the shelves that lined the walls.

"I had a duplicate," he said, sitting down heavily and leaning his elbows on the table. "Sherman gave it to me years ago, and I forgot all about it."

His eyes were dull, and his face lacked its usual ruddy color. Even his hair seemed to have lost its bounce and shine.

"So how's it going?" asked Lucy, seating herself opposite him. "You look a little tired."

Bob let out a giant-sized sigh. "I worked all weekend," he said. "I didn't get home till after eleven last night. And when I finally do get home, all I want to do is go to bed. Not that it does me any good." He looked at her blankly. "I think I'd be fine if I could just get a decent night's sleep, but I don't. I toss and turn and when I fall asleep I dream about Sherman."

Lucy hesitated. She knew that dreams often held information that the conscious mind was unaware of, but she didn't want to intrude on Bob's private grief. As it happened, she didn't have to ask. Bob couldn't wait to let it pour out.

"It's always the same. It's night and I'm coming into the office. I see the wastebasket is tipped over and I hear voices, angry voices. I know something's wrong and I start running to Sherman's office, to help him. But it's like I'm on a treadmill and I can't get anywhere. I'm so tired, but I know I have to run faster, and I do. I get to the door and it opens, but all I see is a hand holding a gun. And then I wake up." He shrugged. "Actually, it's around this time that Rachel wakes me up. She says I'm tossing and turning and shouting 'Stop!'"

Lucy reached out and covered his hand with hers. "The sooner we get to the bottom of this thing, the better," she said. "Let's see what you found in the safe deposit box. Is there anything interesting?"

"I don't know," said Bob, "I just grabbed everything."

His color was a little better, thought Lucy, watching him as he pulled handfuls of papers out of the bag and spread them out on the chipped porcelain-topped table. It reminded her of the table in her grandmother's kitchen.

"These look like old stock certificates," said Lucy, picking up a sheaf of smooth parchment.

"I better check those out," said Bob, unfurling them. "Maine Motorcar."

He actually chuckled and Lucy smiled.

"Do you think they have any value?"

"You never know. I'll have to do some research." He was sorting through the other documents. "The deed to his house, title to his car, army discharge papers . . . all pretty typical."

Lucy shook her head over the pile of stiff documents, some so tightly furled that it was difficult to unfold them.

"You know, I have the feeling we could be looking at something important and we wouldn't even know it," she said. "We don't really know what we're looking for."

"What's that?" asked Bob, indicating a small yellow volume, about the size of an examination booklet.

"This?" Lucy read the title out loud. "*The Battle of Portland: A Definitive Account* by Sherman Cobb." Her eyes met Bob's. "Did you know he was a writer?"

"I had no idea," said Bob, taking the book from Lucy and flipping through it. "Another thing I didn't know about my partner," he said, slumping even lower in his chair.

"He hasn't made it easy for us, has he? If only he'd scratched an initial in the desk or something. Like in Sherlock Holmes."

"Look at this fellow," said Bob, holding up the open book. "George Washington Tilley. I wonder if he was related to Miss Tilley?"

"Her grandfather," said Lucy, peering at the reproduction of a grainy daguerreotype picturing a distinguished gentlemen with impressive whiskers. "He saved the day."

"Listen to this," said Bob, reading from the booklet. "'It is impossible to know how many lives might have been lost, and if indeed the course of the war and its ultimate outcome might have been tragically different, but for the brave and selfless action of this son of freedom—George Washington Tilley.'" He raised a skeptical eyebrow. "This sounds a lot like the papers Richie used to write for school about his heroes. 'Doug Flutie: a Quarterback for All Time,' was my favorite."

"Better Doug Flutie than Genghis Khan," muttered Lucy, remembering an adulatory paper Toby had once written.

She took the booklet and leafed through the yellowed pages that provided a detailed account of the battle and the people involved. Cobb even offered several speculative explanations of why the Confederates had attempted the raid in the first place and what they hoped it would achieve.

"Listen, do you mind if I keep this for a little bit?" she asked. "This has a lot of good information. It would really help with the story I'm writing about the reenactment."

"It's all yours," said Bob, shoving the rest of the papers back into the shopping bag. "I'll take the rest of this and look through it when I get the chance. Unless you want it?"

Lucy shook her head. "I'm sure you can make better sense of it than I can. Besides, I know where you are in case I need anything."

Bob picked up the bag and stood, pausing at the door. "I don't want to pressure you, but have you made any progress on the investigation?" he asked.

It was the question Lucy had been dreading.

"I've still got a few leads to check out, but to be honest, I'll be amazed if anything turns up."

Lucy watched as his shoulders sagged. He seemed five years older.

"I'm sorry," she said.

"It's not your fault. I know you're doing your best." He pushed open the door and the bell jangled, incongruously cheerful, considering the circumstances.

He cocked his head, studying her face in the sunlight. "You ought to try some cortisone."

"Coming right up," said Phyllis, waving a plastic bag with the drugstore logo.

She was wearing a bright plaid jacket and had tied a matching yellow scarf around her head, leaving the ends free to flutter in the spring breeze. Compared to Bob, she looked like a ray of sunshine.

"You're a lifesaver," said Lucy, grabbing the bag and heading for the dingy little hole that was *The Pennysaver*'s employee bathroom.

Phyllis had done her best to brighten the place up, donating a crocheted cozy for the spare roll of toilet paper and hanging up a set of framed prints depicting kittens and puppies. Somehow it all just made the cracked plaster and curled linoleum look worse.

Lucy yanked the string that turned on the bare lightbulb that hung from the ceiling and leaned into the mirror, smoothing the cream on her face. She looked awful, she felt awful, but for once, she realized, she had too much on her mind to bother feeling sorry for herself. She had just gotten back to her desk when the phone rang.

It was Rachel and she was too upset to indulge in any niceties. She brushed aside Lucy's greeting and her mention of having seen Bob.

"They wouldn't let me in! They told me I'm fired."

"Shirley fired you? I can't believe Miss T would let her do that."

"I know!" exclaimed Rachel. "But when I asked to see her, they told me she was unavailable. She slammed the door in my face!"

"Have you tried the phone?"

"Shirley wouldn't let me talk to her."

"Maybe she was taking a bath or napping or something." Lucy didn't really believe what she was saying, but she didn't think she could handle Rachel's problems on top of her own. Not right now, anyway.

"Why don't you believe me, Lucy? That woman and her motorcycle maniac are keeping me out for a reason, and I don't think it's a good reason. I'm really worried they'll do her some harm."

Unbidden, the image from the elder abuse pamphlet of the frail old woman and the looming shadow popped into Lucy's head. She relented. "Why don't we go together, in a few hours? Say, just before lunchtime? See what happens then?"

"Will you do that, Lucy? I'd really appreciate it."

"No problem," said Lucy, adding another item to her packed agenda.

When the noon siren sounded, Lucy was feeling a lot better. Her face didn't itch so much, thanks to the cortisone cream, and the swelling and redness had gone down. Her face was still pretty puffy, though, she decided as she peered into the rearview mirror of her car, like little Shirley Temple on steroids. At least the wrinkles were gone. Countess Irene had kept her promise.

She went through the McDonald's drive-through on the way to Rachel's, polishing off a small cheeseburger and a container of milk as she drove. She'd read somewhere that fast food wasn't actually that bad for you if you skipped the fries, but she had to admit she missed them. She honked as she pulled into the Goodmans' driveway and Rachel came out of the house, buttoning her jacket as she ran.

"What happened to your face?" asked Rachel, buckling herself into the passenger seat.

"Allergic reaction. I tried that face cream Sue recommended."

"Isn't that just typical." Rachel sighed. "Stuff that works for Sue never works for anybody else. I tried to make her flourless chocolate cake once, but it came out like pudding. I don't even try anymore. Face it, she exists on a higher plane than we mere mortals."

"I wasn't trying to look like her," said Lucy, whipping around the corner a bit too fast. "I was just trying to get rid of the wrinkles."

"Well, you did," said Rachel. "Would you mind slowing down? I'd like to live to see another day."

"Sorry. It's just I've got so much to do. Bill's in the hospital. . . ."

Rachel listened as Lucy recounted the story.

"I never would have bothered you with this if I'd known," Rachel said, feeling rather ashamed.

"It's okay," said Lucy, pulling up in front of Miss Tilley's. "How long can it take?"

She was out of the car and halfway up the walk before Rachel had figured out how to unlatch her seat belt. Lucy was knocking for the second time when Rachel joined her on the stoop.

"No answer?" Rachel's voice was worried.

"I hear noises. Somebody's in there." Lucy banged louder.

Rachel nudged her and pointed toward the side of the house where a large motorcycle was standing.

Before Lucy could say anything, the door opened and they

were confronted by Shirley, a rather different Shirley. The white, curly wig was gone, revealing short hair dyed a brassy shade of red. Silver dream-catcher earrings trimmed with feathers dangled from her ears and she was wearing a T-shirt that proclaimed her a "Motorcycle Mama."

"Hi," said Lucy, taken aback. "We just stopped by to visit with Miss T for a bit."

She stepped forward, hoping to breeze past Shirley.

"Not so fast," said Shirley, blocking her way.

"I brought some cookies," said Rachel, holding up a bakery box. "Her favorite kind."

"I'll make sure she gets them," said Shirley, taking the box.

"Can't we see her?" persisted Rachel.

Shirley looked past them, shaking her head.

Lucy followed her gaze, recognizing the heavyset Hell's Angel she'd seen arriving a few days ago strolling down the driveway as if he owned the place. Rachel threw a questioning glance Shirley's way.

"That's my boy, Stanley. I named him after his pa, but he don't like it much. He likes to be called Snake."

Rachel swallowed hard. "He would be Miss T's nephew?" she asked.

"That's right," Shirley said, proudly. "My son, her grand-nephew."

"And he's staying here with you?" inquired Lucy.

"Just to help out."

They glanced at Snake, who was squatting next to his motorcycle, revealing most of his buttocks.

"Snake!" bellowed Shirley. "Hike up yer pants!" She leaned toward Lucy and Rachel. "Boys will be boys," she said.

From her darkened bedroom, Miss Tilley heard voices outside. She recognized Shirley's voice, of course. Who could miss that strident yell? But there were other, lower voices, too.

Rachel's, she thought, and Lucy's. They must have come to visit her.

She tried to get up, to go out and see them, but she couldn't. Her body wouldn't work. How odd. Maybe she could call out to them. They could visit in her room. But when she tried to raise her voice, all that came out was a faint little squeak. What was the matter with her? Had she been taken ill? That was a worrying thought. She was never sick. Strong as an ox, that's what they always said. Not today. Today she felt as weak as a kitten. Her lips twitched at the thought. She was smiling when she fell asleep.

"She's taken a little turn," said Shirley, plucking the string on the box of cookies.

"You mean she's sick?" asked Rachel. "Have you called the doctor?"

"Not so much sick as tired, I think. Nothing you wouldn't expect, considering her age."

"Well, just to be on the safe side, why not have Doc Ryder take a look at her?"

"I don't think it would do any good," said Shirley. "She's that weak."

Shirley glanced at Snake, who was now standing beside his motorcycle, holding a heavy wrench in one huge hand and tapping it against the other.

Lucy wasn't sure why, since Snake hadn't made any overt signs of hositility, but she felt threatened.

"Maybe she'll be better tomorrow," said Lucy. "We'll come back then."

"I wouldn't bother, if I were you," said Shirley. "Considering her age and all, I don't think she's going to be improving."

"Well, I hope she'll be back on her feet in time for her birthday—we're planning a party," said Rachel.

Snake had come closer and was leaning against the house.

"It's too bad, really," said Shirley. "But I wouldn't be at all surprised if she didn't last until then."

"You mean she's dying?" exclaimed Rachel.

"It looks that way," said Shirley, looking suitably downcast "Don't it, Snake?"

Snake tossed the wrench across the yard, where it clattered against some other tools. He scratched his stomach and hitched up his pants.

"Sure do," he said.

Back in the Subaru, Lucy and Rachel debated what to do.

"I don't like it one bit," fumed Rachel. "How do we know she's sick? And why won't they call the doctor? It seems pretty fishy to me. We don't know what they're doing to her in there."

"At the very least they seem to be taking advantage of her, moving in like that." Lucy shook her head. "It's hard to believe that Miss T would welcome someone like Snake into her home, even if he is her grand-nephew."

"And Shirley isn't quite the little old lady we thought she was at first, is she? I wonder why she's showing her true colors now?"

"Why not? She wheedled her way into the house and now she's in control. They could have locked Miss T in her room. They could have her drugged or tied up."

The thought made Lucy feel sick to her stomach. "I don't have a good feeling about this."

"We have to do something. We have to help her," said Rachel. "But how?"

"I know how. There's that new elder abuse program. I did a story about it last week. It's designed for situations like this. Liz Kelly at Senior Services is running it."

"Oh, Lucy, you're a lifesaver. Let's go over there right now."

Lucy's face fell as she braked in front of Rachel's house and she let out a long sigh. "I wish I could go with you, but I really can't. I've got to finish up a couple of stories for Ted because I don't know when I'll get back to work. As it is, Bill's waiting at the hospital for me to take him home."

Rachel gave her arm a squeeze. "Don't worry about it. You take care of Bill. I can handle this."

Lucy still felt guilty, despite Rachel's assurances. "Let me know what happens," she said, as Rachel got out of the car.

Then, giving her head a little shake and shifting into drive, she sped back to the office.

Chapter Twenty

Lucy was finishing up the reenactment story when Rachel called. She sounded furious.

"You won't believe this," she began. "After you dropped me off at the house, I decided to go over to Elder Services instead of calling. I thought the direct approach would be the best. So off I went. Turns out, this fancy new program is just a lot of nothing. I told Liz Kelly about Shirley and Snake and how they'd fired me, and that was a big mistake because I could almost see her writing up a report with me as a disgruntled employee. And then when I asked how soon she was going to look into it, she said she really couldn't do anything because families have rights and I didn't have any proof."

"That's outrageous," said Lucy. "It's time to go to the police."

"That's what I think, too." Rachel paused. "I was going to go myself, but then I started thinking that maybe because of Sherman and all, maybe someone else should go. I mean, I'm already involved in one case and it might look kind of funny."

"I'm almost finished here," said Lucy. "I'll go."

Rachel let out a big sigh of relief. "Thanks, Lucy."

"I'm leaving a little early," she told Ted, when she filed her story. "And I don't know if I'll be in tomorrow."

"Right." His eyes were fixed on the computer screen; he was editing a story. "Give Bill my best."

"I will," she replied, already out the door.

The police station was only a few feet down the street, so she decided it would be faster to go on foot. She wasted no time, loping along at a fast clip. She was panting hard when she went up to the receptionist's counter.

"I would like to report a case of elder abuse," she said.

"Fill out this form," said the bug-eyed receptionist, sliding a sheet of paper under the glass partition.

Lucy stuck her reading glasses on her nose and started to fill in the blanks. She had completed one side before she even got to the line asking for the "alleged victim." Finishing with a flourish, she slid the paper back.

The receptionist actually smiled at her, then glanced at the paper.

"I'll pass this along to the captain," she said. "But first, maybe you'd want to put down something a little more concrete. Evidence of bruises. Financial misappropriations. Something like that."

"I don't have evidence," said Lucy. "I suspect something is wrong."

The receptionist raised her eyebrows and added the complaint to a pile of papers.

"Will someone look into this? Will they at least send an officer out to investigate?"

The receptionist shrugged. "Are you still planning on writing that story about night workers?" she asked.

Lucy went blank for a minute, then remembered inventing the story as a way of getting the receptionist's sympathy the last time she was in the station.

"Uh, yes, well, some things have come up so I've had to postpone it, but I'm definitely planning to do it sometime, uh, soon."

"Well, like I said, I'd be happy to help."

Lucy wanted to growl something about if she really

wanted to be helpful she'd make sure somebody saw her elder abuse complaint and acted on it, but instead she gave the receptionist a smile.

"Thanks. I'll keep that in mind."

Lucy had pushed the door open rather harder than was necessary when she bumped into her friend, Officer Barney Culpepper.

"Whoa!" he exclaimed. "Where's the fire?"

"I've got to get Bill out of the hospital and I'm late."

"I heard about that. Some fall he took. He's lucky he wasn't hurt worse."

Barney removed his blue cap and ran his fingers through his brush cut. He squinted at her as he replaced it on his head.

"Poison ivy?" he asked.

"Yeah," said Lucy, unwilling to explain about Countess Irene. "Listen, Barney. I'm worried about Miss Tilley. These scummy relatives have moved in with her. They won't let me or Rachel in the house to visit. They won't even let us talk to her on the phone. Rachel went to Elder Services but they weren't any help. I filed a complaint here, but there hasn't actually been a crime that I know about and I don't think—"

"Probably not," agreed Barney.

"Could you stop by, unofficially? Just see what's going on?"

"Sure," he said, reaching for the door. "And you—stay out of that poison ivy!"

"Right." Lucy gave him a little salute and hurried down the sidewalk to the Subaru. Only two hours late, she decided, checking her watch. Not bad. Just try to convince Bill.

She circled the parking lot at the cottage hospital seven times before a spot opened up and she could park the car. *Make it two and a half hours,* she told herself, dashing through the automatic door too fast and crashing into it.

"Take it easy, ma'am," admonished the security guard.

What was he doing there anyway? wondered Lucy. Was he there to keep the patients in?

Fortunately, Bill had told her his room number when she

spoke to him on the phone that morning, so she didn't have to cope with the morons at the information desk.

Stop it, she admonished herself as she waited for the elevator. She didn't know they were morons, they were probably perfectly nice ladies who volunteered one afternoon a week. She had to stop this negative thinking. Just because Liz Kelly was a lazy bum and the Tinker's Cove Police Department was useless didn't mean everyone in the whole world was stupid. It just seemed that way.

"Well, it's about time. . . ." began Bill, when she marched into his room. "What happened to you?"

Seeing his horrified expression, Lucy began to sniffle. She sat down in the Naugahyde visitor's chair and, reaching for a tissue, told him all about Countess Irene.

"I just wanted to look like Isabella Rossellini," she sobbed.

"That's the funniest thing I ever heard," he said, roaring with laughter.

Chapter Twenty-one

"Lucy, could you get me something to drink? And can you fix the window shade? I can't see the TV because of the glare."

In the kitchen, Lucy bit her tongue and counted to ten before she plonked a couple of ice cubes into a glass and filled it with tap water. Then she breezed into the family room where Bill was seated in the recliner.

"Water? Is that all we've got?"

"Unless you want milk or margarita mix. Those are your other choices."

"That margarita mix has been around since last summer," grumbled Bill.

"I've been trying to get out to the store all day," said Lucy, staring at him rather pointedly, "but things keep coming up."

It had been a very long morning. Bill had insisted on breakfast in bed, and Lucy had run up and down the stairs several times—"Just a bit of jelly?" "I'd love to look at the morning paper, if you're done with it." "Can you get some paper towels or something? I spilled the juice"—while also trying to get the girls ready for school. Bill had also required help showering and getting dressed before settling himself in the recliner, where the TV clicker had apparently become an integral part of his hand.

"That's not fair, Lucy. I need your help. It's very hard to do things when your leg's in a cast, especially when you're sore all over from falling off a ladder."

Lucy brightened up. "Shall I fill that prescription for painkillers while I'm out?" she asked. If they were strong enough, they might knock him out for a few hours, giving her some peace.

"Don't go to any trouble for me," he said. "I'll just take some Advil."

"Okey-dokey," said Lucy, trotting upstairs to the medicine cabinet.

When she came back down, the phone was ringing. There was an extension on the table next to Bill's chair, but he was ignoring the ringing. She handed him the bottle and reached over him for the receiver.

"Hi, Mom. It's me."

"Hi, Toby," she replied. "What's up?"

There was a pause.

"I talked to my advisor and she said I should drop Chinese and she's arranging for some tutoring in economics. I just wanted to let you and Dad know."

"So you won't get any credit for Chinese?"

There was another pause.

"I was failing, Mom. I wasn't going to get any credit anyway, and this way I won't have an F on my transcript. Plus, I'll have more time for economics, and hopefully I'll bring my grades up there."

"I just don't see why you're having so much trouble this term," said Lucy. "You've always been a good student. What's going on?"

"Mom! Chinese is crazy. It's one of the most difficult languages in the world."

"I told you that when you registered for the course. But you said you could handle it."

A huge sigh came through the phone line. "I was wrong, Mom. You were right."

Lucy immediately felt guilty. Maybe she wasn't being fair. And besides, he was under a lot of pressure and it wouldn't do any good to add to it. It might even backfire. What if he just couldn't take it and threw himself off the top of a building, like the poor kids you read about in the newspaper?

"Well, I guess it sounds like a plan," she said. "Do you want to talk to your Dad? He's right here—he fell and broke his leg."

"Uh," hedged Toby, "I'd love to but I've got to run or I'll be late for my tutoring session. Just tell him for me to get well soon, okay?"

"What's going on?" demanded Bill as she replaced the receiver.

"Toby says he hopes you get well soon."

"No! Before that—when you said he wouldn't get credit for Chinese."

"He's dropping the course."

"What?" Bill was sitting up straighter and his eyes were popping out of his head.

Lucy immediately felt defensive. She called on a higher authority.

"His advisor recommended it. He was going to fail anyway and this way he won't have a bad mark. Also, he'll have more time for his other courses."

Bill humphed. "Of course the advisor said that. This way that bunch of thieves running the college get more money. We've paid for this course, you know, but Toby won't get any credit. He'll have to take something else to get his degree."

"Well, I don't think we can fault the college for requiring that students pass courses to get credit," said Lucy, huffily. "The problem isn't the school—it's Toby. I'm worried about him. Why is he having so much trouble?"

"Because he's not going to class and he's probably messing with drugs and booze and women."

"Not Toby," said Lucy, defending her firstborn. "I think he's just overwhelmed with all the pressure. Maybe he's depressed. They say it's the hidden disease of adolescence."

"Speaking of disease," he said, handing her the Advil bottle, "would you mind unscrewing this cap for me?"

Lucy twisted the cap off and handed him the bottle. She was on her way to phone Ted, to tell him she wouldn't be in today and probably not tomorrow, when Bill called her back.

"Would you get two out of the bottle for me? I don't want to spill them all over."

She looked at him. Maybe she'd better ask Ted for a week.

"Can't you work from home?" asked Ted, when she stopped in at the office on her way to the grocery store.

"I wish. He's really kind of helpless. He says he's sore all over and I have to help him with everything."

Phyllis was skeptical. Lucy saw her eyebrows shoot up over her rhinestone-trimmed eyeglasses and she pursed her Fire and Ice lips.

"Put yourself in his shoes," suggested Lucy. "If you were injured, you'd want Pam to take care of you."

Phyllis was now rolling her eyes, but it made perfect sense to Ted.

"Take as much time as you need," he said.

Lucy stopped at Phyllis's desk on the way out.

"So Bill's not a patient patient?" she asked, her bosom jiggling with laughter.

"I'd love to tell you all about it, but I don't have time. We're out of ginger ale."

"A tragedy," said Phyllis.

"You better believe it."

An hour later, Lucy tossed the last of the grocery bags into the Subaru and dutifully trundled the wire cart back to the corral in the parking lot. She gave the cart a final shove and walked slowly back to her car, wondering why she felt so tired. She would have expected spending the day working at the paper and chasing stories all over town would be more tiring than nursing one invalid. Especially an invalid who wasn't really sick. Just injured.

There was never a good time for an accident, she told herself as she settled behind the wheel, but Bill's accident had come at an especially bad time. It wasn't as if she didn't have enough on her mind worrying about Toby. Plus, there was the odd situation with Miss Tilley, not to mention the investigation of Cobb's death.

She certainly hadn't made much progress there, and now it didn't look as if she ever would. The more she got to know about Cobb, the odder he seemed. She thought of his tightly clipped forsythia bushes, his relationship with Phyllis that never went anywhere, and she wondered if it had something to do with the fact that he was adopted. Having been given up by his birth parents, perhaps he feared further rejection. She was no psychologist, but it made sense to her that an adopted child, unlike her own children who took her love for granted, might very well feel he had to be very neat and very good so that his new parents wouldn't decide to send him back to the orphanage. It was no wonder he'd settled for the rather formalized relationships the Civil War brigade offered, based on similar interests rather than the spontaneous discovery of kindred spirits. Even his best friend, Chip Willis, had spoken of Sherman's contributions to the brigade, rather than his personal qualities.

And now there was the monograph he'd written about George Washington Tilley. Bob had been right on target when he'd pointed out its adulatory tone. It had contained some useful background material for her story, that was true, but the main purpose of the monograph was to lionize old G.W. Tilley. Lucy chuckled at the memory of some of the flowery phrasing. But why? she wondered. Why had Sherman Cobb chosen him for a hero?

Spotting the turn for Red Top Road, and recalling what awaited her there, she made a resolution. The demands of the living would simply have to take precedence over those of the dead. Bill needed her, Toby needed her, the girls needed her, and it looked as if she was going to have to get involved in the situation at Miss Tilley's.

She flicked on the signal, resolving to wrap up the Cobb investigation. She had a few phone calls to make, to the cleaning lady and the cop, and she doubted very much that they had anything to tell her that would be helpful. She'd go through the motions, she'd make the calls, and that would be it. Finito. Over. Done.

Energized by her decision, Lucy got the groceries unloaded and put away in record time. Then she dialed the number Rachel had given her for Maids to Order. The owner listened patiently to her explanation for the call, but was afraid she couldn't be of much help.

"Ginger North cleans that law office," she said, "but she's on vacation. Took three weeks to go to Florida."

"Lucky her," said Lucy, enviously. It seemed as if everyone, except the Stone family, was vacationing in the Sunshine State.

"Not so lucky. Her mother's getting frail and Ginger's trying to figure out what to do. The old lady doesn't want to make any changes, but she can't live by herself anymore."

From the family room, Bill was calling for something to eat.

"That's too bad. Would you ask her to call me when she gets back?"

"Sure," said the woman, but Lucy didn't really expect her to follow through. She wasn't a customer, after all, so why should the woman bother to pass along her message?

"Just a minute, Bill," she yelled back. "I'm just making a phone call."

She quickly punched in the nonemergency number at the police station. The voice on the other end informed her that Officer Wilkes was indeed back from his vacation, but he was not in the station. She left her number and the dispatcher promised that Officer Wilkes would return her call.

Duty done, Lucy turned her attention to Bill, fluffing up a pillow for him and rearranging the afghan over his legs.

"What do you want for lunch? Peanut butter and jelly? Ham? Tuna?"

"You know what I'd really like?" he asked, managing a weak smile. "I'd love a nice turkey sandwich."

Lucy counted to ten.

"Let's try that again. Would you like peanut butter and jelly, ham or tuna? We don't have any turkey."

Bill's voice was small and sad. "Ham."

Lucy was guilt-stricken. "I'll get you some turkey tomorrow. I promise."

By the time Thursday rolled around, nothing short of a natural disaster could have kept Lucy from her weekly breakfast with the girls. Even Bill agreed it was a good idea.

"Maybe it will cheer you up," he said. "You haven't exactly been Miss Congeniality."

"I'm not Miss Congeniality," snapped Lucy. "I'm Nurse Nancy. Now here's your ginger ale, your Advil, your clicker—do you think you can cope for an hour?"

"I have news for you," said Bill. "You're no Nurse Nancy."

Lucy didn't pause to reply as she hurried out of the house. When she arrived at Jake's, however, the others all looked pretty glum, especially Rachel.

Lucy patted her hand as she took the empty chair next to her.

"Have you been able to talk to Miss T?" she asked.

Rachel shook her head.

"Shirley always answers the phone and says she's sleeping."

"That doesn't sound like Miss T," said Sue.

"Maybe she had a stroke," offered Pam.

"Is that supposed to make me feel better?" asked Rachel. "If she had a stroke, why aren't they getting her medical care? She ought to be in the hospital. I don't think she's sick at all. I think they're keeping her from talking to me."

"How could they do that? If she was awake, she'd be demanding to see you."

"Pam's right," said Sue. "Miss T is a strong-minded woman. She doesn't let anyone take advantage of her."

"I just have a bad feeling about it," grumbled Rachel. "I wish I knew what to do. First it was Sherman, now it's Miss Tilley. I feel like I'm losing everyone who matters to me."

"I guess the birthday party's out of the question?" inquired Sue.

Lucy's eyes met Rachel's.

"Yeah," said Pam, speaking for them. "The guest of honor's unavailable. No Miss T, no party."

"And I guess that means no *Norah!* TV show, either," added Lucy.

"Why not?" Sue raised a delicately arched eyebrow and lifted her cup of black coffee. "Sidra told me everyone on the show is very pleased with the material Lucy sent, especially the photos. They're going to use them, like in that Civil War documentary. They've almost finished the segment, but they need one more thing."

Lucy shook her head, like a two-year-old in the throes of a tantrum. "I can't. I can't. I absolutely can't do another thing and I won't."

"Mature, Lucy. Very mature," observed Sue, sarcastically. Reaching into her bag, she took out a narrow cylinder and withdrew a pair of tiny reading glasses, propping them on her nose. Then she leaned a little closer, studying Lucy's face.

"Did you get Countess Irene? Your skin looks fabulous."

"It's the cortisone. Countess Irene gave me hives."

The news didn't faze Sue in the least. "Cortisone. I'll have to try that," she said, removing the glasses and tapping the table with them. "Now, back to business. All Sidra wants is some old newspaper stories to use as graphic elements." She turned a wide-eyed gaze on Lucy. "Now, that's not too hard, is it?"

In spite of herself, Lucy was intrigued. "You mean her birth announcement, stuff like that?"

"Sure. Anything involving Miss T or her family. Or local history. Blizzards, hurricanes. Anything noteworthy."

"We can use *The Pennysaver* archives," said Pam. "They go back over a hundred years and pretty much cover everything that happened in town."

"The Pennysaver is a hundred years old?" Rachel looked doubtful.

"It wasn't called *The Pennysaver.* It was *The Courier,* and then *The Advertiser.*"

"Okay," said Lucy. "I'm stuck home anyway with Bill. I might as well have a project."

"Better yet," suggested Rachel, with a wily smile, "have Bill do the research. Give him something to do that will keep his mind off his boo-boo."

"I'll toast to that," said Lucy, raising her coffee cup.

Chapter Twenty-two

When Pam cruised up to the old farmhouse on Red Top Hill in her aged boat of an Oldsmobile later that day, Lucy ran out to meet her. She stopped in her tracks, however, when she noticed the car was filled to the gunwales with old newspapers, all neatly bound in oversize volumes.

"Golly, I had no idea there'd be so many," she exclaimed.

"Me, either. It took forever to load the car. So, where do you want them?"

"In the family room, I guess. That's where Bill is holding court."

Bill wasn't exactly thrilled when the two women marched into his sickroom with their arms full of books.

"What are those?" he demanded.

"Old newspapers." Lucy nodded toward a corner. "I guess we can just stack them here."

They dropped the books on the floor, creating a cloud of dust.

"I don't want those dusty things in here," complained Bill.

"I think we should line them up against the wall under the windows," said Pam. "That way it will be easier to get at the volume you need."

"What am I? Invisible? Can't you hear me? I don't want them in here." Bill was on his feet, leaning on a crutch.

"You mean stack them as if this end of the room is a shelf?" asked Lucy, ignoring him.

"Exactly," said Pam.

"Let's get started," said Lucy. "I don't imagine there's any way we could get them in chronological order?"

"Hey!" Bill was tapping Lucy on the shoulder. "This is not a good idea. What about allergies?"

"I did put the most recent ones in the car last, so they're on top," offered Pam. "And I only brought the ones from 1910 to 1985."

"You don't have any allergies," said Lucy, waving away his objections. "Let's start at this end and work our way back."

Unable to refute this, Bill stumped back to his chair and clicked on the TV.

"Okay," said Pam, picking up one of the volumes and checking the date stamped on the spine. "July to August 1980; I'll put it here for the time being. We can move it over when we find later ones."

"I've got January to February here, I'll put it next to it."

"You keep stacking 'em and I'll go out and bring in another load," suggested Pam.

"Okay."

"What about my lunch?" whined Bill. "I haven't had lunch yet."

"Neither have we," said Lucy, who was on her knees. "I'll fix something for all of us when we're done."

"I'm starving," said Bill, hollowing his stomach. "I'll probably be dead of hunger by then."

"Here comes 1976," said Pam, staggering in under the weight of six books.

"Ah, the Bicentennial. There's probably good stuff in there. Oops, this is 1913."

"Don't mix it in with the others," said Pam. "We ought to keep it separate."

"Yoo-hoo! I'm here. I'm sick and I'm hungry."

"Just put it on top of Bill," suggested Lucy. "Maybe it will shut him up."

"You mean kind of wall him off, like in that Poe story?"

"That's the idea," said Lucy.

"Not very funny at all," snarled Bill.

"Instead of carrying on like a big baby, why don't you take a look inside? See if you can find any stories that mention Miss Tilley."

"In your dreams," said Bill, changing the channel.

Pam and Lucy looked at each other.

"I bet he'll change his mind," whispered Pam.

Lucy glanced at Bill, who had let the volume slide off his lap and onto the floor, and back to Pam.

"I hope so."

An hour later, the books were neatly lined up in close-to-chronological order along the wall. Pam was shifting them around, trying to get the order straightened out, and Lucy was in the kitchen mixing up tuna salad. Bill had given up on daytime TV and was idly turning the yellowed pages of the 1913 issues of the Tinker's Cove *Advertiser*.

"Ho-ho," he said, suddenly becoming interested. "You'll never guess what I've found."

"What?" inquired Pam, panting as she switched the first half of 1954 and the second.

"The old witch's birth announcement. 'Born to Judge William T. Tilley and his wife, Sarah, a daughter, seven pounds and two ounces.'"

So this is what it's like to die, mused Miss Tilley, blinking at the bright light that surrounded her. Everything was so white and she had the strange sensation of floating in a white cloud. This was what she'd always imagined death would be like. She waited expectantly for the clouds to part revealing Saint Peter and the Heavenly Host.

Oddly enough, she wasn't afraid. Of course, she had committed no sins that Saint Peter could reproach her for. She had been a dutiful and obedient daughter; she had willingly taken on the responsibilities of the post of librarian at Broadbrooks Free Library; she had worked hard, observed moderation in all things and followed the Golden Rule. All that was well and good, she told herself, but her trump card for admission through the Pearly Gates was the fact that she had remained a maiden lady throughout her long life.

She smiled with satisfaction and opened her eyes wide in anticipation of the marvels that would soon be revealed to her. Instead, she saw the ceiling light fixture.

She blinked in disbelief. Was she not aboard the express to heaven? Was she in fact lying in her bed, in her room, under a bright ceiling light? This couldn't be true. And what was that light doing on anyway? She hated ceiling fixtures and much preferred the natural light of day or the soft light of lamps.

She turned to her left. The Sandwich glass lamp was still on her nightstand, but it was off. She squinted, focusing on the wall beyond. The window shade was down. Now that was wrong. She never pulled the window shades. She would have to get up and open it, and while she was at it, she would switch off the ceiling light. She tried to rise from her bed but found she couldn't do it. She couldn't move.

She was tired, she realized. So tired. The room was growing fuzzy again. The window and the walls receded into the bright whiteness that surrounded her. Once again she felt as if she were floating. It was like being in a pool of warm water. She felt so light, so weightless. All her aches and pains were gone. She felt entirely relaxed. She didn't have any worries, either. Not a care in the world. Just this blissful sense that she was complete unto herself and utterly at peace. She felt divine.

From the distance, she heard chimes. The music of the spheres. Or perhaps the grandfather clock. How many times did it chime? She'd lost count.

"Just lift your head, dear."

She felt a hand slide under her neck, pulling her out of her cloud. She squinted and saw Shirley, dear Shirley, looming over her. She thought it was Shirley, but what had happened to her hair? When had it turned red?

"Open wide, now. Just a little bit of medicine."

It wasn't Shirley. What a silly mistake. It was Mother. She was sick with rheumatic fever and she had to take the bad-tasting medicine. Obediently, she opened her mouth, but instead of the vile liquid she felt a tablet of some kind followed by a splash of water. She swallowed and soon the warm, fuzzy feeling returned. She was back in the clouds.

Chapter Twenty-three

Friday was rainy. It wasn't supposed to rain in May, thought Lucy, as she belatedly turned the kitchen calendar to a new page. April showers were supposed to bring May flowers, but the flowers were few and far between in her yard. The forsythia had dropped their petals and were putting out green leaves. The daffodils had also gone by and were yielding to the aggressive daylilies, whose spiky green leaves asserted their right to the flower bed they shared.

Apart from those few patches of green, however, the yard presented a dismal sight. The trees hadn't leafed out yet, so they were still gray, which also happened to be the color of the garden shed and the gravel driveway. The grass wasn't gray, it was a dull, flat brown, and Lucy knew from experience that the soil beneath it would be squishy and slippery underfoot.

Spring in New England was the season that wasn't. Summer was hot and green, fall was crisp and gold, winter was cold and white. But spring was generally a cold and wet continuation of winter until the lilacs bloomed, when just like that, it turned to summer in an instant. Spring was over before it began.

Not that she was complaining. These clouds definitely

had a silver lining. Today she had been assigned to cover Team Day at the middle school. Team Day was the new, politically correct version of the old-fashioned Field Day that was designed to foster cooperation rather than competition. Lucy hadn't been looking forward to spending the morning at the middle school and now she wouldn't have to. Thanks to the rain, Team Day would most certainly be postponed.

Which meant she could take her time this morning. She'd already started a load of wash, and while she waited for the machine to finish its cycle she'd called the police station, looking for Bob Wickes. He was out on assignment so she hadn't been able to talk to him, but she had paid the bills and called the disability insurance company and requested the necessary paperwork so Bill could file a claim. It was great not to feel rushed, she thought, as she loaded the wet wash into the dryer and prepared Bill's lunch.

She took the tray into the family room, setting it down on a little table beside Bill's recliner.

"I made you a sandwich and you've got a thermos of milk and another thermos with hot soup, plus some cookies and fruit. I guess that should hold you till the girls get home from school."

"No problem," said Bill, who was keeping himself busy with the old newspapers.

Whenever he found something pertaining to Miss Tilley, or anything particularly interesting, he marked the page with a Post-it note. The growing stack of volumes next to his chair was bristling with the little yellow bits of paper.

"You're sure it's okay if I go to work?" Lucy was hesitant to leave him alone.

"I'll be fine," he said.

Lucy bent down and kissed him on his head.

"Stay out of trouble," she said.

"Don't worry about me. The only place I'm going is down memory lane." He tapped the papers. "And I can't get in trouble there."

* * *

Lucy was still congratulating herself when she arrived at *The Pennysaver.* Giving Bill those papers to look through had been a stroke of genius; not only was it keeping him busy while his injuries healed, but he was finding plenty of interesting material that Sidra could use to put the final touches on the *Norah!* show about Miss Tilley.

"What are you doing here?" asked Ted, as Lucy walked through the door. "Aren't you supposed to be over at the middle school?"

"Uh, in case you didn't notice, it's raining," said Lucy, shaking out her coat before hanging it up. "They can't have Team Day in the rain."

"They are having it. Indoors, in the gym. The principal even called, wondering why you're not covering it."

"Say no more." Lucy put her coat back on and went back out into the rain.

Lucy could hear the din coming from the gymnasium as soon as she stepped inside the middle school. It grew louder as she walked down the vinyl-tile hall and exploded when she pulled open the door. No wonder. The gymnasium was packed with the entire eighth-grade class, divided into teams, and all the team members were yelling and screaming encouragement to each other. From what she could tell at a glance, the yellow team seemed to be winning a race that involved forming a human chain and passing along towels that were used as stepping-stones to cross the gym floor. The person at the front of the chain couldn't step forward until the person at the end cleared the last towel, which could then be passed forward, allowing everyone to advance one step.

As she surveyed the scene, it occurred to Lucy that each team looked like a different-colored worm, inching its way across the floor. The Parent-Teachers Organization had raised money for team T-shirts, after a presentation by the phys-ed teachers. They had explained that the teams would be chosen randomly, to discourage cliques, and that all the races would involve cooperation by team members. Furthermore, the competition would draw upon a wide variety of skills and attributes, so that all the team members would be able to contribute and not just the most athletic.

It had all sounded great, and Lucy remembered being quite convinced that Team Day would be a lot more fun than the traditional Field Day, which had been dominated by the class athletes. She clapped her hands and cheered when the yellow team did, in fact, win the caterpillar race, then watched in dismay as the caterpillars immediately dispersed when the various team members went in search of their friends.

Sara, she saw, had wasted no time leaving the orange team to which she'd been assigned and had hooked up with Katie Brown, in green, and Jennifer Walsh, in blue. The three had formed a tight little knot and were giggling about something.

Lucy suspected this failure to maintain team spirit wouldn't be tolerated for long, and it wasn't. A piercing electronic shriek gave notice that the public address system had been turned on and Ms. Boone, the assistant principal, took the microphone.

"Attention! Attention! All students must remain with their teams."

This was met with a general groan. Lucy smiled at the students' reaction, and the woman standing next to her spoke up.

"Frankly," she said, "I don't know why they bother with all this noncompetitive stuff. Competition is a fact of life. The SATs aren't a group effort, are they? And colleges certainly don't recruit the purple team—they give sports scholarships to the kids who score points and make the all-stars."

"Do you mind if I quote you on that?" asked Lucy, pulling out her notebook and pen. "I'm Lucy Stone and I'm covering Team Day for *The Pennysaver.*"

"You're Lucy Stone?" The woman's eyes widened. "I'm Donna Didrickson. My daughter Davia spent Saturday night at your house."

"Davia! That's right," exclaimed Lucy, taking a closer look at the woman.

She was blond and athletic looking, and she reminded Lucy of Video Debbie, with her well-proportioned and toned body. And considering the nylon warm-up suit she was wearing, she was on her way to, or from, a sports club.

"Davia's a lovely girl," continued Lucy. "You must be very proud of her."

"Of course I am," asserted Donna, ticking off her daughter's accomplishments. "She's captain of the field hockey team and its leading scorer for the second straight season. She's ranked number two according to grade-point average and she played on the varsity basketball team this past winter. Not even in high school yet and she was on the starting team! But frankly, just between you and me, we're pinning our hopes on her balalaika lessons. That's what really impresses college admissions officers, you know—something different, something that makes your child stand out."

Lucy watched as the teachers began sending kids back to their teams, getting them organized for the next competition—a three-legged race. Sara, she saw, had been paired with a boy who only came up to her chin and she didn't look very happy about it. Lucy wondered if she knew her class rank, and what it was.

"Isn't it a little early to start thinking about college?"

Donna's eyes widened in disbelief. "It's never too early, not if you want your child to go to a top-notch school!"

"Attention! Attention!" It was Ms. Boone again, attempting to get the students' attention. She was somewhat more successful this time, probably because a uniformed police officer was standing next to her.

"Students! We're going to have the three-legged race in just a moment, but first, I want to introduce you to Officer Wickes, who's going to announce the winners of the caterpillar race."

Lucy couldn't believe her luck. She'd been trying to contact Bob Wickes for weeks, and here he was in the same room with her—and about a hundred excited eighth graders.

No matter, she should certainly be able to have a word with him before the event was over.

Lucy joined in the applause for the red team, which placed third in the caterpillar race, and the blue team, which placed second, and put her hands over ears when cheers erupted for the winning yellow team. It occurred to her that the three-legged race would make a good photo, so she pulled her camera out of her bag, intending to snap a few pictures. She was just about to explain her intention to Donna when she was interrupted.

"You know, Lucy, I was very surprised when Davia told me Jennifer Walsh was at the party," said Donna.

Lucy didn't understand. "What do you mean?" she asked, letting the camera dangle from the cord around her neck. "They've been in school together since kindergarten."

"I know they're in school together, but heavens, that doesn't mean they have to socialize. I can assure you I'm very selective when it comes to choosing friends for my children."

Out of the corner of her eye, Lucy caught sight of Bob Wickes's navy blue uniform. It was moving toward the doorway.

"Jennifer's a very nice girl," said Lucy, starting to follow him.

"Doesn't she live on Bumps River Road?" whispered Donna, referring to a rather run-down part of town.

"What if she does?" Wilkes was almost at the door and Lucy was afraid she would miss him.

"Have you been down there? Do you know the sort of people who live there?" demanded Donna, grabbing her arm.

"People like what? *Poor people?* Because I can assure you that Jennifer is a very sweet girl!"

Lucy was thinking back, trying to remember if there had been trouble at the party. She remembered finding Davia and Sean Penfield making out behind the couch. At first blush she'd blamed Sean, assuming he'd pressed himself on Davia, but now she wasn't so sure. Middle-school-aged girls could be quite aggressive. Things had gone pretty smoothly after she'd broken up the amorous couple, but she did remember that Jennifer had been upset. She'd thought at the time that one of the boys had tried something with her and had separated the kids by sexes, but maybe it had been one of the girls who had upset her. Maybe it had been Davia.

"Did Davia and Jennifer have some sort of fight?" asked Lucy, relieved to see that Wilkes had paused in the doorway, where he was talking with the president of the P.T.O.

"Are you accusing my Davia? Let me tell you, she is a young lady. She has been brought up very carefully and knows how to conduct herself properly at all times."

Lucy suppressed the urge to laugh.

"I'm sure she does. Look, I'm here as part of my job and I have to do some interviews. I really can't talk to you any longer."

"Well, I can see you're just not getting it," said Donna, in a huffy tone. "I don't see any reason to continue this conversation. Good-bye!"

Finally free of Donna, Lucy sped across the gym, but when she got to the doorway Officer Wickes wasn't there.

"So, tell me," said Lucy, smiling at the president of the P.T.O. "Why did your organization decide to donate the T-shirts for today's Team Day?"

Lucy couldn't get Donna Didrickson out of her mind as she ducked the raindrops and hurried back to her car. Who did Donna Didrickson think she was, anyway, to go around deciding that Jennifer Walsh wasn't socially acceptable? The Walshes had lived in Tinker's Cove for over a hundred years. In fact, she realized as she passed the Civil War memorial on the school lawn, at least five Walshes were listed on that very piece of carved granite.

She chuckled, thinking of the irony of the situation as she started the car. After all, her conversation with Donna had taken place during Team Day, an event specifically designed to break down social barriers among students. But while the teachers were working to get the kids to look past their differences and to appreciate each other for their strengths, Donna Didrickson had been busy drawing social distinctions. Jennifer Walsh was poor, so Jennifer couldn't be friends with Davia.

The more things change, she mused as she drove down Oak Street, the more they stay the same. What would Donna Didrickson do if Davia fell in love with a black man, or an Asian? A Jew? Would she disown her the way Judge Tilley had disowned his daughter?

That must have been quite a scene, thought Lucy, remembering Judge Tilley's stern visage in the painting that hung over Miss Tilley's mantel. With that hawk nose, those piercing brown eyes and that thin line of a mouth, he didn't seem like a man you would want to cross. He looked, she had to admit, like a very unpleasant fellow. A man who probably didn't smile much, considering those long lines that ran from each side of his nose to the corners of his mouth.

Funny, she thought, as she waited for a break in traffic so she could join the line of cars snaking down Main Street, that face reminded her of someone. But who? She knew she'd seen someone recently who looked remarkably like the judge, but a kinder and gentler version. Someone with the same coloring, the same brown eyes, but someone who hadn't been afraid to smile.

Sherman Cobb, she realized, just as a driver flashed his brights at her indicating he would let her into traffic. She gasped, grabbing the steering wheel tightly and making the turn. It was definitely Sherman Cobb. *Sherman* Cobb. Chap Willis had told her that when his parents adopted him, the one condition they'd agreed to was to name him Sherman. This couldn't be a coincidence, thought Lucy. Sherman Cobb had been related to the Tilleys. No wonder he'd been so interested in the Battle of Portland and the mayor, George Washington Tilley. He was a Tilley, probably the judge's illegitimate son. No wonder the judge had taken such an interest in him and had even left him money for his education.

She was pursuing this line of thought when taillights flashed red in front of her. She slammed on the brakes, but it was too late and she smacked into the car ahead of her with a jolt. Seconds later, she felt the impact when the car behind her smashed into her rear.

Miss Tilley's eyes opened. Her heart was pounding, she realized. She must have had a fright. Probably just a reaction to the shock of transferring from one mode of being to another. Shuffling off your mortal coil must certainly take a toll, not to mention the ascent to the heavenly sphere. She felt sorry she'd missed it. Had it been rapid, like the thrusting ascent of the space shuttle, or had angels gently guided her through the firmament?

A distant crash made her muscles tighten, and then she heard another. That must have been what woke her, she realized, with a sense of annoyance. What was all that crashing and banging? She certainly hadn't expected heaven to be this noisy. Choirs of angels, of course, cherubim and seraphim, but not all these thuds and bumps.

The other place? Her jaw dropped at the idea. She quickly reviewed her life. Not possible, she decided, unless there'd been some sort of administrative mistake. It would no doubt be cleared up. The Creator certainly wouldn't tolerate slipshod bookkeeping and neither would Saint Peter. Where was he, anyway?

"You could get off your lazy butt and help me!"

Oh, dear. Not at all the sort of thing you expect to hear in heaven. And that voice was so familiar. It sounded like Shirley, but of course, it couldn't be. Not dear Shirley. Besides, Shirley was much younger than she and quite hale and hearty. What would she be doing in the hereafter? No, she was back on earth, most likely attending to the funeral arrangements. What a shame she couldn't be there, but of course, you couldn't attend your own funeral.

She heard a door open and turned her head, expecting to finally see Saint Peter. Instead, she saw a heavyset, bearded man in black clothing decorated with chains.

She was in the wrong place! She would most certainly have to straighten this out.

"She's awake, Ma!" yelled Snake.

Julia wanted to speak up, to clear up this confusion, but discovered she couldn't make a sound. Her body simply would not work. Not surprising, she decided, considering her situation. No doubt there was some other form of communication. A higher form. She'd soon get the hang of it.

There was a quick patter of footsteps and Shirley's face floated above her.

"There's my good girl," cooed Shirley, straightening the covers and tucking them in.

So, she wasn't dead yet. She was alive, in her own bed. She was quite comfortable, but she was very thirsty. She wanted to ask for water and struggled to speak. All she managed to produce, however, was a faint groan.

Shirley's response was to shove a pill into her mouth. It felt like a cotton ball, sitting on her swollen tongue. Next came a splash of water and she took it greedily. She heard Shirley set the glass on the table and then the door closed.

The pill, she realized, was still on her tongue. It hadn't gone down. She didn't want to risk choking on it, so she spat it out. She'd try again later when Shirley came back. In the meantime, there was nothing to do but lie there and wait, listening to the banging and crashing. Whatever were they doing? It sounded as if they were searching the house.

Her vision was clearing, she realized, as the crack on the ceiling above the bed came into focus. She glanced around her bedroom, wondering what time it was. What day was it? The shades were down, but it didn't seem very bright outside. Dusk?

A sudden grating, dragging sound startled her. They must be up in the attic, going through the trunks. Whatever could they be looking for?

Her gaze fell on her bedside table. The daffodils Rachel had put there in a vase had withered and dried up. She must have been lying here for days, she realized, spotting the glass of water. She wanted to reach for it and, to her surprise, her arm responded. She could move her arm.

It took great concentration and she was quite clumsy, but she finally managed to wrap her fingers around the glass. Her next task would be bringing it back to her lips. It seemed to take forever, but finally she was able to rest the glass on her chest.

Focusing her eyes on the glass, she slowly lifted her head and tilted back the glass. She spilled some, but she got a good swallow or two. Then, exhausted, she let her head fall back on the pillow and the empty glass slipped from her hand and rolled off the bed onto the scatter rug.

Chapter Twenty-four

The rain, which had been little more than a light drizzle, turned into a downpour when Lucy hauled herself out of the car. She wasn't hurt, and a quick glance at the Subaru's front end didn't reveal any damage. Miraculously, the car she hit, an older-model Jeep, didn't seem to have any damage either.

She pulled her hood up over her head and went round to the back of her car; it seemed to be fine, too. But when the driver of the little Hyundai that had hit her reversed a few feet, the bumper fell to the ground and dragged along, making a hideous scraping sound.

Other drivers who were stuck behind them were honking impatiently, and Lucy realized that traffic would be blocked unless they moved their cars.

"Why don't we just exchange names and addresses and get out of here?" she suggested to the driver of the Jeep, a young woman with curly blond hair.

"Okay," agreed the woman. "I don't have any damage that I can see, and I want to get home before the kindergarten bus."

"Not so fast," said the driver of the Hyundai, a middle-aged man Lucy recognized from the IGA, where he worked behind the meat counter. "I've got damage here. I say no-body moves until the cops get here."

"But we're holding up traffic," said Lucy. "We'll give you all our info and you can just pull into this parking spot right here until the tow truck comes."

"I don't care about traffic, I care about my car," grumbled the man. "Women drivers!"

"Hey," said Lucy, feeling her hackles rise. "You hit me, you know."

"Well, you hit me," said the woman. "But I did hit the brakes kind of suddenly when I saw a pedestrian in the cross-walk. We all should have been more careful, with the rain and all." She pulled a cell phone out of her purse. "I'll see if my neighbor can meet the bus."

They could already hear a siren and see the flashing lights of an approaching police cruiser. Lucy went back to her car to get her registration card, and when she joined the others, they were already talking to one officer. A second was di-recting traffic.

"Officer Wickes," she exclaimed, reading his nameplate. He seemed impossibly young, with red hair and a freckled face. "This is lucky."

They all looked at her as if she were crazy.

"It's just that I've been trying to reach him for quite a while," she explained. "I have a question, but we can take care of that later."

"Let's step under this awning and get out of the rain," suggested Wickes. "I have to fill out an accident report."

The awning provided some protection from the rain, but it was still dank and cold. Lucy was shivering by the time Wickes began questioning her.

"Your license expired three months ago," he said, care-fully examining her documents.

Damn, she'd forgotten all about renewing the darn thing. Even worse, she'd already been cited once and it would cer-tainly show up on the computer when he ran her license number.

"I know," she said, adding a huge sigh. "But my husband's been sick and I've been real busy lately and I haven't had a chance to—"

He waved away her explanation. "Don't waste your breath. I've got to cite you. But I'm going to put the accident down to the rain and road conditions. That way it's nobody's fault, nobody's insurance goes up."

"Thank you," said Lucy, taking the fistful of papers he was giving her.

"If I were you, I'd get that license taken care of today."

"Good idea," said Lucy

He was turning to go when she remembered her unfinished business.

"Stop!" she shouted.

He turned slowly. "There's something else?" he asked.

"I understand you were on duty the night of March seventeenth. Do you remember anything unusual that night?"

The young officer gave her a curious look. "March seventeenth was weeks ago, before I went on vacation," he said. "How am I supposed to remember?"

"It was the night the egg truck crashed."

"That was unusual," said Wickes. "Nastiest thing I've ever seen."

"What I mean is, was there anything else unusual that night?"

He'd taken a step or two backward, getting some distance between them.

"No. Lady, I don't remember anything more unusual than the egg truck. Now, I've got to get back to work and you've got to get your license renewed. Have a nice day."

"Right," muttered Lucy, hurrying back to the shelter of her car. She'd got rear-ended and would probably be wearing a cervical collar tomorrow for whiplash, she'd gotten a second citation for her expired driver's license and it was raining. Having a nice day didn't really seem to be in the cards. Especially if she added in Bill's accident and Toby's problems at school.

She drove along Main Street to *The Pennysaver* office in the next block, but there were no empty parking spaces at all. Not a nice day, not a nice day at all, she decided, driving around the block to the municipal parking lot behind town hall.

"Honey, you look like something the cat wouldn't even bother to drag in."

Lucy gave Phyllis a dirty look. "You really know how to make a girl feel good."

"Are you having a bad day?" asked Phyllis, adjusting her cardigan and settling in for a listen. "Why don't you tell me all about it?"

"I wouldn't know where to begin," said Lucy, removing her sodden coat and hanging it on the coat stand. "I think I'll just try to put it all behind me."

Phyllis smoothed her ruffled feathers and replaced her half glasses. "Well, if you need a sympathetic ear, I'm here."

Lucy started to answer but Phyllis held up a chubby finger tipped with orange nail polish and reached for the ringing phone. "It's for you," she said, transferring the call.

Lucy waited for her phone to ring, then picked up. She didn't recognize the soft, breathy voice on the other end of the line.

"This is Ginger North, returning your call."

Lucy's mind was blank.

"From Maids to Order."

"Oh, right. You're the one who cleans Cobb and Goodman, right?"

"Right. I've been away in Florida. My mother's getting on and she needed some help. But now I'm back home, for a while, anyway." There was a pause. "I hope it'll be a while, but I really don't know. She's so stubborn. She keeps firing her helpers, says they're stealing her blind. I just don't know. I'd like to move her up here, but my husband refuses to let her live with us and she doesn't want to come anyway. I don't know what to do."

Lucy thought of Miss Tilley. She didn't know what to do either.

"I know how hard it is," said Lucy. "All of a sudden you've got to be your mother's mother."

"You said it," agreed Ginger. "And then I came back and found out Mr. Cobb had died. I swear you could have knocked me over with a feather. He was such a sweet man. Very obliging, grateful for everything you did for him. And he always gave me a very generous Christmas check." There was a pause. "Of course, I would have liked him anyway. Isn't that the way it is, though? The ones who are difficult and picky give you last year's fruitcake and the ones who are sweeties give you a big tip. Somehow it ought to be the other way round." Again there was a silence. "I can't believe he killed himself."

"The police say that's what happened, but Bob Goodman has asked me to investigate. He doesn't believe it was suicide."

"But if he didn't kill himself . . ." began Ginger, interrupting herself with a gasp.

"Someone must have murdered him," said Lucy, finishing the sentence. "That's why I wanted to talk to you. You may have been the last person to see him alive. Do you remember anything at all unusual that night?"

"He died that night? After I left?" Ginger's voice had gotten louder; she was practically shouting.

"Did you notice anything? Did he seem anxious or distracted?"

"Not a bit. He talked about this battle reenactment, the Battle of Portland, I think it was. He was looking forward to that. You know they wear costumes and pretend to be Civil War soldiers. He got a lot of enjoyment out of that."

"He was working late?"

"Sometimes he did, you know. When he had cases coming up. He said he'd be burning the midnight oil, getting ready for circuit court."

"That doesn't sound like a man who was planning to kill himself. Did he have any visitors?"

"No. He was by himself when I left. He told me to have a safe trip and to call him if I needed any legal advice. I'd told him I wanted to make sure my mother's affairs were in order, and he'd told me what I needed to do. He was great that way. Never charged me a cent."

"You didn't see anyone at all? No extra cars in the parking lot, for example?"

"That reminds me. I did see a motorcycle."

Lucy stiffened and her grip on the receiver tightened. "In the parking lot?"

"No. On the road."

Lucy's interest ebbed. Even if it had been Snake, there was no evidence he had gone to Cobb's office.

"Did you recognize the rider?"

"No. It was dark, of course. I just saw the lights and heard the motor. Very loud. It kind of startled me because you don't usually see anybody on the road that time of night. It was one o'clock in the morning. Nobody's out and around then except me, and sometimes I see a cop car parked out by the interstate exit. That's it."

"So it was just a typical motorcycle rider with a big helmet?'

"No, come to think of it. He wasn't wearing a big plastic helmet. He had on one of those small ones like Hell's Angels wear, and I thought he must be pretty stupid if he thought his beard was going to protect him in a crash."

Lucy's spine tingled.

"He had a beard?"

"Yes. A big, bushy one. My headlights picked it up. And there was a coiled snake on the back of his jacket—I saw it when he turned by the Quik Mart sign. That sign gives off quite a bit of light, you know."

"Thank you," said Lucy.

Chapter Twenty-five

Lucy punched out Rachel's number and waited impatiently while the phone rang. *Answer the phone, answer the phone,* she repeated, like a mantra. She didn't want to leave a message, she didn't want to wait for Rachel to return her call. She wanted to talk about this right now.

"Hello."

Finally.

"It's me. You'll never guess what I found out. Snake was spotted not far from the office the night Sherman was killed."

"Really?" Rachel's voice was breathy.

"According to the cleaning lady, Ginger. She saw him."

"Do you think he killed Sherman?"

"I think it's a definite possibility."

"I don't like this at all," said Rachel, sounding deadly serious. "He's over there at Miss Tilley's. God knows what he and Shirley are up to."

"I'm pretty sure there's a link between Miss T and Sherman Cobb," said Lucy, struggling to put all the pieces together. "I'm not positive, but I think the judge was Sherman's father, which would make him Miss T's half brother. My guess is the Hendersons wanted him out of the way so they could go after Miss T."

"Oh, my God," gasped Rachel. "He's a killer and he's in her house."

"We've got to go to the police," said Lucy. "Meet me there."

Lucy was shrugging into her clammy jacket when Phyllis snatched it away from her.

"You'll catch your death in that. Here, wear mine."

She thrust her raincoat at Lucy and handed her an umbrella.

Lucy gave her a quick smile and dashed out the door, raising the umbrella as she ran down the street. She knew she must be quite a sight, rushing along the sidewalk in Phyllis's oversized, puffy-pink down coat waving the flowery umbrella, but she didn't care. When she got to the police station Rachel was just pulling into the parking lot in her aged Volvo.

"Do we have a plan?" asked Rachel, meeting Lucy on the stoop.

"Let's start with Barney. Maybe he's in."

"And if he isn't?"

Lucy didn't have a plan B. "Let's hope he is."

The receptionist gave Lucy a big smile and was only too happy to call Barney, the community relations officer, to let him know that two citizens wanted to speak with him.

A moment later, the security door opened and Barney ushered them down the hall to his little office.

"Come on in, ladies," he said. "Have a seat." He took his own seat on the other side of the desk and folded his hands on the blotter. "What can I do for you?"

Lucy hesitated for a moment; then the words poured out. "I have some new information about the Cobb case that indicates Miss Tilley is in danger," she said.

"Whoa there, Lucy. Cobb case? I didn't know there was a case," replied Barney.

Rachel gave him a glance that would wither a turnip. "Don't play coy with me, Barney Culpepper," she snapped. "You know damn well that Sherman Cobb did not commit suicide, and we're trying to prevent a second murder. Shut up and listen to Lucy."

"Yes, ma'am," said Barney.

"Ginger North, who cleans the law office, told me she saw Snake Henderson riding his motorcycle near the office on the night Cobb died. And now we're worried because Snake and his mother have moved in with Miss Tilley and aren't letting anyone see her. We think there's some sort of mischief afoot."

Barney's forehead folded like an accordion. "What kind of mischief?"

"Well, it's obvious," said Lucy, impatiently. "He killed Sherman and now they're after Miss Tilley. God forbid she may even be dead already. We don't know because they won't let us see her or talk to us on the phone."

"You think these two things are related somehow?" asked Barney, scratching his head with an enormous hand.

Lucy sat up bolt upright. "Yes! Judge Tilley was Sherman's father. He arranged for the court bailiff to adopt him and insisted he be named Sherman. Why would he do that if he wasn't his son?"

"And Miss T's brother," said Rachel. "Half brother."

"Hold on," cautioned Barney, holding up one hand in the gesture he used when he was directing traffic. "Maybe the old judge did have some fun on the side, but what's that got to do with anything? And I gotta tell you, just because somebody saw this Henderson guy in the vicinity doesn't make him Cobb's murderer." He scratched his head. "Why would he kill him? Somehow I don't think he was worried about the shame of it all, the disgrace of his extremely respectable grandfather having an illegitimate son."

"Very funny," snapped Lucy. "I don't think Snake gives a damn what people think about him. I think it's got something to do with money. Inheritance. That's what's at the bottom of this. They want something. They didn't get it from Cobb so they killed him, and now they're trying to get it from Miss Tilley."

"But what?" Rachel's dark eyebrows had shot up. "Sherman didn't leave anything to the Hendersons, or Miss Tilley."

"What about Miss Tilley? Do you know what the terms of her will are?"

"Actually, I do," said Rachel. "According to Bob, she left everything to the library, and everything isn't much."

"Maybe they'll make her sign a new will," suggested Lucy "A will in their favor. It's been done before."

"I never thought of that," said Rachel, looking down at her lap. She raised her head and leaned forward, practically on her knees, hanging on to Barney's desk like a prayer rail. "You've got to get in that house and check on Miss Tilley," she said, pleading. "I know it's probably against department policy and everything, but think how you'd feel if you did nothing and all this time she's been suffering. What if she dies?"

"There, there," said Barney, leaning across his desk to pat her hand. "You don't need to worry on that score. I was there yesterday and Miss T was sleeping peacefully."

"You actually saw her? Shirley let you in the house?"

He nodded. "Nothing was out of order. Miss T was tucked in bed. Shirley seems to be taking good care of her." He leaned back in his chair, which creaked. "She's very old. She's dying, but she's home with her family and they're taking care of her." He folded his hands across his potbelly. "I think this is the way she'd want it. I really do."

"Well, you can pretend everything's okay, but I'm not convinced," said Lucy, jumping to her feet. "I have got to see for myself."

"Whoa, there," said Barney, hauling himself out of his chair. "You sit back down and listen to me."

Resentfully, Lucy did.

Barney leaned over her, grasping the arms of the chair and sticking his face into hers.

"There's a fine line here between concern and meddling. The Hendersons are Miss T's family, her only family. They have the right to decide what's best for her and you have to abide by it. I've told you she's at peace, and that's going to be the end of it. Do you understand me? I don't want to have to arrest you for trespassing and harassment. Are we clear on this?"

Lucy nodded.

Barney let go of the chair and stood up.

"Ladies, you go on home now. Your families will be wanting their suppers."

Lying in bed, Miss Tilley heard voices. A deep, rumbling male voice and a shrill female voice. First one voice, then the other. Sometimes both together, trying to outshout each other. It was almost like music, some modern, discordant type of music. The bass fiddle and the kettle drum, then the squealing, shrieking violins. Occasionally the percussionist banged out a beat or hit the cymbal. She had never liked modern music much.

Of course, she knew it was Shirley and Snake, arguing. If only she could hear what they were saying, then she might understand what was going on. It was too bad they had such poor diction. Apparently Harriet hadn't been a careful mother; Shirley seemed lacking in the most basic social skills. As for Snake, it seemed incredible to her that she could actually be related to this man. Tattoos!

There was a loud crash and she winced, wondering which of her antiques had been smashed to bits. What was going on out there? What was it all about?

Shifting her position, she encountered something hard under her shoulder. A pill. She had avoided swallowing them for some time by holding them in her mouth and spitting them out when Shirley wasn't looking. She reached under her shoulder with her opposite hand and retrieved it, slipping it under the rug. There must be quite a collection under there, she thought. Maybe she should find some other hiding place. It wouldn't do to have the pills crunch under Shirley's sneakered feet. She shuddered, thinking of the X Shirley had cut in each sneaker to accommodate her bunions.

The voices were quieter now and she wondered if she

dared risk eating a cookie. She had a package of *petit beurre* biscuits in her nightstand drawer because she sometimes woke up hungry in the night. She had been eating them sparingly, waiting until her hunger pangs became almost unbearable. She was hungry now, but she didn't want to risk being discovered. It was better, she thought, to let Shirley think her plan, whatever it was, was working. That she was indeed drugged. It was just a matter of time, she told herself, until someone came to the house. Lucy, perhaps, or Rachel. Or even that social worker from the Council on Aging. Then she would call out for help.

The problem was, she admitted, that even without the drugs she tended to drift off into sleep. She hoped she hadn't missed a potential rescuer when she nodded off.

Hearing the voices growing louder once again, she decided to risk eating a cookie. Shirley, she had learned, was much more likely to pop in on her when the house was quiet and not when she was busy arguing with Snake.

Moving slowly and carefully so the bed wouldn't squeak, she reached her arm out from under the blanket and grasped the crystal knob of the nightstand drawer. It slid open and she felt inside for the paper packet, wincing as it crackled under her fingers. She withdrew a cookie and bit off the tiniest bit of scalloped corner.

She sighed in ecstasy. It was delicious. She rolled the fragment around on her tongue, making it last as long as possible. Only when it had completely dissolved did she take another tiny bite.

When she had finally finished the cookie, Miss Tilley stretched. The movement made the plastic on her adult diaper crinkle. Lord, how she loathed these things. She had been shocked when she discovered Shirley had put one on her, outraged in fact. But as things had turned out, they had been a blessing in disguise. It would have been impossible for her to use the bathroom without alerting Snake and Shirley to the fact that she was clearheaded and awake.

Sitting up, she swung her legs over the side of the bed and stood up. They were really going at it now; she doubted they would disturb her. She walked over to the door and put her ear against it.

"You motherfucker!"

She jumped back as if scalded.

"You son of a bitch!"

She clucked her tongue. Papa had been right. Profanity was the sign of an uncultivated mind. She made her way around the bed to the opposite side of the room. There she put her feet together and reached her arms above her head, stretching. She would do a few sun salutations, she decided, just to stay limber. She placed her hands together in prayer position and took a deep breath, exhaling as she raised her arms above her head and leaned back

A loud bang, like a gun firing, startled her and she almost lost her balance. Frightened, she scampered back into bed. The silence pounded against her eardrums as she trembled.

Chapter Twenty-six

"I can't believe he actually said that," fumed Lucy, as she and Rachel left the police station.

The rain had stopped but the sky was still overcast and there were puddles on the sidewalk.

"'Your families will be waiting for their suppers!'" mimicked Rachel, marching right into a puddle and splashing herself and Lucy. She was so angry she didn't even notice. "Why can't I get them to take me seriously? It was the same thing at Senior Services."

"They didn't help you at all?"

"Oh, she made a few phone calls; she even checked with the bank. There was no unusual activity, she said, so she couldn't do anything."

"You know, Snake and Shirley are playing this pretty smart. They're being careful not to arouse suspicion by emptying out her bank account; they even managed to fool Barney when he visited. I think this is a plan they've been working on for a while. Remember, Snake was in town the night Sherman died, which was a full week before Shirley showed up at Miss T's."

"They must have known about Sherman's relationship to the family, too, don't you think? How could they know that?"

"From Shirley's mother, maybe? She was the older sister, remember. She might have been aware of things that went right over Miss T's head."

"And she might have nurtured a grudge against her father," added Rachel. "Imagine how she must have felt, disowned by a father who was unfaithful to her mother. A double betrayal."

The thought made Lucy feel sick. Snake and Shirley weren't just out for gain, their motivation was far deeper. They wanted to even old scores. They wanted revenge.

"I wish there was something we could do," she said, pausing next to Rachel's car.

Rachel squeezed her arm. "We've done everything we can. We've gone to the authorities; we've told them everything we know. It's out of our hands."

"I guess you're right," said Lucy, watching her drive off.

Lucy was still wearing Phyllis's coat, so she headed back to *The Pennysaver*. Phyllis looked up when she yanked the door open, making the little bell jangle.

"No go?" she asked, seeing Lucy's downfallen expression.

"We couldn't convince them that anything's wrong," said Lucy, replacing Phyllis's coat on the rack. "Thanks for the coat."

"It's like the time Elfrida's little boy, Howie, had appendicitis. She was in and out of the doctor's office telling him that Howie had appendicitis. She was sure of it but they wouldn't believe her because the tests came back negative. Howie kept getting sicker and sicker and she didn't know what to do."

"What did she do?"

"Well, he finally got so sick that she took him to the emergency room and that time the tests came back different. They operated and the surgeon told her that if she'd waited any longer he might not have lived."

"That's an awful story," said Lucy.

"It gets worse," said Phyllis. "Turned out the lab made a mistake on the first set of blood tests."

"Good Lord."

Lucy sat down at her desk, staring at the computer. Behind her, she could hear Phyllis preparing to leave.

"Bye now. Have a nice weekend," said Phyllis.

Alone in the office, Lucy knew it was time to go home. It was time for her to get in the car and drive on up Red Top Road to the house. Kudo was probably sitting in his usual spot on the porch, waiting for her. Bill and the girls would be getting hungry, waiting for her to bring home the usual Friday night pizza. It was just like Barney said, they were waiting for their supper.

She got up and put on her still-damp coat; she turned off the lights and locked the door behind her. She got in the Subaru, started the engine and drove down Main Street. But instead of continuing on the way home, she took the turn that led to Miss Tilley's house.

If the police wanted hard evidence before they would act, if Senior Services needed some sort of proof, well, she'd get it for them. She knew in her gut that Snake and Shirley were up to no good and she was going to trust her instincts just like Elfrida did. She wasn't going to wait until it was too late.

She started to brake as she approached Miss T's little house, then realized it would be smarter to park the Subaru a bit farther down the street, where Snake and Shirley couldn't see it. That meant she had to walk back along the road, where she would certainly attract notice. Pedestrians were a rare sight in Tinker's Cove; it would be far better to appear to be a runner, out for a jog.

Shivering, she shrugged out of her jacket. At first glance her jeans, turtleneck and sweater might pass as athletic wear. Fortunately, she was wearing her usual running shoes. Leaving her purse and jacket in the car she jogged in place, then set off down the road at an easy pace. Her intention was to run past Miss Tilley's house, looking for signs of occupation. This was what burglars did, they cased a house before they attempted an entry. A bad analogy, she decided. She preferred to think she was on a reconnaissance mission, like one of Charlie's Angels.

She tried not to be too obvious and kept her head straight, only allowed her eyes to wander as she trotted past the little Cape Cod house. There was no sign of Snake's motorcycle, which had, until now, been parked in front of the garage. Lucy thought he must be out; she knew there was no room for the Harley in the garage because that was where Miss Tilley kept her huge old Lincoln. She didn't drive anymore, but Rachel occasionally chauffeured her around town.

Reaching the corner, Lucy had to stop to catch her breath. She bent over, hands on her knees, and rested, panting like Kudo after he'd chased a rabbit. The difference was, she realized with dismay, that Kudo could run for miles and she had only gone a few blocks. Thank goodness she hadn't tried this before she began her exercise program.

Straightening up she ran back the way she had come, keeping an eye out for homecoming traffic and neighbors. The street was sparsely settled, with only a few houses, and from outside she could see the flickering blue light of television sets through the windows. No children played outside, no curtains twitched. Everybody was watching TV.

Back at her car, Lucy wished she had X-ray vision. Miss Tilley's house could be empty; it certainly looked deserted with the shades drawn and the morning paper lying on the front path. If only she knew what was going on inside.

She considered another trick used by burglars and reached inside the car for her cell phone. She would call and see who answered the phone. Of course she wouldn't identify herself; she would just push the end button.

She punched in the number and listened to the rings, growing more hopeful with each ring. Maybe Snake and Shirley had both gone out. For groceries or cigarettes. Maybe they'd left town altogether. A girl could hope.

She was about to stop the call herself when she heard a click and a hello. It was Shirley; she recognized her voice.

It was as if an icicle had slid down her back and she shivered. Remembering she'd taken her jacket off, Lucy climbed in the car and started the engine so she could warm herself while she considered her options. If she wanted to play it safe, she decided, she could just go up to the front door and knock. If Shirley wouldn't admit her she could force her way in. Just march in as if she were welcome, breezing her way through the house to Miss Tilley's room.

Problem was, Shirley had managed to deflect that approach in the past. She might get as far as the living room but, unless she was willing to physically manhandle Shirley, Lucy doubted she'd get any farther.

No, she decided, a less direct method would be better. She knew the house well. If luck was with her she could slip unnoticed through the back door and into Miss Tilley's downstairs bedroom. It wouldn't be that difficult, not in an old house like Miss Tilley's where the small rooms all had doors and there were plenty of pantries and bulky old pieces of furniture. Why, she herself had been surprised more than once in her own house by a meter reader, come to check the water meter in the cellar, or one of the kids' friends come to retrieve a forgotten jacket or school book. In fact, that was one reason she liked having Kudo—he always barked and let her know when anyone came to the house.

Hopefully there were no dogs here, she told herself as she got out of the car and cut through the Wilsons' backyard. The Wilsons were Miss Tilley's longtime neighbors and they always spent the winter in Florida. They probably wouldn't be back for a couple of weeks but Lucy stayed away from the house and close to the lilac hedge that marked the end of their property.

Her heart began to pound as she pushed her way through the privet into Miss Tilley's yard. She paused and stood very still, checking the windows. The shades were drawn tight on every one; only the glass pane on the kitchen door, which was only covered with a white muslin curtain, offered the possibility of a peek inside.

Attempting to look natural, Lucy approached the back door. It was only when she was at the little wooden step that she crouched down, then carefully raised herself just enough so that she could see between the curtain panels. Her view was limited because the back door opened into an ell, a shed that was an intermediate space between inside and outside. In winter it offered an airlock between the heated kitchen and the frigid outdoors; in summer it was a handy place to store garden tools and flowerpots.

Peering through her little peephole, Lucy saw nothing but the expected clutter of newspapers waiting to be recycled, a bag of deicing crystals and a couple of snow shovels, several pairs of boots neatly lined up against the wall and a few jackets hanging from nails.

Her hand was steadier than she expected as she turned the knob, but then she was half hoping the door would be locked. It wasn't. Obligingly, it swung inward, practically inviting her to enter.

Lucy slipped through soundlessly and shut the door carefully behind her, listening intently. She listened not just with her ears but with every fiber of her body; even the hairs on her arms were raised and alert to the slightest vibration. But all Lucy heard was the hum of the refrigerator and, from upstairs, she thought, the indistinct rise and fall in volume of a TV show. Good, she thought. Shirley was watching TV.

Cautiously, Lucy pushed the kitchen door open a crack. She couldn't see much, just the bulky electric stove with its automatic timer that had been the ultimate in cooking technology in 1952 and the old-fashioned refrigerator with its round top. She pushed the door a little farther and her view now included the kitchen table, which was covered with old, yellowed documents.

Lucy rushed forward, her breath catching in her throat. She began rifling through the papers, greedily hunting for information. Then, remembering the need for caution, she snatched her hands back. She hoped she hadn't disturbed them too much. Moving as quietly as she could, she sorted through them. As far as she could tell they were a jumble of everything from old savings account books to product warranties to more of those old Maine Motorcar stock certificates. With a start she noticed a preprinted will, the sort you could buy in a stationery store, naming Shirley the sole heir and signed by Miss Tilley in a weak, wavering hand.

A burst of canned laughter reminded her of her mission. She tiptoed across the kitchen to the door that led to the dining room and pressed her ear against it. All she could hear, louder now, was the television set. It sounded like one of those daytime talk shows, with loud bursts of clapping and booing. She sent up a silent prayer that Shirley would be fascinated by "Mothers Who Steal Their Daughters' Boyfriends" or "Men Who Love Their Cars More Than Their Wives."

Lucy waited for a loud burst of applause and opened the door a crack, recoiling in shock at what she saw. Miss Tilley's prized rosewood dining table was covered with a scattering of dirty dishes, ashtrays and beer cans. Even worse, the pottery rabbit that served as a centerpiece was broken, smashed into bits. The room was empty, though, and so was the living room beyond. The way was clear to Miss Tilley's bedroom, right next to the living room.

Lucy stepped over the bare wood floors and onto the thickly cushioned oriental rug and hurried past the messy table. Not a good sign, she thought. If Miss Tilley were in control, she would never have allowed something like that to happen.

Lucy was sure the living room was empty but she paused when she reached the connecting archway, just to make sure, and stepped into a shadowy corner. From her vantage point she could see the entire room and it wasn't an encouraging sight. Books had been tumbled from the shelves, cushions had been yanked from the chairs and sofa and thrown on the floor, pieces of old china had been thrown onto the floor. Lucy winced at the sight of the smashed Coalport teapot, which had once held pride of place in the china cabinet.

This was worse than she had expected. She had suspected something was wrong in the household, she had even been worried for Miss Tilley's safety, but she hadn't admitted to herself the possibility of violence. She wasn't sure exactly what she thought had been going on, but she hadn't thought it would involve broken china. Stealing, maybe, even threats, but not wanton destruction. There was no longer any doubt about it, she had to get Miss Tilley out of here.

Lucy's heart was pounding as she reached for the knob on Miss Tilley's door. "Please, please, please let her be all right." She was saying it out loud, she realized. Over and over, as if the phrase had some magic properties.

"Let her be all right; let her be all right." She grabbed the knob and twisted it.

"Hold it right there."

Lucy flinched and snatched her hand back, as if the knob were on fire. She whirled around to face Shirley.

"This is outrageous," Lucy began, spitting out the words, only to sputter to a halt when she spotted the handgun Shirley was pointing at her.

"Just do what I tell you and nobody will get hurt," said Shirley, directing her away from Miss Tilley's door and back into the dining room.

Lucy didn't believe her, but her options were limited. She obeyed, keeping a wary eye on Shirley and the gun.

"Stop right there."

Lucy was in front of the door that led to the old buttery, or pantry, in the days when the dining room was the keeping room. Then the members of the household gathered around the keeping room's massive fireplace to warm themselves, to cook meals and to heat water. In those days food was stored in the buttery but now, Lucy knew, Miss Tilley used it to store china and glassware.

"Open the door."

Lucy felt a faint flutter of hope in her chest. Maybe Shirley intended to lock her in the buttery. She could handle that. Why, the buttery even had a window. Shirley would tie her up, of course, but Lucy was confident she could eventually manage to escape.

Lucy opened the door and waited for further instructions.

"Now, pull up the trapdoor."

Lucy's heart sank. Shirley was going to lock her in the root cellar. No doubt the root cellar had been less frightening in the days when potatoes and turnips and carrots and other garden produce had been stored there. But now, if it was anything like her own root cellar, it was a damp, cold and dark place where spiders and mice and maybe even snakes lurked. She didn't want to go down there. Damn it, she wasn't going to go down there.

"Hurry up," snarled Shirley. Lucy felt her press the gun into her back. "I haven't got all day."

She bent down and grasped the ring, giving the trapdoor a tug. It came up quite easily. Lucy peered down, expecting to see nothing but a rough wooden staircase and a dirt floor. What she saw were blue-jean-covered legs, a heavy torso in a torn T-shirt and a bearded face. Snake's body.

Lucy recoiled in shock and horror, involuntarily whirling around. She saw Shirley's eyes narrow and her mouth harden into a thin line, she saw a flash and heard the gun fire, and then she was falling into the darkness.

Chapter Twenty-seven

From far away, Lucy heard someone calling her name. It was too early to get up. She wanted to stay in bed where it was warm and comfortable.

She shut out the voice, clinging to unconsciousness.

The voice was louder.

Something was the matter with her bed. It was tilted somehow, and her head was lower than her chest. She must have lost her pillow. She lifted her arm to reach for it and a sharp, stabbing pain ripped through her shoulder.

She heard a groaning sound, then realized she had made the sound. And with good reason. Her shoulder was killing her and she had a splitting headache. Not to mention there was something seriously wrong with her bed. Something was definitely very wrong and she had to find out what. She opened her eyes.

Miss Tilley's wizened face was floating above her, she realized with a shock. She closed her eyes and opened them again. Maybe she was still dreaming. Maybe it was a nightmare.

"Lucy! Are you all right?"

It was definitely Miss Tilley. She was dressed in a nightgown and her white hair was sticking out all over her head. The silver sneakers were on her feet, twinkling madly.

Lucy tried to lift her head and groaned again.

"Hold tight," said Miss Tilley, squinting as she peered down at Lucy. "I've called the rescue squad."

"Where am I?" Lucy couldn't produce much more than a whisper.

"You're in my cellar. Shirley shot you and you fell through the trapdoor."

Lucy began to remember. Shirley had pointed the gun at her and ordered her to open the trapdoor. She'd looked down and seen Snake's body.

Snake's body.

She wasn't in bed. She had fallen through the trapdoor onto Snake's body. Involuntarily, she cringed in revulsion. Her shoulder hurt like hell and she was dizzy. Damn it, she couldn't move. She was just going to have to wait for help. She began to feel very queasy.

Heavy footsteps shook the floor above her, and a face shiny with sunburn looked down at her.

"We'll have you out of there in no time," said a hearty male voice.

"Good," said Lucy, in a weak voice.

The EMTs made rather a production of getting Lucy out of the cellar. The smallest was elected to lower himself through the trapdoor and check her vital signs. Then a large basket sort of contraption was slid through the opening and Lucy was strapped into it. The trapdoor wasn't large enough to lift the stretcher up straight so they raised one end—the one with her head—and slid her through at an angle.

Lieutenant Horowitz greeted her when she appeared aboveground.

"Well, Mrs. Stone, this is a first even for you," he said, stroking his elongated upper lip.

From his tone, Lucy suspected he thought her predicament was amusing. She didn't see the humor.

"How's Miss Tilley?" she asked.

"I'm fine," exclaimed Miss Tilley. Lucy painfully turned her head and saw that she was seated at the kitchen table, slurping away at a big bowl of soup. "All that bed rest did me a world of good. I'm raring to go."

Lucy wished she felt half as good. She knew she needed to get to the hospital, but she had to ask one last question.

"Where's Shirley?"

"Right behind you." Miss Tilley sucked up a noodle and nodded. "I conked her with the bust of Lincoln."

The EMTs lifted Lucy's stretcher and carried her out of the kitchen. Their path took them past Shirley, who appeared to be out cold on the floor with a third EMT crouching beside her. Then Lucy was in the ambulance, the door slammed shut and they began to move.

In Miss Tilley's kitchen, Shirley began to stir.

The EMT, a young woman, stroked her forehead and told her she would be fine.

Shirley's eyes flew open and she slapped the EMT's hand away.

"Get your hands off of me!" she shrieked.

Officer Barney Culpepper snapped into action, reaching for his handcuffs.

"We can do this the easy way or the hard way," said Barney, wrestling the woman facedown onto the floor.

He placed his knee in the middle of her back and snapped the cuff on her right hand, then pulled her arm back so he could cuff her left hand.

"Owww," screamed Shirley, as if she were being killed.

Miss Tilley clucked her tongue in disapproval.

"Officer Culpepper is only doing his job. If you're not willing to cooperate, he has no choice but to use force," she said.

"Shut up, you old biddy," hissed Shirley. "My big mistake was—"

"You made a lot of mistakes, dear," said Miss Tilley,

placidly. "For example, you never caught on to the fact that I wasn't taking the sleeping pills. I heard everything. I know Snake killed Sherman, and you were trying to get me to sign a will leaving everything to you. Signing that, I suppose, would have been signing my own death warrant. I even heard you shoot your own son." Her voice slowed. "And of course you shot dear Lucy."

Miss Tilley put down her spoon.

"Quite frankly, it's hard for me to believe that you could really be a member of my family. Are you in fact Harriet's daughter, or did you make that up?"

Shirley snorted in contempt. "Mother was right about you. You are a self-righteous prig and so was my grandfather."

Horowitz held up a cautionary hand. "Before this goes any further, I think I'd better read you your rights. You have the right to remain silent—"

"Aw, shut up. I know my rights." Shirley faced Miss Tilley. "And for your information, you old fool, you did sign that will."

Miss Tilley recoiled, as if she'd received an electric shock.

Shirley was on her feet now, standing between Barney and another police officer.

"You're a sad, pathetic old woman." She laughed. "You were so eager to have some family, to have somebody care about you, that you never checked me out. Sure, I've been to jail before, and you know what? It doesn't scare me one bit." She tilted her head toward the trapdoor. "Snake, there, he was getting soft. Getting all snively. He was getting to be a liability. I mean, if I had to do everything myself, what did I need him for?"

Miss Tilley raised her big, china-blue eyes and leveled them on Shirley. "Before you take her away, I have one question."

"Go ahead," said Lieutenant Horowitz.

"Why did you kill Sherman? What was the reason?"

Shirley's thin lips twisted into a triumphant sneer. "You think you're so smart, but you never figured it out, did you?"

She chuckled. "Precious Sherman was dear Papa's bastard son. The old buzzard knocked up his secretary. I had to get him out of the way, just so there wouldn't be any messy inheritance issues after I finished you off."

For once in her long life, Miss Tilley was genuinely shocked. She watched as Shirley was hustled out of the kitchen and the EMT shut the door behind them.

"Good riddance to bad rubbish," said the young woman. "Now, how are you feeling? Maybe we should take you to the ER for a checkup? Just to be on the safe side?"

"That won't be necessary."

"Is there someone who could stay with you for a bit? Is there someone I can call?"

Miss Tilley smiled. "Rachel. Her number's by the phone."

While the EMT was dialing on the old rotary phone, Miss Tilley slowly stood up. Walking slowly, almost as if in a daze, she made her way into the living room and lowered herself into her favorite Boston rocker. Letting out a long sigh, she turned and looked up at the portrait of her father that hung over the fireplace.

He looked the same as always, still dressed in his judicial robes. His eyebrows bristled; his nose was sharp and hooked; his lips were set in a thin line.

In the deep recesses of Miss Tilley's mind a memory stirred. She remembered visiting Papa's office with Mama. Papa's secretary, Miss Kaiser, had given her a small piece of chocolate wrapped in shiny foil. She had often asked if they could visit again, but Mama had always said no. Maybe Mama had suspected something; maybe she'd known that Papa's relationship with Miss Kaiser wasn't all business.

Julia gazed up at the portrait, and she noticed something she hadn't seen before. There was definitely a twinkle in Papa's eye.

"You old devil," she said, winking at the portrait.

Chapter Twenty-eight

Rachel Goodman gave a perfunctory knock and walked right into Lucy's kitchen; she knew Lucy had joined Bill on the sick list and Rachel didn't want to put them to the trouble of answering the door.

"We're in here," called Lucy.

Rachel pushed open the door to the family room, which had been turned into a temporary sick bay. Bill was in his usual place in the recliner and Lucy was stretched out on the couch. They made a touching picture, with matching red afghans spread over their laps.

"Well, you two are the cutest pair of invalids I've ever seen!" Rachel declared. "Matching blankies!"

"They're from Norah," explained Lucy. "Monogrammed."

Her fleece blanket was embroidered with a huge blue *hers* while Bill's had a *his*.

Rachel raised her eyebrows and shook her head in disbelief. "Can I get you guys anything?"

"No." Lucy shook her head. "We're doing pretty well. I got shot in the shoulder, so I can't use my arm, but Bill's arms are fine. He can't use his leg, but mine are fine. Together we're a complete person."

"More than one," said Bill. "About one and a half, I'd say."

"Make it one and a quarter," said Lucy. "I don't really have much energy. Getting shot takes a lot out of you."

"I'm sure it does," said Rachel, taking a seat in an arm-chair. "You had a close call."

"And I hope she's learned her lesson," said Bill. "She should mind her own business and stop sticking her nose in where it doesn't belong."

"If I hadn't gone to Miss T's that day . . . Well, I don't even like to think about what could have happened."

"You wouldn't have got shot, that's what would have happened."

"Now, now, children," Rachel scolded. "Play nicely or your friend will have to leave."

Bill apologized by way of a crooked smile.

"So, how's Miss T doing after her ordeal?"

Rachel smiled. "She is doing great. She lost some weight, but I've been making things like tapioca pudding and milk-shakes for her and she's gaining it back. She swears the bed rest did her good and she's got more energy than before. She works out with a TV show every morning now."

"Miss Tilley?" Bill couldn't believe it.

"Honest to God. She modifies some of the exercises, but she's pretty good at the yoga portion of the show. She makes me do it with her." Rachel flexed her arm, exhibiting her newly firm biceps muscle.

"I guess Shirley didn't realize who she was taking on," said Lucy.

"And a good thing, too," said Rachel. "If they hadn't been convinced the drugs were working, I'm sure they would have used force. That Shirley is one mean woman."

"What did they want?" asked Bill. "She couldn't have much money. She was a librarian."

"A rich librarian, as it turns out. Bob did some research and found out that some old shares of Maine Motorcar—Sherman had some too—are actually worth a bundle."

"Maine Motorcar, that sounds familiar," said Bill, reaching for one of the bound volumes of newspapers. He flipped through the pages until he found what he was looking for. "Here it is. An advertisement offering shares in the new company. It lists Judge Tilley as the chairman of the board, and Sheriff Wilbur Cobb is the treasurer."

"That's Sherman's father!" exclaimed Lucy, quickly remembering to correct herself. "Adoptive father, I mean."

"Yup. He and Judge Tilley were lodge brothers. Honorable and esteemed Beavers."

"I guess the Beavers never caught on," said Rachel. "I've heard of Moose, Elk, Lions, Eagles—"

"Even Odd Fellows," inserted Lucy.

"But never Beavers."

"The Beavers were an industrious lot," said Bill, smiling at his own joke. "Quite a few of the brothers invested in the company. They were going to build the cars right here in town."

"You're kidding. Did they ever do it?" asked Lucy.

"I don't think so," said Bill. "It was 1929."

"The stock market crash," said Lucy. "They probably lost it all."

"Not exactly," said Rachel. "It seems that Maine Motorcar was bought by New England Tool and Die, which did a huge business during World War Two and eventually became part of General Avionics. Those old stock certificates mean Miss Tilley owns thousands and thousands of shares of General Avionics."

"Well, good for her," said Lucy.

Rachel shrugged. "I think she feels she paid a high price, if you know what I mean. She was really quite delighted when Shirley showed up. She even liked Snake. She really wanted to reestablish her family. She yearned for that connection, but Shirley still felt very bitter toward her mother's family. She wanted to get even. I honestly think revenge was more important to her than the money."

"I think you're right," agreed Lucy. "The sad thing is that Miss T really did have family here all along, but she just didn't know it. I think Sherman was going to tell her—remember he'd asked to meet with Miss T? I think the one thing he wanted before he died was to be acknowledged as a Tilley, the judge's son and the grandson of the hero of Portland. He really idolized them."

Rachel nodded. "The cops think he actually may have started this whole thing by contacting Shirley. Horowitz told Bob that her Florida phone number was scribbled on his desk blotter."

"It wouldn't surprise me. I always thought Shirley's story about seeing a TV commercial for nationwide information was pretty fishy." Lucy sighed. "Isn't it funny how people in the same family can be so different? Maybe Shirley inherited some bad genes or something. Family means nothing to her. She killed her own son, for goodness' sake."

"Well, it turns out he wasn't actually her son. He was her husband's son from an earlier marriage—one of her husbands, that is. She had several, a couple of them at the same time. She raised him with the predictable result that he ended up in jail. She thought she could use him in her scheme, but apparently he wasn't willing to take orders from her anymore and she got rid of him. She wasn't taking any chances that he might give evidence against her." She paused. "Bob says she'll spend the rest of her life in jail."

"Couldn't happen to a nicer person," said Lucy, reaching to answer the ringing phone.

"Hi, Toby," she said, catching Bill's eye.

She tried to make her voice sound cheerful, despite the fact that these days Toby rarely called home with anything except bad news.

"Mom," he began in a firm voice. "I've come to a decision."

Lucy's eyebrows shot up and Bill leaned closer, trying to hear.

"I'm going to finish out the term—finals are next week—but then I want to take some time off next year. I need some time to decide if college is really the right thing for me. I've been thinking I could work with Dad. What do you think?"

"I think you better talk to your father," she said, handing over the handset.

"Hey, Toby," said Bill, using his hearty father voice.

Lucy and Rachel watched as he listened, his expression growing cheerier with every word of Toby's.

"Sounds good to me, son. I could really use the help."

He was beaming by the time he said good-bye.

"He wants to take a year off from school and work with me." He held up his hand, cautioning her. "I know what you're going to say and—"

Lucy had initially tensed, ready to argue that Toby shouldn't interrupt his studies, but she was surprised to find the anxiety that had been accumulating for months, growing with each miserable phone call, was draining from her body. She suddenly felt light and buoyant, almost giddy.

"It's okay. I think it's a good idea."

"You do?"

Lucy nodded, gravely. "Let's face it, you're not getting any younger. He can keep an eye on you."

"I admit I had an accident," said Bill, "but I only hurt my leg. I'd like to remind you that the rest of me is in perfect working order."

"Ahem," said Rachel, clearing her throat. "It sounds like it's time for me to get going. Are you sure I can't do anything for you?"

"We're fine," said Lucy.

"And getting finer," said Bill. "The cast is supposed to come off next week."

"That's great," said Rachel. "So I can count on seeing you both at the big birthday bash?"

"Wouldn't miss it for the world," said Lucy.

Chapter Twenty-nine

"Mom, how much longer are you going to be?"

Sara's voice on the other side of the bathroom door was polite, but even through the century-old pine Lucy could discern a note of impatience. She had been in the bathroom for quite a while, she realized. Smoothing the hypoallergenic moisturizer she'd bought at the natural foods store under her eyes hadn't taken more than a minute; the problem was the assortment of antioxidant vitamins she'd bought. They were supposed to fight aging and guard against a host of ills, but Lucy couldn't figure out how many tablets to take. The directions were printed in very tiny type on the label and she couldn't make them out, even when she squinted and took them over to the window where the light was bright. She was definitely going to have to buy some cheaters, but in the meantime she knew what to do. She opened the door.

"It's about time," fumed Sara. "We're going to be late for the party."

"Hold on a minute, miss," demanded Lucy, blocking the doorway. "Can you read these directions for me?"

Sara looked at her oddly. "You can't read?"

"I can read, I just can't see. It happens when you get older. Presbyopia."

Sara took the bottles. "Two of these, one of this and one of that."

"Thanks."

Lucy took the pills and hurried into her bedroom to get dressed. It was May 20, Miss Tilley Day, and she knew Sue was counting on her to be prompt. Despite all the work and planning that had gone into the gala celebration, Lucy had a case of pre-party jitters. Maybe it was because they had all worked so hard, especially Sue, that she so desperately wanted the day to be a success.

Lucy flipped through the clothes in her closet, looking for something to wear. She should have thought of this earlier, she admitted, as she discarded one garment after another. Jeans were too casual, her little black dress was too dressy and her good wool slacks were at the cleaners. The only pair that were left had been too tight the last time she wore them.

She eyed them doubtfully as she slipped them off the hanger, but when she pulled them on they fit easily over her thighs and fastened neatly at the waistband. Astonished, Lucy looked at her reflection in the full-length mirror. She knew she hadn't lost any weight, but she did look trimmer. Working out with Video Debbie had made a difference. And, she admitted to herself, she felt better, too. Less tired and more energetic. More cheerful, too. Maybe she had found her own positive personal paradigm.

The parking lot at the community center was full, so Lucy dropped Bill and the girls off at the door. His leg was healing nicely and the cast was off, but he still found walking long distances difficult and was using a cane. Toby's decision to spend a year working with his father couldn't have come at a better time, thought Lucy, as she steered the car down the street using her good arm, looking for a place to park. Her shoulder was still a little stiff, but otherwise she'd suffered no long-term ill effects from the gunshot wound, which the ER doctor had dismissed as a scratch.

From the number of cars parked along the road, it seemed

the whole town must have turned out for Miss Tilley Day. She had to park some distance away, and the celebration was in full swing by the time she arrived, pink and breathless from hurrying. Lucy paused in the doorway to catch her breath and to take in the scene.

The utilitarian hall had been transformed, thanks to Sue and Corney Clark, into a festive bower. White and lavender crepe-paper streamers looped from the sides of the room and gathered in the center with an enormous bunch of pastel balloons served to hide the acoustic tile and created a tentlike atmosphere. Bunches of lilacs, Miss Tilley's favorite flower, were everywhere: on the windowsills, on the refreshment tables and in wicker stands set in the corners and along the walls. In the center, under a white arbor covered with ivy and roses, sat Miss Tilley. She was wearing a brand-new dress, and her white hair had been freshly curled, topped with a sparkling rhinestone tiara. It matched her silver shoes, which twinkled whenever she moved.

Lucy made her way through the crowded room, winding around groups of chatting adults and dodging the kamikaze tactics of the kids, fueled with too many sugary cookies and cupcakes snitched from the long tables filled with food. Finally reaching Miss Tilley, she took her hands, gave her a peck on the cheek and wished her a happy ninetieth birthday.

"Did you see the TV show? I'm a star." Miss T indicated a television set placed in one corner that was playing the tape from the *Norah!* show.

"I've known that all along," said Lucy. "You've always been a star to me."

Others were waiting to great Miss Tilley, so Lucy gave her hand a final squeeze and took her leave. "I'd better report to Sue; I'm sure she has something for me to do. Enjoy your day."

Lucy made her way to the kitchen, keeping an eye out for Bill and the girls. Zoe was one of the zooming kids, either chasing or being chased by boys. Sara was chatting with a group of girls gathered around Davia Didrickson, and Bill had taken a seat along the wall, joining Bob Goodman and Sid Finch, Sue's husband. Reassured that they were all behaving themselves, she reported to Sue.

"It's about time," muttered Sue, who was mixing up a huge vat of punch. "What took you so long?"

"Hey, I'm still on the injured list," joked Lucy.

Sue gave her a once-over. "You're looking pretty good for someone who got shot." She narrowed her eyes. "Actually, you're just plain looking good. You go, girl. Whatever you're doing, keep it up. It's working."

Lucy was temporarily flummoxed. "Uh, thanks," she said. "How can I help?"

"Refresh the sandwich and cookie platters, okay? Keep 'em looking full."

For the next hour or so, Lucy was kept busy running between the kitchen and the buffet tables, which were covered with Corney's pale pink linen cloths and loaded with platters of fabulous food. Everyone in town had brought something: plates of finger sandwiches, bowls of shrimp bristling with toothpicks, assorted cheeses, fruit salads, vegetable crudités and dip, bite-sized quiches and savories, enormous bowls of chips, homemade cookies and cupcakes. Lucy had never seen so much food, or such appetites. No sooner would she put down a fresh platter than she'd notice something else needed to be refilled. She couldn't keep the food coming fast enough.

She was only distantly aware of the program taking place on the stage, where a steady stream of townsfolk were coming up to the microphone and sharing their stories about Miss Tilley. She had been the town librarian for so long that everyone knew her, and she knew them. Lucy didn't catch the details, but there was plenty of laughter.

"Here, take a break," said Sue, handing her a cup of punch.

Lucy took it and drank gratefully; she hadn't realized how thirsty she was.

"We're going to have the cake soon, so I think we'll hold the rest of the food while people eat that." Sue was nervously scanning the room, making sure everyone was having a good time, when her eyebrows shot up. "Who's the tall, dark and handsome stranger in the Armani suit?"

"I don't recognize him," said Lucy. "He can't be from around here. Maybe he's a—"

"Shh!" admonished Sue. "He's going up to the microphone."

"You may not remember me," said the stranger, "but I grew up right here in Tinker's Cove. My name is Richard Mason."

"I remember you!" declared Miss Tilley, raising a gnarled finger. "You still owe an overdue fine at the library!"

Everyone laughed, including Mason.

"That's why I'm here," he said, reaching inside his beautifully tailored jacket and pulling out a white envelope. "That fine has been on my mind for a long time. It really bothered me because the library was a very special place to me. I spent a lot of time there when I was a boy. I wasn't welcome in a lot of homes in town because I came from the wrong side of the tracks and my father was the town drunk."

Lucy couldn't resist looking for Donna Didrickson. She finally found her, standing next to the field hockey coach and wearing a thoughtful expression.

"I was always welcome at the library," continued Mason. "Miss Tilley not only provided me with an escape from my unhappy childhood, but she gave me a glimpse of the world beyond Tinker's Cove. She always believed in me, and I couldn't let her down. I put myself through college, went to work for a paper company and now I'm proud to say Mason Industries is the largest producer of quality paper in the world."

There was a buzz in the room, as people compared their recollections of Richard Mason and his father.

"Well, Richard, are you going to pay the fine or not?" snapped Miss Tilley, holding out her hand.

"I think this will cover it."

Mason placed the envelope in her hand, and everyone was silent as she opened it with trembling fingers.

"But, Richard, you only owed fifteen cents. This check is for a million dollars."

Everyone gasped.

"Consider it interest," said Mason, smiling. "It's for a scholarship fund, to be named after you, for Tinker's Cove kids who wouldn't otherwise be able to get the education they need to succeed in life."

"Yes, Richard," said Miss Tilley, blinking furiously to stem her tears. "That's what we'll do. Thank you."

"Thank you," said Mason, bending down to hug her.

The room exploded in applause and Sue dimmed the lights, giving the signal for the cake to be brought in. It was carried aloft, ablaze with candles, by four uniformed members of the Civil War reenactment group, and set in front of Miss Tilley. Her face was radiant in the candlelight, her eyes bright with joy. She took a deep breath and, assisted by the cake bearers, blew out all ninety candles.

"That was some party," Bill said to Lucy, as they drove home. "And you were the prettiest one there. I couldn't keep my eyes off you."

Lucy felt her cheeks grow warm.

"Daddy says Mommy was the prettiest one," said Zoe, giggling in the backseat.

"She *was* the prettiest one," said Bill, firmly. "She looks just like she did when she was in college. Hasn't changed a bit."

"So, Mom, does that mean you're going to give up your creams and vitamins?" asked Sara.

Lucy reached into her purse and pulled out her wallet, withdrawing her new driver's license and studying her photograph. It was very small, of course, too small to capture the wrinkles around her eyes and the fine lines on her upper lip. Still, the clerks at the Division of Motor Vehicles weren't known for taking flattering photographs and she had been pleasantly surprised when she saw the new picture. She looked pretty good.

"No way," she said. "I've just begun to fight."

Please turn the page for an exciting sneak peek

of Leslie Meier's next Lucy Stone mystery

FATHER'S DAY MURDER

coming in June 2003

wherever hardcover mysteries are sold!

Maybe going to the newspaper convention wasn't such a good idea after all, thought Lucy, carefully folding her best dress and tucking it in her suitcase. It was a flowery-print silk sheath that she'd bought at Carriage Trade's end-of-season sale last August. It was perfect for an occasional summer theater show or cocktail party, the sort of event she was likely to attend in Tinker's Cove, but she wasn't convinced it would do in Boston. It screamed summer resort wear rather than urban sophistication.

Too bad, she told herself firmly; it would have to do. According to the schedule Ted had given her, there would be only one dress-up occasion at the conference: the awards banquet. She was certainly not going to buy a new outfit for one event, especially when she had a perfectly good dress in her closet. A lovely dress. A designer dress. A dress splashed with gaudy pink and fuchsia and orange blossoms.

Lucy gave her hair a good brushing, studying herself in the mirror. She saw an average sort of person—average height, average weight, not as young as she used to be and not as old as she hoped to be—someday. Her shining cap of dark hair was her best feature, she thought, mostly because she didn't have to do much with it. She got it cut once a month, rinsed in some hair color now and then to cover the gray that had begun to appear and that was it.

Lucy gave her reflection one last look and decided she looked presentable, dressed for comfort on the bus in jeans and an oversize white shirt. She slipped the brush into the suitcase and was zipping it up when she heard a thunderous crash outside.

Involuntarily, her stomach clenched. What now? she wondered, as she ran to the window to see what had happened. At first nothing seemed different, only that the backyard looked rather empty. Then she realized that the toolshed, which had been covered with climbing rambler roses, had somehow collapsed. The roses were still there, still in bloom, but not as high as they used to be.

Bill and Toby were standing in almost identical positions, arms akimbo, examining the damage. Kudo, the dog, was running in circles and barking furiously.

"Shut up!" yelled Bill, advancing at the dog.

Kudo gave a protesting yelp or two, then scooted off in search of safer ground. Toby was thinking of following him—Lucy could tell by a slight shift in his weight and a definite angle toward the house—but Bill had him in his sights. She'd better get down there fast, she decided, before things got nasty.

Bill had already worked up a good head of steam when she stepped out onto the back porch.

"Why'd you say it was all set when it wasn't?" he yelled at Toby.

Toby shook his head, shrugged his shoulders and held out his hands. "I thought it was set."

"How could you think that? There was nothing to hold it up once I took out the corner post. How stupid can you be? Did you think the air would hold it up? Did you think Newton's laws have been repealed? Dr. Gravity took the day off?"

Toby's face was red, and Lucy knew he was struggling to keep his temper.

"I didn't understand," he said, shaking his head. "I thought you'd done something. I thought you had it under control."

It sounded reasonable enough to Lucy. Kids expected their parents to take care of things for them. There was a roof over their heads, dinner on the table, clean clothes in the drawers. Dentists' appointments got made; all they had to do was show up and open wide. That dynamic had changed, of course, when Toby started working for his father. Now he was supposed to earn his keep.

"No!" barked Bill, pointing a finger at him. "That was your job." He jabbed a finger at him. "You! You were supposed to put in a brace."

Toby's face was beet red and his chin was quivering.

"Why didn't you explain that to me, Dad? Why?"

Bill threw up his hands. "God almighty, do I have to explain everything? This is a job your average idiot could do with his eyes closed and one hand tied behind his back."

Toby didn't answer; he fled to the rattletrap Jeep he'd bought with money borrowed from Sara, the family miser, and sped off, spraying gravel.

Bill turned to Lucy. "Can you believe that kid?"

Lucy didn't want to answer. She figured anything she could say would only make Bill madder, so she just shook her head.

"Can't you say something?" demanded Bill.

She was spared having to answer by Kudo, who suddenly ran by with a limp chicken in his mouth. Proof positive that once again he'd gotten into Mrs. Pratt's chicken house.

"I'll call and find out how much damage he did," said Lucy, heading for the house.

"You'd better catch him and tie him up first," said Bill, picking up the crowbar. "You know, Lucy, I can't guarantee that beast will be here when you get back from Boston."

Lucy had heard these threats before and didn't take them seriously. She knew Bill was really fond of Kudo. She suspected that he pretended to be antagonistic so he wouldn't be asked to help take care of the dog. She shrugged and went inside to get the box of dog treats she kept handy for calling the dog. He could hear her shaking it from miles away, and the sound never failed to bring him home, drooling with anticipation. When she came back out of the house, however, she realized Bill's truck was gone.

"Great," she muttered, shaking the jar furiously. Now she didn't have a ride to the bus.

A half hour later she had locked the dog in the house and had tracked Elizabeth down at her friend Jenna's house. Impressing upon her the gravity of the situation—that she was going to miss the bus unless Elizabeth returned home immediately with the Subaru—took a bit of doing.

"But, Mom, you said I could have the car while you're gone."

"I'm not gone yet, Elizabeth. And unless you take me to the bus stop I won't be gone at all."

"Okay, Mom. I'll be right there."

She had plenty of time, she told herself, trying to stay calm. At least forty-five minutes. Plenty of time. No reason to panic. She'd go upstairs and get her suitcase and Elizabeth would no doubt be pulling into the driveway when she came down. After all, it was only five minutes to Jenna's house.

But when Lucy came out on the porch with her jacket and purse slung over her arm and towing her wheeled suitcase, there was no sign of Elizabeth or the car. She went back in the house and reached for the phone.

"Jenna," she said, struggling to keep a level voice, "is Elizabeth still there?"

"Oh, hi, Mrs. Stone. Yup, Elizabeth is right here."

"Could I please speak to her?"

"Sure thing."

When she heard Elizabeth on the other end of the line, she could barely contain her fury.

"Right now. This minute. Get in the car. Understand?"

Elizabeth understood. Minutes later she rolled into the driveway, loud music pouring from the station wagon's open windows. Lucy threw her suitcase into the back and climbed into the passenger side.

"There are hamburgers for supper. Dad can grill them.

There's macaroni salad all made, and you can slice up some tomatoes."

"Sure thing, Mom."

From her spritely tone and the way her head was bobbing along to a Janet Jackson tune, Lucy doubted she'd heard a word.

"I'm serious, Elizabeth. Don't forget to pick up Sara and Zoe. Sara gets done with her volunteer job at the animal shelter at four, and you can swing by the Orensteins' for Zoe then, too."

"Right, Mom."

"What did I just say?"

"Grill the tomatoes, slice up the gruesome twosome."

Lucy let it go.

"You know, the only reason I'm letting you use my car while I'm away is so you can get yourself to work."

"I know, Mom. I know."

Elizabeth had taken a job as an au pair for a wealthy couple, Junior and Angela Read, who were summering at his family's enormous shingled "cottage" overlooking the ocean on Smith Heights Road. Elizabeth would be responsible for taking care of their three-and-a-half-year-old son, Trevor.

"It wouldn't hurt you to take a look at that old Gesell book I gave you. Trevor's at a tricky age." She remembered that when Toby was three and a half she'd been convinced he had gone deaf because he never seemed to hear what she was saying and insisted on ignoring her and stubbornly going his own way. It was only after consulting the child-care books that she'd discovered such behavior was normal. What the book's authors had neglected to mention was that he might never grow out of it.

"Don't worry, Mom. We'll be at the yacht club most of the time."

"You do understand that the Reads aren't sending you to the yacht club to get a tan and flirt with the boys, don't you? They'll expect you to take care of Trevor."

"I know. I know. How hard can it be to take care of one

little boy? Besides, he'll probably take a lot of naps and stuff."

"Sure," said Lucy, stifling the impulse to burst into hysterical laughter.

The bus was just coming into view when they pulled into the Quik-Stop parking lot.

"Oh, God, I almost forgot Father's Day." Lucy already felt a little pang of guilt. She wasn't going to be home on Friday after all; Ted wanted her to stay for the morning workshops which meant the next bus didn't depart until Saturday morning.

"It's okay, Mom. I know what to do. Honest, I've been around for nineteen Father's Days. In fact, I've already got a great idea for a present."

"Good. Don't forget the cards. He loves them, and they have to be homemade. The funnier the better."

"Of course, Mom."

"Bacon and sausage—he'll want both."

"Right."

"Plenty of eggs."

"Right."

"Doughnuts from Jake's . . ."

"Absolutely. There's not enough cholesterol in bacon, sausage and eggs. Got to have doughnuts, too."

Lucy smiled at Elizabeth's joke and got out of the car just as the bus pulled into the parking lot. She was lifting her suitcase out of the back when she remembered the most important thing.

"Don't forget the Bloody Marys!" she said, leaning on the driver-side door. It certainly wouldn't be the perfect Father's Day without Bill's traditional eye-opener.

"Mom, aren't you forgetting something?"

Lucy's mind went blank with terror.

"My toothbrush? Did I remember to pack it?"

"No, the liquor. I can't buy vodka and neither can Toby. We're underage."

"Right, right." The bus motor was rumbling. "I'll get vodka. I won't forget. You get the rest of the stuff."

"The bus is gonna leave, Mom. You better hurry."

Before she could say good-bye, Elizabeth had driven out of the parking lot.

Lucy felt alone and deserted. It wouldn't have killed Elizabeth to wait a few minutes so she could wave to the departing bus. Maybe even say an encouraging word, like "Have a good time" or "Don't worry about a thing."

Lucy trundled her suitcase around the bus and gave it to the driver, who stowed it in the baggage compartment, and bought her ticket. He punched it when he gave it to her, telling her she would need it when she debarked in Boston. Then she climbed on board and took a seat next to a window. The driver clambered aboard, released the brakes, which gave a huge hiss, and they began to roll.

Alone in her seat, Lucy reached for her cell phone. Things had been so confused when she left that she wanted to make sure everything was all right. Maybe she could catch Bill, just to touch base and let him know she'd left the hotel phone number on the refrigerator. Or Toby, to tell him that his father wasn't really angry at him; he had just been upset about the shed collapsing. Or she could call Zoe, at her friend Sadie's house, just to say good-bye and remind her to be a good girl.

Lucy was fingering the phone, trying to decide which number to call, when the bus began the long climb past Red Top Hill and on toward the interstate. From where she sat she had a clear view of the little New England town with its white church steeples rising above the leafy green trees and the Main Street shops with the sparkling blue harbor beyond.

It looked, she thought, like a picture postcard. Or the opening scene from a movie. The credits had finished rolling, the heroine had boarded the bus leaving her small-town past behind her and the adventure was about to begin.